David Benedictus was born in Kensington during the Munich crisis and was educated at Broadstairs, Eton, Balliol and Iowa. After a brief spell as a private tutor, washing up at Butlin's and writing scripts for the COI, he became a story editor of 'The Wednesday Play'. As a television drama director and a theatre director he specialised, he says, in the rude and obscure, although he did spend a year with the RSC. He is married to the actress Yvonne Antrobus and they live in Twickenham. He also writes a weekly column on antiques in the London *Evening Standard*, and has written nine novels.

Lloyd George

DAVID BENEDICTUS

SPHERE BOOKS LIMITED
30–32 Gray's Inn Road, London WC1X 8JL

First published in Great Britain by
Weidenfeld & Nicolson Ltd 1981
Copyright © 1981 by David Benedictus and Elaine Morgan
based on a BBC series written by Elaine Morgan
Published by Sphere Books Ltd 1981 (Twice)

TRADE
MARK

Set in Monotype Plantin

Printed and bound in Great Britain by
©ollins, Glasgow

Acknowledgements

Obviously my most substantial debt is to the admirable Elaine Morgan, whose scripts form the basis of this book. She and I drew heavily upon Peter Rowland's weighty biography *Lloyd George* (Barrie & Jenkins, 1976). John Grigg's *The Young Lloyd George* (Eyre Methuen, 1973) is extremely valuable and well-researched, while *Lloyd George: Family Letters, 1885–1936* edited by Kenneth O. Morgan (University of Wales Press and Oxford University Press 1973), Lloyd George's correspondence with Frances Stevenson 1913–41, collected, under the title *My Darling Pussy* and edited by A. J. P. Taylor (Weidenfeld & Nicolson 1975), and Frances Stevenson's diary, published as *Lloyd George: a Diary* and also edited by A. J. P. Taylor (Hutchinson, 1971), were other rich seams to mine. But the volumes of Georgiana are so numerous (and so contradictory) that it would be tiresome to list them at greater length.

David Benedictus
1979

Chapter One

Sometimes Davy thought he could remember his father, sometimes he wasn't sure. Betsy, his mother, often spoke of him, and when she did, her slow, soft voice acquired an extraordinary sweetness. She was never the same after her husband died; she had always been serious, now she became solemn. She had always been dignified, now she became remote. Betsy spoke of William George so often that Davy became confused – were his memories truly his, or had they been filtered through his mother's grief?

But he remembered the sale well enough, and how hundreds (it seemed like thousands) of strangers had invaded the farm and carried off his mam's belongings. And he, Davy, eighteen months old, and his three-year-old sister, Mary, had tried to block the gates against those huge and sinister people with their heavy coats and boots, and strange threatening smells. Davy learned then that the forces arrayed against him were many and powerful and not to be discouraged by loud screams or little fists.

So his father was dead, the farm near Haverfordwest, and the contents, were sold, and there was nothing to be done but accept Uncle Lloyd's kind offer of hospitality and load what few belongings had escaped the auctioneer's hammer on to the trap and let the pony take the strain. Betsy said they must take a chest of William's books with them to their new home. William, a schoolmaster until shortly before he died, had laid great stress on book-learning, and it was Betsy's duty to her dead husband to ensure that the children had access to knowledge. As Bacon had written: 'Knowledge itself is power'.

Davy knew nothing of that yet. But he knew that his world had mysteriously altered. The big man with the dark, wavy hair and the whiskers on his face had gone away. And he knew, after all the preparations, that they too were going away. Betsy explained it to Mary and Mary explained it to him.

Of course it was very exciting for Mary and Davy; and the 170-mile journey to Llanystumdwy was an adventure to be dreamed about for many weeks. It was the second long journey of Davy's short life. When just two months old he had travelled from Manchester to Pembrokeshire, but then he had slept, and though Mary tried to explain about the journey to him, she had not the words nor he the comprehension to make very much of it all.

Was Betsy excited? Her unfamiliar black dress was cold and crinkly and her pale face and the dark around her eyes made her look like a stranger. And though Mary and Davy tugged at her hem, she didn't respond as merrily as she used to do.

They drove up and down mountains; there was snow on the roads, and the wheels of the trap turned quietly and the snow creaked under them. Once they drove across the sea, which seemed to be on fire, so powerful were the rays of the setting sun. And when they finally reached Llanystumdwy, the children were fast asleep.

Over 'Highgate', Uncle Lloyd's cottage, hung a painted sign. It depicted a boot and a top-boot and Davy liked watching those two boots wave in the wind. He had no idea why they were there, but they looked very jolly against the blue sky. There was also some lettering on the sign, but what 'Richard Lloyd – Gwneuthurwr' meant not even Mary could tell him. Later he came to suppose that Uncle Lloyd must be a most important personage to have his name above the door. Indeed he was, for Uncle Lloyd was not just an ordinary cobbler, but a master shoe-maker who employed other cobblers, and he was not just Llanystumdwy's shoe-maker, but a shoe-maker to most of Caernarvon. Nor was he just a master shoe-maker; he was a man of letters, a patriot, president of the local debating society, and celebrated throughout North Wales as an inspired Baptist preacher. That was something to be proud of, for whereas a boot-maker concerns himself with a man's feet, a preacher is concerned for the whole man.

Davy was lucky in his Uncle Lloyd.

Mary skipped past the welcoming arms of her uncle Richard, and Rebecca, her granny, and dumped herself straight down in her uncle's rocking chair. There she sat and sniffed and sucked her thumb. She didn't care about anything just so long as she could rock herself in this lovely chair. Davy was much embraced; his frock was much admired and his hair was much stroked, but he tolerated it, since there was little else he could do, and in due course – if his experience of grown-ups was anything to go by – they would put him down and leave him to get on with the real business of exploring.

Betsy couldn't help but cry, and Rebecca comforted her, glad of the opportunity.

'*Ah, tyrd nawr, paid ag wylo, merch i,*' said Rebecca, 'hush, there's a good girl, time to dry your eyes now. And pull yourself together. You have the children to think of.'

'It's the thought of leaving him there, all those miles away in Pembroke. I won't even be able to visit his grave. Oh Mam!'

Richard remarked that since his chair was evidently unlikely to be free for some time he might as well get on with carrying the luggage upstairs, but the women were too busy talking to pay much attention to him. Davy too found serious talk tiresome stuff, and as soon as he felt floor beneath his feet he scuttled off into his alarming but exciting new territory.

'He should never have given up the school,' Rebecca was saying, 'he was doing well enough at that. What did he want a farm for?'

Betsy was too tired to argue much, but felt she had to say: 'It was so sudden, Mam. He caught a chill and within a week . . .'

'Oh Betsy,' said Rebecca, more to fill the silence than anything else. Betsy's telegram had just said: 'Come Richard'. Neither Richard nor Rebecca could make it out, but telegrams were always bad news. Rebecca had thought it strange that her daughter had been so brusque, but Betsy had not had enough money for a longer message. And it had achieved its object, for Richard had set off at once.

'I couldn't have managed,' said Betsy, 'not with all those strangers around, arrangements to be made, and the children to be seen to. Richard was wonderful.'

'I always hoped he'd settle down and get himself a family. Little did I think he'd get one quite so soon.'

Whether her mother approved or disapproved of the new arrangements, Betsy was not to discover for the noise of hammering from the workshop interrupted the conversation.

The woman looked up sharply but Mary just kept on rocking. If it were Richard it seemed an unlikely time for him to start work. It didn't sound like Richard. But if it were not Richard . . .

The boy was happy. He had found a place more wonderful than he could have dreamed of. A room with such a smell to it, and wooden beams arching away into spidery darkness. A room full of marvellous and astonishing things to be seen and touched and banged together. Lasts and heel-balls, rows of leather strips, knives and nails, candles, thongs, soles, uppers. And the sound of a hammer on a last was such a grand sound to be making all by oneself: it seemed a shame for *them* to have come in and spoil it all.

Later when the children were sleeping Rebecca asked Richard, 'Will she be staying, do you think?'

Richard closed the Bible slowly before asking: 'Where else could they go?'

'You realize what it means, Richard, I'm sure. You'll have to work harder. You'll have to start earlier and finish later.'

'I'm prepared for that.'

'Did he leave her anything?'

'The estate is worth less than a thousand pounds. And there are a few hundred in a building society. But she'll need every bit of that with two children to bring up.'

'Three', said Rebecca.

There was a brief pause. Richard's hands, as tough as the

leather he worked, lay on the black Bible. 'I didn't know,' he said.

'And what if you want to get married yourself? How would you manage with two families?'

'If the Lord has laid this task on me he will give me the strength to carry it through.'

Betsy came in and sat down at the table. She looked older than her thirty-five years. Her mother said: 'You should be resting.'

'At least the children are. They were worn out.'

'What's the idea of bringing all those books here, Betsy? Poor Richard!'

'They were Will's books,' replied Betsy with pride.

'They'd have fetched a bit surely? Better than carting them all the way up here to gather dust.'

'Mam, they are not going from here! They are very near all I have left that belonged to him. Anyway, they will come in useful for the children to read.'

'But when will they read them? It's not story books, is it? It's deep stuff, and all in English.'

'The boy will read them,' said Richard.

'How do you know what he'll do?' Rebecca was not angry, but the bulk of the work would have to be done by her. With Richard working and Betsy pregnant she was not going to find it easy.

'Because he is Will George's son: and if I am to take Will's place it is for me to bring him up as near as I can the way his father would have wanted.'

Betsy had been in domestic service in Pwllheli but you would not have thought it. Though frail, she had a calm dignity and seriousness which was not easily shaken. She had cried once; that was enough. Maybe Davy will take after his father, Rebecca thought, and read deep books in English, and much good may it do him. But the boy is not yet eighteen months old. The thought of two, no three, more babies in the house, alarmed her. How would they ever manage?

Richard clasped his hands and said: 'Before we go to bed

we will have a prayer.' The women shut their eyes as he said: 'Lord God of Hosts, we beseech thee in the name of thy Son, who taught us to have compassion on the widow and the fatherless: give us the strength and the resolution to take up the burdens each day brings, to live together in peace and harmony, and to bring up these thy little ones in the knowledge of thy word . . .'

But all Betsy could think of was a lonely grave and in it all that remained of her handsome, witty husband.

It was a good place and a good time to be young. What if money were short? It cost nothing to look across Tremadoc Bay to the misty outlines of Harlech Castle. It cost nothing to hide in the apple-tree in the garden, to sway in the wind and smell the blossom. It cost nothing to pick your way from boulder to boulder up the Dwyfor River while the noisy waves splashed your ankles, and to leap ashore for blackberries. Oh the Dwyfor was a great place to play! When one grew tired of skimming stones across the water one could lie on the bank and dip one's arms deep down into the sparkling soda that was the Dwyfor. And if one was lucky a trout might nestle on one's palm and could be tickled ever so gently with the pads of one's fingers. Then up the hill through the Tynewydd woods, for among the rowans and silver birches were nuts, and sloes, and fungi, leaf-mould and who knew what?

Davy was the pioneer, but Bob, William and Evan were usually there close behind him, and a scruffy dog or two running this way after rabbits or that way after sticks. And rather further behind the boys they could sometimes hear the panting of the squires' keeper. The squire was Sir Hugh Ellis-Nanney, very grand and very English but grown fat on Wales; not a man to be crossed for he lived in a castle.

And then in the evenings there was food to be eaten with Uncle Lloyd saying grace in that soft baritone voice; and Betsy, a little partial perhaps, choosing the choicest morsels for David, who enjoyed his food; and then the best time of all, the evenings. For then there were Will George's books to be read, as well as Uncle Lloyd's. Davy read them all, making notes on whatever caught his fancy. Richard was impressed by the boy's intensity, but Rebecca did not survive long enough to see the fine use to which the chest of books was being put. She died when Davy was just five and was buried in the tiny graveyard of Pen-y-maes chapel in Criccieth. She should have lived another twenty years. She would have been the proudest woman in Wales – after Betsy.

All three children went to the village school, a substantial building (vast to the children) just across the old stone bridge. It was an Anglican 'National' school in which English was spoken, and Davy found it unnatural to pray in a foreign language to the god of an English church. What a watery language and what feeble prayers! For twice a day on Sundays and every Wednesday evening Davy was accustomed to walk the couple of miles or so to Pen-y-maes where Uncle Lloyd would preach the sermon and lead the prayers. That *was* religion! For then the cobbler's voice would become a potent instrument of the Lord and make such holy Welsh music that the Anglicanism taught at school seemed little better than the sound of a penny whistle.

One night when the two boys were practising the Apostles' Creed, which was to be recited before the School Inspectors, Richard was unable to conceal his resentment and rushed off into the workroom where he could be alone with his shaped leather, his faith intact. The older boy followed him.

'Uncle Lloyd?'

'Mmm.'

'We *do* believe in God the Father, don't we? Maker of heaven and earth?'

Richard removed the last nail from his mouth and emphatically confirmed that we did. Then he continued: 'Davy, you have heard me in the pulpit since you were old enough to understand. Now have you ever heard me use words of controversy or condemnation concerning any other man's faith so long as he is a follower of our Lord Jesus Christ?'

Davy shook his head. The smell of the leather and the shape

of the last would always be associated in his mind with good-ness and spirituality. In such a place and at such a time Davy would have believed that the Queen of England was a rein-carnation of the Virgin Mary had his uncle told him so in that gentle voice, those musical phrases.

'If I have thoughts on other matters,' Richard continued, 'the pulpit is not the place to give vent to them. And I do not believe that a child's mind ought to be moulded prematurely in these matters. They are things we must each decide for ourselves.'

'But you were angry. I could see. I want to know why.'

'We will discuss these things when you are older.'

Richard relished the prospect. Regular meetings of the local debating society (known as he 'village parliament') whetted his appetite for dialectic, and it was always an anticlimax to come home to a house in which words were functional and conversation lacked the finer points of intellectual display.

Davy's voice became shrill with entreaty: 'But how will you know when I am old enough? If I am old enough to ask you, am I not old enough to be told? And if you think a child should not be influenced – although other less scrupulous people may be influencing him all the time – you are not really leaving him to decide for himself, Uncle, you're only giving the other side their own way.'

At this Richard turned to the boy and put his hands on the thin shoulders. Davy's face was solemn, the eyes unflinching.

'Well then, Davy, I shall ask you some questions and you can think about them in your own time.'

'Yes, Uncle Lloyd.'

'What do you understand by the Communion of Saints?'

'Sounds like people with haloes drinking wine. No, I don't know.'

'I didn't suppose you would. Do you think it is pleasing to God that a class of children should be asked to stand up in his name and recite a string of words which is meaningless to them? *Do* you, in fact, believe in the Holy Catholic Church?'

'No, we're disciples of Christ.'

'And the others in your class?'

'Mostly Methodists.'

'Exactly. And do you suppose it's pleasing to God or to man that they be made to stand up and say things that neither they nor their parents believe to be true? Or that tenant farmers who can barely afford to pay the landlord should have to find still more to pay tithes to a church which they do not support? Or that if they withold those tithes they should be turned out on to the road with their wives and children?'

'No!' cried Davy.

'Well, well,' said Richard more calmly, 'those are big questions for you to ponder, and you must find your own answers to them.'

Davy already had his answers. 'But something ought to be *done*! What can people *do*?

'That's a bigger question still. For the moment, nothing, I'm afraid.'

But David Lloyd George had other ideas.

It had been the custom on church festival days for the fifty or so students at the Llanystumdwy National School to process from the school playground to the church. A few weeks before Davy's conversation with Uncle Lloyd, Davy and Willie and some other children had broken free of the procession and sprinted into the woods. Not only did several others join them, but to their surprise nothing was said in condemnation by Mr Evans, the headmaster, the following morning. A fine headmaster, David Evans, a Greek and Latin scholar, a mathematician, an astronomer: more to the purpose, a man who did not believe in interfering unnecessarily. It had been pleasant in the woods, pleasanter than in Church, and all the pleasanter for feeling oneself to be part of a popular revolution. The success of this exercise and Uncle Lloyd's words prompted Davy to another experiment in youthful dissent.

The diocesan inspector was tall, dark and gaunt, with pince-nez. The rector was rubicund with a fringe of fluffy white hair round a large bald patch. ('Like a ruff round a dog's neck', whispered a child. 'Like a frill round a cake,' whispered another.) The squire was upright and fierce, with a blond moustache. The squire's sister was stout, with jet beads on her imposing bosom. The children were nervous, because Mr Evans was uncharacteristically nervous, but they were also nervous because of what Davy had told them to do. Disaffection in the open air seemed as natural as breathing; the same sort of behaviour within the four bleak walls of the school was alarming to contemplate.

Mr Evans had warned the boys and girls of the senior classes to be on their best behaviour and had had them recite the first lines of a prayer to clear their throats. He disliked this sort of ceremony as much as the children did, but he showed his dislike in a kind of strained formality. It was difficult to be sure what sort of a mood his pupils were in, they seemed so queer.

Said Sir Hugh in his voice which was not just English, but *English* English: 'Well, here we are then, Williams. All ready and waiting for you, eh?' From the Inspector's face it would appear that he was the most nervous of them all.

The rector said: 'Good afternoon, children.'

'Good afternoon, Reverend Ellis,' said the children.

The rector introduced the squire and the squire's sister. On any other occasion their strange names and voices might have induced a titter or two amongst the children. But not today. Then Mr Evans made a small encouraging gesture with his hand and the children said in a slightly ragged chorus, but much as rehearsed: 'Good afternoon, sir. Good afternoon, ma'am.' The boys bowed from the waist and the girls dropped demure curtseys; Evans looked relieved, the squire and the squire's sister benevolent.

The rector continued with his introductions. 'And this is Mr Williams, the new diocesan inspector, who has come to see how well you have learned the creed and catechism, and to test your understanding of the gospels.'

'Good afternoon, Mr Williams,' came the chorus of children.

Mr Williams adjusted his pince-nez: 'I think we'll begin with the creed, Mr Evans. Whenever you're ready.' And the diocesan inspector smiled benignly from a great height.

'Now then, boys and girls, all together: "I believe . . ." '

The children stood up, but said not a word. Mr Evans looked at the rector. The rector glanced surreptitiously at Sir Hugh Ellis-Nanney and at Miss Ellis-Nanney and then back at Mr Evans, who said: 'Come along now, children. There is nothing to be nervous about. But I want no more shilly-shallying. When I raise my finger, begin. "I believe . . ."'

The children's eyes were not on the distinguished visitors, not on the rector, or the inspector, not on the headmaster. The eyes behind Davy were on Davy, those level with Davy and in front of him looked into space. Davy's face was rigidly determined, his lips so tightly together that they looked like one of Uncle Lloyd's shoes when he pressed the upper to the sole ready for stitching.

The rector stepped forward. He had often suspected that Mr Evans was too weak a man to make a successful headmaster. Moral authority was what it took, and moral authority was part of a rector's stock-in-trade.

'Now then, boys and girls, all you have to do is to recite the creed. I have heard you say it on many previous occasions, so I know you are perfectly familiar with it: there is no need to be afraid. All these people are your friends; that is why they have come here, to hear you give of your best. So when your headmaster gives the word . . .'

The children remained impassive. But it was evident from their faces that some were not as resolute as others. Willie especially, seated in the very back row, kept glancing around him; there were even tears in his eyes. And now, when Mr Evans announced: 'On a count of three: "I believe . . ." One, two, three,' it was the voice of a man who knew he was beaten, a general awaiting the surrender documents to sign. But then came the cavalry, riding out of the sunset, for Willie could no longer restrain himself and shouted in a tearful voice: 'I believe! I believe in God the Father, maker of heaven and earth . . . ' And now the spell had been broken. The other children – most of them a little relieved – joined in the familiar words in voices which were unnaturally loud and strangely pitched. All, that is, except Davy.

That evening at Highgate Davy was full of contempt and indignation for his younger brother, but Willie refused to apologize. Betsy was amused at the earnestness of her two young sons in their knickerbockers and scarlet stockings, while Uncle Lloyd looked proudly on.

'I stuck up for *you* though, didn't I,' cried Davy, 'when those boys from Criccieth punched you in the stomach? It was four of them and all! Only *I* wasn't afraid. I didn't let *you* down, did I?'

'I wasn't afraid, either,' said Willie sullenly. He didn't want to be put on the defensive but it was hard to avoid it with Davy in this mood.

'You wouldn't have copped it any worse than the rest of us.'

'I've *told* you! You don't ever *listen* to me. I *wasn't afraid*!'

'Why did you do it then?'

'Because I was sorry for Mr Evans. It was awful for him. And he has always been very nice to you.'

There was a pause as Davy saw the advantage sliding away from him.

'That's beside the point, Will.'

Willie felt his position powerful enough to call in an adjudicator. He turned to Uncle Lloyd. Said Richard: 'You have always had a soft heart, Willie. Certainly we should never pursue any action to the point of vindictiveness. And you are right to point to Mr Evans as a good man. He was only doing what he saw as his duty, carrying out the orders of those set above him.'

Betsy said: 'Remember, Richard, that they pay by results. Mr Evans could never live on just the pennies from the children. Which might have some effect on where he sees his duty to lie.'

Betsy's comment was typical, for her mind ran constantly these days on money and how little of it there was to go around.

But Richard would not accept his sister's pragmatism: 'No, no, I believe the man to be sincere. We must respect his faith, even if he doesn't respect ours. But he should have asked himself two questions: whether it can ever be right to get children to make public declarations which are contrary to their own and their parents' beliefs; and, if not, whether a man can do a wrong thing and exonerate himself by pleading that he is ordered to do it.'

To an independent observer – and to Will, who was not independent – Davy's expression was more than a little smug as he said: 'I think he *will* start asking himself these things now, Uncle Lloyd.'

'Then we must pray that he finds the right answer.'

Betsy asked: 'What did Mr Evans do after those other people had gone?'

'Nothing,' said Willie.

'He didn't punish you in any way? What did he say?'

'Nothing,' said Davy.

Richard looked proudly at his favoured nephew as he delivered his verdict: 'In my opinion he never will say anything. I think you may well find that in future that little ritual will simply be dropped from the school curriculum.'

And Richard was right. Headmaster, inspector, gentry and the Established Church itself, had been put to rout by the determined opposition of a thirteen-year-old boy.

Davy was determined and Davy was bright, but there remained the question of what he was to do when his schooldays came to an end in a year's time. It is always a problem when a genius has to prove to the world that he is a genius – and at the same time make some money. Davy had no doubts that he was a genius: he used to climb to the top of an oak-tree and read Euclid in leafy seclusion; obviously nobody but a genius would behave in such a way. Equally he did not doubt that money was an urgent necessity. The Georges may have been the richest family in Llanystumdwy, but that sort of money would not go far in London. The small sum which Betsy had had invested in a building society had been swallowed up in the massive debts revealed when the building society ceased to build. An attempt by Betsy to establish that her family owned the land upon which the Stumble Head Lighthouse was built and to make a claim accordingly against the authorities, was as ineffectual as the waves which battered against the Stumble Head. And Mary had been sent away to Miss Wheatley's school, and Miss Wheatley would need to be paid. The anxiety affected Betsy's health, but a fourteen-year-old cannot concern himself with money when the world is waiting to be saved from its own follies – at least not all the time.

The world was being saved two or three times a week by the 'village parliament', which met at the smithy, where Hugh Jones, the blacksmith, presided. He was a man with the proper physique for saving the world; also a deep bass voice. Here, sitting on tree-trunks with a leather-bound Bible resting on the anvil, the world of men admitted Davy to their company, and agreed that he had every right to be there, for when he engaged Hugh Jones in debate, the words blew around like sparks from the furnace and the air grew hot.

'It is all very well, *machgen i*, for you to sit there like a Daniel come to judgement, quoting from the second gospel and thinking to confound us all. But we've had this argument with your uncle more than once in the last nine years. You object to a service of infant baptism because the baby can't answer for itself, then I must ask you – ' and the blacksmith pointed the huge forefinger of his huge hand at Davy – 'why don't you object to the burial service? The corpse can't answer for itself either.'

Hugh Jones smiled around him at his audience then put a taper to the fire and lit his clay pipe from it. Davy was nodding his head in appreciation.

'He has a quick brain though, Richard,' Hugh continued. 'The Methodists are not going to have it all their own way here from now on.'

Another blacksmith, Myrddin Fardd, whose greatest joy was the study of tombstone inscriptions, remarked: 'Metho-dists or Baptists, we can all give him a pat on the back for his stand in the school last month. What are you thinking of putting him in for when he finishes school – next year, is it?'

Said Richard: 'I have been giving it a lot of thought.'

'Law perhaps?'

Hugh Jones exploded with anger, his huge voice filling the room with fury: 'Lawyers, never! Rogues the lot of them.'

Davy stood up from his tree-trunk and faced his Goliath.

'Abraham Lincoln was a lawyer! We have a picture of him at home. *He* wasn't a rogue – he was one of the best men who ever lived!'

'Was he now? And where did you pick that up from, Davy?'

'You won't flat him on history, Hugh,' said Richard. 'He's been working his way through all those books his father left, and he writes out a precis of each one of them.'

'Sounds like a lawyer to me!' said Myrddin, adding in a more serious tone: 'Should I put in a word for him with Mr Breese of Breese, Jones and Casson in Porthmadog?'

Richard thanked the tombstone-fancier, and sighed. That Davy should be articled to a firm of lawyers was what he'd always wanted for the lad. But whether Davy *could* be articled was another matter. For the preliminary law examination he would need two foreign languages and Welsh, of course, did not count as foreign. Mr Evans from the school would have liked Davy to have been enrolled as a pupil teacher, but for that he would have had to join the Church of England. Nonetheless Evans promised to do what he could to coach the boy in the rudiments of Latin, though he admitted that French was a closed book to him. Uncle Lloyd and Davy acquired some French books and opened them together in the front room; whatever Cassell's *Popular Educator*, a French *Aesop's Fables*, a battered grammar and a tattered dictionary could teach, Davy would learn. And the moonlight streamed through the windows of the cottage, the Dwyfor murmured and a vixen barked, while uncle and nephew worked together at declension and conjugation, verbs regular and irregular until . . . well, until hard work and determination were properly rewarded.

Llanystumdwy was on the Dwyfor, but Porthmadog was on

the sea. From the harbour sailing-ships took slate from the Blaenau Ffestiniog quarries to Germany and returned with cod from Newfoundland. Llanystumdwy was part of Wales, but Porthmadog belonged to the world.

The offices of Breese, Jones and Casson, were not so romantic, however. Gabled and half-timbered, the square, respectable-looking building suggested lace curtains and Gentleman's Relish, propriety and moderation in all things. It discouraged levity though it could not curb Davy's exuberance.

He had a way with him, all the girls said so. A look in his eye which meant mischief and fun. They spied him as he walked from Mrs Lloyd Owen's lodging-house in the morning and they giggled at him as he walked home at night. When he raised his hat to them they whispered together and hid their faces; when he flourished his cane, it was almost more than they could bear. Each week-end he would travel back to Llanystumdwy to see Betsy, Willie and Pollie (which was Mary's nick-name), and to hear Richard preach and to report to him on his progress in the legal profession.

They thought he looked tired. He did look tired. He *was* tired. He was up before six each morning reading Hallan's *Constitutional History*, Williams' *Real Property*, Stephens' *Commentaries*, and other such dusty books, and he stayed up burning Mrs Owen's candles until she felt impelled to protest; and then there were those beastly girls. It wasn't what he did with them, for the opportunities to do anything wicked were rare indeed, but what he thought about doing, what he dreamed about doing, what he planned to do with them, that was what sapped his strength and made those huge, dusty volumes seem larger and dustier than ever. He was a handsome young fellow, but he did look tired.

The practical work was interesting, for besides being clerks to the justices. Breese, Jones and Casson handled all the litigation which Porthmadog could supply. Collecting fire insurance premiums and tackling ratings appeals was less romantic than leading for the Crown in a murder trial at the Old Bailey. but time was on Davy's side and he was sensible enough to be patient. At the end of a six-month probationary period he was articled in the sum of £100, plus £50 stamp duty, which Richard was at some pains to raise. But the sacrifice was good practice for Uncle Lloyd. Although Davy helped in the garden at week-ends. Richard's favourite nephew was to be a drain on the family resources for some time to come.

With the failure of Betsy's building society it became necessary for Uncle Lloyd to think radically about the family's finances. There were four mouths to be fed (five at week-ends) and work as hard as he might, there was a limit to what a cobbler could earn in a village like Llanystumdwy. Besides there were the spiritual needs of the congregation at Pen-y-maes to be supplied as well. When G. P. Williams, a friendly ironmonger, offered Richard a small house at nominal rent in Criccieth on condition that he became a full-time pastor, the cobbler had little choice. Highgate and the business were speedily sold, Davy dug up the fruit bushes and the move to Morvin House was completed.

In his diary Davy wrote: '10 May 1880. Left Llanystumdwy without a feeling of regret, remorse or longing.'

But the move to Criccieth brought mixed blessings. Davy would no longer have to pay Mrs Owen her weekly rent, but he would have a five-mile walk night and morning through the dreadful Criccieth weather. (Years later Davy was to write: 'I know no place where it rains so incessantly. Hundreds of well known doctors go there and appear to die soon after. The air is too fresh, the water too pure, and there's too much of it.') Morvin House would be a good deal more suitable for an ambitious young solicitor than Highgate, but how was he to share sweet nothings with the local girls with suspicious Willie and disapproving Pollie alert for every creak of stays, every squeak of excitement. It was some consolation perhaps to recollect that less time with the girls would mean more time to cram for intermediate law exams. But exams don't blush as charmingly as girls do, nor is the law so susceptible to a young man's flattering tongue.

Mr Breese, senior partner in Breese, Jones and Casson, was Liberal agent for Merioneth and part of Caernarvon, and encouraged by Uncle Lloyd whose own political ambitions had been frustrated, Davy undertook some canvassing work prior to the 1880 election. Later in the same year a by-election offered Davy the chance to engage in some real political dialectic and he started to contribute pieces to the *North Wales Express*. He was just seventeen years old, but the vigour of his attacks as 'Brutus', fearless observer of the political scene, first on Lord Salisbury, and then on Ellis-Nanney, Tory squire of Llanystumdwy, who had the temerity to stand for South Caernarvonshire in opposition to William Rathbone, the Liberal, was remarkable and the arguments shrewd. Uncle Lloyd was profoundly impressed, and, more to the point, Rathbone was elected by a comfortable majority.

Davy was working to capacity. Besides wielding his pen as a lassoo to rope in and bring back to order any roguish politicians who needed chastening, he started to preach in the small, granite Pen-y-maes Chapel ('Oh my own dear boy spoke well!' Richard noted. 'Never more striking and effective . . . Thy protection over him, O Lord!'). He became secretary of the local branch of the United Kingdom Alliance for Temperance Reform, and made a deep impression upon all the members of the Porthmadog Debating Society, for he defended the rights of the Irish peasants and denounced Gladstone for sending troops to Egypt, with equal potency. He was not a demagogue, his speeches being witty and ironic rather than violently passionate, but a vigorous and assured debater.

In November 1881 Davy visited London for the first time, to sit for his intermediate law exams. He was alarmed neither by the city nor by exams. A phrenologist felt the bumps on his head and assured him that he was going to be Prime Minister. His diary entry records his visit to the Houses of Parliament:

'Grand buildings outside, but inside they are crabbed, small and suffocating, especially the House of Commons. I will not say but that I eyed the assembly in a spirit similar to that in which William the Conqueror eyed England on his visit to Edward the Confessor, as the region of his future domain. Oh, vanity!'

He told William about London, how he had felt so much at home there, about the theatres, the electric lights, the girls, and was disappointed that William seemed to take it all so coolly.

'When we've made our mark here, Will,' he said, 'We can set up in partnership in London. Lloyd George and George. How does that sound?'

'Very grand,' said William quietly. He never told his brother how it rankled that Uncle Lloyd had insisted on David taking both names. There was so much that he never told Davy.

After the news that Davy had passed his exams reached the family in Criccieth, Davy, exhilarated, reopened the subject: 'You can take *your* finals in another two years, Willie. I'll help you all I can, but you must work very hard; everything hinges on that.'

'I'm not sure it's what I want to do,' said his brother. 'I wondered once about medicine.'

'Oh, but that's ridiculous! You'd never pass. Besides it would take too long and cost too much. And what about Uncle Lloyd? Somebody's got to stay and look after him. I won't always be here. I'll tell you what I've done though, Willie. I've kept all my notes and the exam papers; you'll find them very useful.'

'Like your clothes,' said William, but so quietly that Davy didn't hear.

On 10 June 1884, Davy recorded in his diary that he had met 'a sensible girl without any fuss or affectation about her'. This was remarkable since 'Margaret Owen Mynydd Ednyfed', as Davy referred to her, lumping together the girl with the substantial farm she was sole heir to, had been sent away to a smart girls' school in Dolgellau, where she had learnt a number of genteel accomplishments, and was adored by both Richard, her prosperous and proud father, and Mary, her imposing though illiterate Welsh mother ('*bonedd gwlad*' they called her in Wales).

The courtship was a gradual affair, Davy taking Margaret home 'the short way' after meetings of the Criccieth Debating Society and leaving notes for her in the holes in an accommodating wall. By night at the top of the Foel he talked to her seriously about his ambitions for himself and his plans for her, and his letters made his intentions plain enough. ('My supreme idea is to get on. To this idea I shall sacrifice everything – except, I trust, honesty. I am prepared to thrust even love itself under the wheels of my juggernaut, if it obstructs the way, that is if love is so much trumpery child's play as your mother deems courtship to be. I have told you over and over that I consider you to be my good angel – my guiding star. Do you not really desire my success?')

Richard Owen of Mynydd Ednyfed Farm was of very ancient family. (Well, all families are ancient but Mr Owen liked to fancy that his was one of the most ancient in Wales.) His wife was jealous of her husband's heredity and regarded Davy as 'a penniless fortune-hunter without two pennies to rub together.' Having invited Davy to Mynydd Ednyfed for tea, indelicately she pointed out that the Lloyds and the Georges lived rent-free by the charity of an ironmonger called Williams who belonged to the same obscure Baptist sect as Richard Lloyd, and that Betsy George, Davy's mother, took in summer lodgers. Davy was profoundly embarrassed and extremely angry. Penniless he was, and, if Maggie brought a fortune with her, he would not refuse to take it, but there was more to it than that. He had protested in frequent letters that he loved her and some of those letters she had actually acknowledged. Since she continued to see him, Davy reasoned, though not as frequently as she promised, she could not be entirely averse to his courting, and in this lay his defence to any of the cruel insults which that formidable mother of hers was so quick to spit across the front room.

'They have been meeting secretly,' cried Mrs Owen, 'I found letters from him hidden under the lining of her handkerchief drawer.' And from her tone it was not easy to judge whether she objected to the liaison, the letters or Margaret's choice of a hiding-place. 'Furthermore,' the mistress of Mynydd Ednyfed continued, 'You will see from what he writes that she kindly presented him with one of our prize asters – and that he could not be sure of the colour of it because – and here her lip trembled – "*it was dark at the time*".'

'Is this true, Mr George?' asked the gentleman farmer, hoping devoutly that it wouldn't be, because if it were, he would have to do something about it and he couldn't for the life of him think what.

'My name is *Lloyd* George, Mr Owen,' said Davy, whose experience of public speaking and heated exchanges in the debating chamber was going to prove most useful, 'and I am totally astonished by the tone and expressions which Mrs Owen has seen fit to employ! I don't deny having meetings and conversations with Miss Owen – why should I? Why should either of us wish to deny it? I cannot believe that you, sir, have to be assured that you daughter is incapable of doing anything of which she need be ashamed, and I am shocked beyond words to learn that her own mother could even hint at such a possibility!'

'Should she not be ashamed of deceiving her own parents?' asked Mrs Owen, whose habit it was only to take from an argument that which suited her point of view. It was not an easy question to answer – so Davy asked *her* one.

'Are you implying she has *lied* to you? Mrs Owen, it is *you* who should be bitterly ashamed of voicing such an accusation. It is only a few months since I first had the honour of making Miss Owen's acquaintance, but there is one thing I would gladly stake my life on: she is incapable of uttering an untruth.'

Mrs Owen looked at her husband as though it was his fault that her daughter's name was being cleared in this infuriating way. 'You are twisting my words! I never said she has actually told lies – '

'I thank you for confirming that,' Davy interrupted. And

then he turned to Mr Owen, who had been hoping that he wouldn't. 'I hope, sir, we may resume our discussion at a later date. Would next week be convenient?'

'Now, look here, it's all very well, but this puts a rather different complexion on things, you know.'

Such a reasonable attitude incensed Mrs Owen still more. Davy was quite fearful for a number of china ornaments within easy reach of her trembling hands as she cried: 'It's perfectly obvious why he comes sneaking around here! She's an only child; she'll have a handsome dowry and a hundred acres of the best land in Criccieth. That's all *he* cares about!' And then she turned on her house guest as she continued: 'Do you really suppose all that will be thrown away on an upstart like you? Don't you realize that my husband can trace his ancestry back to Owain Gwynedd, Prince of North Wales?'

Davy felt almost sorry for her as he replied: 'Mrs Owen, I have always understood that people of truly gentle birth can be recognized by their magnanimity and good manners. Yet within two minutes of my entering this room you have sneered at my mother on the grounds of her tragic bereavement and her endeavours to bring up her children by honest hard work, and insulted the religious beliefs of my uncle, whose faith is every whit as sincere and honourable as your own.'

It was at this point that Mr Owen, alarmed at the savage turn the conversation was taking, announced that he could take no more bickering. 'Mr George – Mr Lloyd,' he mumbled in excusable confusion, 'I'm sure your family are very good and respectable people, but the fact is that I've made my plans for Maggie's future and am not going to see them upset. I'm afraid I must ask you not to come here again.'

Davy made a fine and dignified exit, which impressed the Owens' maid, Margiad, so deeply that she found herself hoping that the young man would nevertheless call again. Maggie was sure that he must. Her father and mother could be brutes, but, when they realized her determination and Davy's remarkable qualities – all he needed was a little time – they would soon come round.

Davy walked slowly back to Morvin House. He had been shocked by the Owens' attitude towards him, but, although it made him no fonder of them, he could see their point of view. After all he did, at least during the summer months, live in a lodging-house.

'Mam,' he announced when he got home, 'I'm very sorry but you're going to have to choose between the lodgers and me.'

Betsy was amazed and demanded to know more. Davy found that he couldn't repeat in front of his family what Mrs Owen had said to him; it was too hurtful. So he merely said that it wasn't convenient, that it wasn't fair on him when he had documents to study, nor on Willie who was working for his law exams, to be kicked upstairs to an attic.

Willie remarked mildly that he didn't mind where he worked; what made it all so difficult was that Davy kept over-loading him with clerical jobs from the office.

'Am I to turn work away just because I haven't got a clerk? It's not easy starting up a new practice.'

'It's not all that easy for me either,' said William, still mildly. 'Casson knows I'm working for you in the evenings while he trains me during the day time. And then he finds out you're taking business away from him, and it's me he takes it out on.'

'The thing that worries me,' said Davy, thinking how selfish Will was always to be concerned with himself, 'is the impression clients will get when they come here. They'll wonder which it is, a solicitor's office, or a common lodging-house. And, after all, who is the chief breadwinner in this house?'

'Mam is,' said William defiantly. Davy was taken aback, but William explained: 'Last summer the visitors brought in a lot more than . . . ' (he was about to say Davy's work as a solicitor, but restrained himself).

'He's only building up the practice yet, Will. Don't be too hard on the lad. He may be right. We'll see how we manage without the lodgers.'

They didn't manage. Davy and Will came down from the

29

attic . . . and then went up there again. Betsy and Pollie put away the extra towels and linen . . . and took them out again. That summer one of their lodgers was H. Rider Haggard. The presence of a literary gentleman made the whole undertaking seem just a little less squalid.

Davy was twenty-two when his association with Breese, Jones and Casson terminated. He had decided to set up in private practice. He could barely afford the cost of the brass plate. He could not afford the gown and bands, without which it was not permissible to appear in the County Court, and had them on credit from the shop. But when you are twenty-two it is better to be independent and live on credit than to be rich and servile. He had three offices; at Morvin House, Criccieth, in Porthmadog at the house where he had lived five years before, and at Blaenau Ffestiniog. His first jobs on his own account were debt-collecting: depressing and time-consuming work, but necessary. His first appearance in court was to defend a poacher charged with assaulting a railway porter. He worked hard, had a good courtroom manner, and was intelligent: it did not take him long to make a reputation, or as much of a reputation as could be made in the local courts before biased magistrates and on behalf of feckless criminals.

It was easier to become celebrated in the rumbustuous world of politics and there too Davy had his triumphs. Chamberlain was his idol and Davy followed his career with a mixture of admiration and envy. His programme was properly Liberal, advocating free primary education, Home Rule, Land Reform, the payment of MPs and other radical steps. Certainly the paying of MPs must be high up on a list of priorities; however else would Davy manage to represent his constituents as and when the call came? So during the autumn months of 1885 he toured the election meetings of North Wales, speaking with a vigorous energy in favour of Chamberlain, and ridiculing what he called the unholy trinity of Liberal demonology, the brewer, the bishop and the squire, Ellis-Nanney. It was when the Conservatives singled him out for attack that he knew he was beginning to worry them, and, when his life was threatened in Criccieth he raised a troop of vigilantes in Porthmadog and continued on his way.

The result of the election was that the Liberals won thirty of the thirty-four Welsh seats, but did less well elsewhere. The number of seats held by the Liberals was equalled by the combined totals of Conservatives and Nationalists. Hardly a stable political situation, but Davy was not dismayed. If more elections were necessary, more speeches would have to be made and Davy was in good voice.

There were days when Davy felt there was nothing he couldn't do, no case too hard to tackle, no one he couldn't impress, and there was no limit to his ambitions. North Wales would fall to him, then the rest of Wales, then England, then Britain, then the world. Phrenologists after all deal in bumps on the head, and that is substance, not superstition. So why should he not be Prime Minister? All he needed was good health, a measure of good fortune, a handful of good contacts and a good wife. And *that* was the trouble.

'Nobody can help you, *machgen i*. The master means her to have Mr Edwards.'

'Ah, but Margiad, the Lord never gave you those velvety brown eyes and that wicked little dimple without a warm and loving heart to match. Would you see me die of a broken heart without lifting a finger to help me?'

The sixty-year-old servant shook her head. It was better not to talk to the young man for he took your words and and turned them inside out.

'Then save me before it's too late!' Margiad remained tight-lipped. 'He may be rich and respectable but I'm poor and in love, and, Margiad, I'll not be poor for ever. By the way *is* he rich?'

'He's a good clean-living man. and a good Calvinist,' said Margiad, wondering why she was defending Mr Edwards, 'and what if he is rich? He's very fond of her and she of him.'

Davy gripped the woman by her arm, and his eyes were irresistible.

31

'Fond!' he cried. 'What does that matter? He's forty-five. And she's not in love with him. Don't you care for her at all?'

'Me not care for her?' cried Margiad, much insulted. Those eyes!

'Well then, give her a letter. Where's the harm in a letter? She no longer collects them from the old place, and if I can't write to her . . . Will you, Margiad?'

'What about Jenny Williams?'

'Jenny who? Oh Jenny *Williams*. Last I heard she was engaged to the postman.'

'Liza Jones, the singer, then? And Morwen Price from Porthmadog? And those Irish girls after the Pentecostal dance? And – '

'You're talking about a past that is dead and gone. I'm talking about Maggie Owen, who is far above all other women as heaven is above the earth! You'll take her a letter, won't you, Margiad?'

And suddenly she finds herself hugged and kissed by this strange, enthusiastic young man, although she is not aware of having committed herself in any way. But what harm *could* there be in a letter?

'And you can tell her that here's a Baptist who can out-kiss any of those Calvinist louts, hey?'

Just a letter, after all. But now he is at her again, squeezing and kissing and – oh!

'And if you like you can tell her how you know!'

And yet the letters were not so much full of kisses as: 'You will appreciate my anxiety to bring the matter to an issue with your mother. I somehow feel deeply that it is unmanly to take by stealth and fraud what I am honestly entitled to. It has a tinge of the ridiculous in it moreover.'

And: 'Believe me – and may heaven attest the truth of my statement – my love for you is sincere and strong. In this I never waver. But I must not forget that I have a purpose in life. And however painful the sacrifice I may have to make to attain this ambition I must not flinch – otherwise success will be remote indeed.'

And: 'You seem to think that the supreme function of a

wife is to *amuse* her husband – to be to him a kind of twin or plaything to enable him to while away with enjoyment his leisure hours. Frankly, that is simply prostituting marriage. My ideas are very different – if not superior – to yours. I am of the opinion that woman's function is to soothe and sympathize and not to amuse. Men's lives are a perpetual conflict. The life I have mapped out will be especially so – as lawyer and politician. Woman's function is to pour oil on the wounds – to heal the bruises of spirit received in past conflicts and to stimulate to renewed exertion. Am I not right? If I am then you are pre-eminently the girl for me.'

Maggie was puzzled. She loved the lad; more than a hundred Mr Edwardses. But he asked too much of her. How could she all at once sacrifice her family and friends on the altar of his ambition? Was there not some way in which she could avoid hurting her parents? He seemed to think she could only prove her love for him by behaving heartlessly to everyone else. Was love meant to be like this?'

So she tried ignoring him. She tried breaking the appointments they made. She tried being ill. But whatever she did or tried to do, her parents were angry, and Davy was angry and even Margiad was angry.

She told him so. 'Why,' she said, 'do you have to make enemies of everyone?'

And he said that making enemies, being attacked, was what his life was about, that if he was to succeed he had to accustom himself to that; therefore it was imperative to have someone by his side to support him. So she asked: 'But what will I tell them?'

'Tell them you are going to meet me. Tell them before they ask.'

'They'll suggest something different.'

'And you'll say it's dishonourable to break a promise. Oh tell them, Maggie, that you love me, that you're going to marry me, and be done with it.'

She said she needed more time and that it was cruel to be so blunt with them, but, he asked, why was it cruel to go against their wishes and not against his? And he said it was they who were cruel. And he went on and on at her so that at length she agreed to be plain with them, and then he took her in his arms and for a while all the pain was forgotten.

The Owens came round. The Owens began secretly to feel a little proud of their future son-in-law, although they didn't tell Maggie that. And Uncle Lloyd was astonished, doubly astonished, when he learned that Betsy and Will and even Pollie had known about the liaison for some time. Uncle Lloyd tried his best. When Davy was not back by midnight he would pull on his boots and climb the hill in search of him. So Davy hid his uncle's boots which put a stop to *that*. So then Esgob (the bishop), Davy's new nickname for Uncle Lloyd, tried another tactic, inviting a series of the better-favoured Baptist girls to tea at Morvin House. Davy countered this by flirting with the girls encouragingly but keeping his serious love-making for the plump and decidedly Calvinist Maggie. So then Uncle Lloyd asked his friends about this Maggie Owen and was told that his nephew had done pretty well for himself. And when people one respects say something often enough there is a strong tendency to believe them; so Richard did.

As many problems were created by this pragmatic and ecumenical love-match as were solved. Where were the couple to live? And on what were they to live, if not on dreams? And what sort of wedding ceremony should they have? It was decided that they would live with the Owen family at Mynydd Ednyfed, since Davy felt it more fitting that he should live in a big house than that Maggie should live in a small one. It was further decided (by Davy) that they should live off Will – plus whatever Maggie brought with her (about which it would not have been polite to speculate). To this end it was necessary that Will should pass his finals, which he obligingly did with first class honours. That was good news, although Davy wondered whether it would not have been more suitable for the younger brother to have done just a little less well. One genius in the family, thought Davy, was quite enough. As for the wedding, the solution was simple.

The Owens wanted a Calvinist ceremony: Davy suggested a Baptist one. So they settled on a Methodist chapel at Pencaenewydd. Margaret was twenty-one, Davy twenty-five. On the morning of the wedding Davy wrote in a letter to a friend: 'I'm setting off for a far-off land – a *better* one too I hope.'

The service was conducted jointly by Uncle Lloyd and the Methodist minister from Criccieth. It was a quiet wedding – exceptionally so for Betsy, Willie and Pollie, who stayed away. The couple caught the midday train to London. Before retiring to bed in Parker's Hotel, Davy wrote: 'I'm very glad the whole business is over. Never felt so anxious.'

But in Criccieth, where as usual it was raining, there was a bonfire and fireworks. *Who* was celebrating *what* was not entirely clear, but everyone felt much more cheerful afterwards.

Professionally Davy was feeling restless. Poaching cases were all very well and he was grateful to the poachers of North Wales for helping to keep him going, but he needed rather more than this to bring him fame, fortune, and the premiership of Great Britain.

The opportunity came when an old quarryman, a calvinistic Methodist, died, having requested that he be laid to rest beside his daughter in the consecrated ground of Llanfrothen parish church. The grave was half-dug and the late Robert Roberts quite ready to lie down in it and get some peace, when the rector, the Reverend Richard Jones, instructed the grave-digger to stop digging the hole and start filling it in again. If Robert Roberts wanted to be buried in Llanfrothen churchyard and have a Methodist perform the ceremony he would have to be content with the corner of the graveyard devoted to suicides and bodies washed up by the sea, and other undesirables. The son of Robert Roberts was incensed – for so far as he was concerned his father had been by no means 'undesirable' – and inconvenienced, for he had relatives, cousins from Wrexham even, coming specially for the funeral. So he knocked on the door which bore the spanking new brass plate proclaiming 'Lloyd George & George'.

There was a particular reason for calling on Davy to deal with the matter for he it was who had been proclaiming in public speeches the implementation of the Burial Act of 1800, whereby nonconformists could be buried where and, within Christian reason, by whom they pleased.

It was the sort of case to make a lawyer's eyes gleam, for the points at issue were nice ones. The rector argued that the disputed part of the graveyard had been donated to the church on the strict condition that all burials there would be Church of England ones. (Indeed he was sure that was the case for had it not been he who had persuaded the widow, whose land it was, to convey it to the dean, the archdeacon and himself with a proviso to just this effect?) Roberts countered that since his sister was buried there surely his father could be too. But Davy discovered that Roberts's sister had been buried after the land had been given to the church *but before the proviso had been added*. Things looked black for Roberts and his cousins from Wrexham and indeed for the corpse who was in some danger of remaining above ground until the lawyers had finished with him, but Davy was able to show that, thanks to the Statute of Limitations the proviso must be invalid. If the land had been in general use for more than twelve years no inserted clauses could change anything, and according to the parish records the land had been in use for twelve years and a week.

Davy was cock-a-hoop, Roberts also, and the corpse must have been quietly satisfied when it heard the lawyer advise the Methodists to break down the padlocked gates of the cemetery, force an entry, and bury the old quarryman there without more ado.

But the Anglican county court judge was unimpressed and found in favour of the rector. He took two months to give his judgement and made inaccurate notes of the jury's findings. At once Davy instructed his client to appeal to the Queen's Bench in London.

The resulting victory for the young Welsh barrister received great publicity and he became the champion of the Welsh nonconformists. The firm of Lloyd George & George was made, and the late Robert Roberts was permitted to remain undisturbed in the ground next to his daughter's body.

It was not long afterwards that the Liberal Associations in the South Caernarvonshire boroughs chose Mr Lloyd George to represent them as prospective parliamentary candidate, nor was it very long before Maggie enjoyed a triumph of her own and introduced another prospective voter into the world. The baby screamed lustily, but that was not an indication of voting intention; just wind.

'Oh Mrs Jones,' said Davy more than once, for the name tripped sweetly off the lips, 'Let us sing another duet together.' Lily Jones had an abundance of chestnut hair and seemed a good deal more amenable than Maggie. Maggie spent all her time with the baby, who was called Richard after his great-uncle, and even when the baby was asleep in bed, Maggie talked about him. Davy had nothing against the baby – indeed he was quite fond of him when he was clean and quiet – but he did feel that Maggie had been taking him, Davy, rather for granted since the baby came. Lily Jones did not take him for granted. And Lily Jones had chestnut hair. They sang another duet, full of love and longing, and then Davy asked a question he had been meaning to ask for some time.

'Isn't anyone else coming to your musical evening, Mrs Jones?'

'It doesn't seem so.'

'Did you – ' and Davy paused, wondering how to phrase the question so that Lily Jones would not be offended – 'did you remember to invite them?'

Lily Jones ran her fingers through her chestnut hair. 'Oh dear, how bad of me,' she murmured, but she didn't sound sincere as she murmured it, although Davy thought it *was* rather bad of her, 'things do slip my mind. I've had that weakness for years now, since my husband died in fact.' Lily

Jones really was forgetful that evening, for having completed a nicely executed *arpeggio* in E flat major she left her slender hand on the high notes at Davy's end of the keyboard and appeared to forget about it. Davy returned it to her, and then – since the amnesia seemed to be infectious – forgot to take *his* away. There were to be no more songs that evening, and in due course both Lily Jones and Davy would suddenly remember just what it was they wanted to do, and each wanted to do what the other wanted, which was wonderfully fortunate, and so they did it. Afterwards Davy ran his fingers through that lustrous chestnut hair, and stopped thinking of the desirable Lily Jones and began thinking of Edmund Swetenham.

Edmund Swetenham had won Davy's home constituency of Caernarvon Borough for the Tories in the election of 1886, and it rankled, for the Liberal candidate ought not to have been beaten. And now four years later the white-haired and kindly old Tory QC was dead; he had had influenza and the exertion of reaching for a book from his library shelf had done for him. Swetenham died so suddenly that all those involved in Caernarvonshire politics were quite unprepared, and Davy, already adopted as the Liberal candidate, had to redouble his efforts to make a name for himself and win votes. (Lily Jones, of course, had no vote, which is why she was being replaced in Davy's thoughts by Edmund Swetenham.)

He decided that the popular issue would be Welsh nationalism and to demand of Gladstone that he implement his promise to disestablish the Church in Wales, and make disestablishment consequent upon the granting of Home Rule to Ireland. Besides dealing with such heavy matters as temperance reform and the antiquated tithe system he was always able to make people laugh. When he referred to the Tories' search for a successor to Swetenham it was better than the music hall.

'So they went to the owner of the Dinorwic slate quarries and begged *him* to stand – and he declined the honour! They tried the youngest son of Lord Newborough, and *he* didn't fancy his chances. They went up to London and drew a blank there too! But finally they found the ideal candidate back home on their very doorstep – the squire of Llanystumdwy, Sir Hugh Ellis-Nanney!'

'No, seriously, now – he's the perfect Tory condidate. He's a landowner, a member of the aristocracy and he's rich!'

And Davy's voice grew graver as he drew a moral to adorn the tale. 'The Tories seem to imagine they are living in the seventeenth century! Don't they realize that the day is dawning when, although people may have to pay their rents to the man in the castle or the manor house, they'll give their votes to a man who understands their problems because he, like them, was born and bred in a *cottage?*'

It was when the election campaign was in full swing and Davy was loving every minute of it that he spied at the back of one of his meetings a rather too familiar face, framed by a great mass of chestnut hair. Had the liberal Lily Jones suddenly become enthusiastic for the Liberal cause? If only that had been the explanation! Lily passed a note up to the platform from which Davy was making his speech. Davy unfolded it. His voice became faint, trailing away into silence. He clutched the arms of his chair for support. Perspiration prickled on his forehead. Later that evening a meeting was held in Lily's parlour in the presence of J. T. Roberts, the Liberal agent. No longer were Davy and Lily singing in harmony. Now their voices were out of tune.

'You know *I* haven't got that amount of money,' said Davy. His mouth was dry, and he couldn't be sure whether his face was flushed or unnaturally pale, but it couldn't possibly have been its usual colour.

'I'm not asking for a lump sum,' said the amateur singer, 'you could pay so much a week.'

'Oh no,' said Davy firmly, 'I'm not letting you hang that millstone round my neck for the rest of my life.'

'You've hung a millstone around mine, haven't you?'

Davy cursed chestnut hair with a terrible silent curse, but

all he said was 'Lily, I just want Mr Roberts to hear you say this. You're not claiming that I in any way – deceived you or . . .'

'No, I'm not saying that. It was six of one and half a dozen of the other. But it's me that'll be landed with the baby. And I don't see any sense in me struggling to bring it up on the parish and you living in clover.' Davy cast a look at Mr Roberts, the sort of look a dog might give its master when its paw is caught in a trap. But Mr Roberts maintained a discreet silence. The mercenary lady continued: 'Oh yes, you are. You might not have any money, but your in-laws have got plenty. Ask them.' Davy grew angry. Lily's voice was gentle and demure as she continued: 'I don't care where it comes from. But where *is* it to come from?' She looked at Davy and Davy looked at Mr Roberts; Lily looked at Mr Roberts, and Mr Roberts looked down at the brief-case in his lap.

The settlement was an unusual one. Lily was to receive an annuity on two conditions: she was never to reveal the identity of the child's father and she was never to permit the child to be photographed. It was a lot to ask of an attractive young widow with chestnut hair, but when she studied the papers she looked up shrewdly: '*Somebody's* digging into their pockets,' she murmured. 'How lucky for me the election came when it did. And how lucky for you, my little politician, that not *all* the rich men are in the Tory party!'

There was an impressive turn-out for the count in Caernarvon town hall. Ellis-Nanney was sitting amongst his friends at one end of the main table. He was recollecting that his Liberal rival was the same young boy who had been responsible for those unfortunate scenes in the school in Llanystumdwy. Mr Roberts was at the other end of the table with *his* friends and was recollecting that the Tory candidate (or certain members of his party at any rate) had been distributing free coal to the electorate. He was also nervously glancing around him (as was his habit these days) for attractive young women in advanced states of pregnancy, but the coast seemed clear.

Near the door Uncle Lloyd was looking ill at ease. He was dreading the silent journey back to Criccieth when words of support and consolation would have to be found. William was more optimistic. He knew from comments made to him in the office and out in the country districts that the support for his brother was deep-seated and arose out of more than mere admiration for an attractive and cheeky young man. But he was anxious too. If Davy were elected and went up to London, he would be earning nothing as an MP and expenses in the big city were bound to be fearfully high. The job of keeping the family fed, housed and clothed would then devolve entirely upon Will. The business was flourishing, but it was only a small business and William sometimes wondered what might happen if he thought to find himself a wife, and settle down and have children. It would not be easy. Why was it, he wondered, that Davy could afford to marry and have children while he and Uncle Lloyd seemed to have abrogated the right to have families of their own? And how was it that Davy got all the girls? Nonetheless he watched the growing piles of votes with mounting excitement. One moment the Tory pile seemed the bigger, then the Liberal; it was evidently a close-run thing.

Davy was nervous, but excited. This was what it was all about. In his father's books the great men were seldom outvoted; their qualities were recognized early and they swam to power on a rising tide of popular support. But should they go under they always bobbed up again; you couldn't keep a good man down for long.

The returning officer was beckoning to him; Ellis-Nanney was already hovering at his shoulder. As Davy left his small band of supporters Richard squeezed his arm and wished him good luck.

'They'll go wild in Llanystumdwy if he's done it,' said Will.

'They won't,' said Richard bitterly. 'Look at the boy's face.'

Davy returned to them. His mouth was screwed up in an unnatural attempt at a smile. He said nothing. William asked

41

'By how much, Dei?'

'Six votes. They're just going to announce it.'

'It was bribery!' cried William angrily. 'Free coal for voting Tory – they'd never have won it fair!'

'It came too soon,' said Richard. 'The Boy Candidate' – that was the wrong slogan. Another year, another six months, Davy, and nothing could have stopped you.'

'It wasn't that,' said the boy candidate. 'I got carried away. I went too far. It's wrong to antagonize the moderates.'

William was almost in tears. 'What a shame, though. After all you'd put into it.'

'They're about to make the announcement.'

But they didn't. A violent commotion had broken out around the table. The Tories and the Liberals were shouting at each other and at the returning officer, and waving sheets of paper in the air. Davy hurried across the hall. Ellis-Nanney was pale; his hands were stiffly by his side.

'I regret to say, Mr Lloyd George, that a small number of the Liberal votes seem to have got into the wrong pile. By mistake of course.' His words were heard by the Liberals, who laughed raucously. I must ask you to take my word that I am totally at a loss to account for it.'

Davy raised a hand to silence his supporters, then turned back to the squire.

'Of course, of course, I accept that without reservation. But I think we had better ask Mr Williams for a recount, and see if the electorate agrees . . . '

There was a recount. Davy had won by twenty votes. The Tories called for another recount. There was another recount. Davy had won by eighteen votes. It was good enough. Mr Williams made his announcement, declaring that Davy had been duly elected.

Later, standing on the balcony of the town hall and with Maggie at his side, Davy acknowledged the cheers. They sounded unlike other expressions of enthusiasm. To Davy they sounded strangely natural, like the wind and the sea and the rain. He made a ridiculous speech. 'The county of Caernarvon today is free,' he cried, 'the Boroughs have wiped away the stain.' He hardly knew what he was saying. The crowds could hardly hear him anyway for all the cheering.

As the couple left the balcony and went indoors to where Will and Richard, who was weeping without shame, were waiting, the cheers turned to singing. The singing was in Welsh and it, too, sounded perfectly natural.

Chapter Two

David's first appearance in the House of Commons caused something of a stir. He took his seat on Budget Day, 1890, and waited, pale with nerves, while Question Time considered such weighty matters as the Boulak Museum, the Portuguese imbroglio and the Indian Factory Law, until he was introduced by Messrs Acland and Rendel. The Liberals cheered him, and while George Goschen, an obscure Chancellor, introduced his obscure budget, David dashed off a letter to Maggie. 'It will interest you to know that Goshen has *taken off* 2d in the pound duty on tea. I am glad now we didn't buy that chest – it will be cheaper now by a few shillings at least.'

Those were good days. Good days for the Liberals, and good days for a handsome twenty-seven-year-old who was lionized wherever he went. On Sundays when the sun shone David and Sam Evans, the young MP for mid-Glamorganshire, recently widowed and by no means disconsolate, took a boat down-river to Kew. The sun sparkled on the water dripping from the blades of the oars and the girls were as pretty as any in Porthmadog. Maggie visited London occasionally but found it dirty and noisy, and David's accommodation so poky and squalid that she couldn't help but count the hours till she was back in Criccieth.

Besides there was cholera in London, wasn't there, and other nameless evils which could assail small babies. Baby Dick needed her more than David did; it was as simple as that.

'It's different for you, Dei,' said Maggie, 'you're busy all day with all your new friends, but what am I to do? And it's costing money, me being here when I could live at home for nothing. I feel that I'm sponging on Will.'

David was outraged. 'Sponging on *Will*? But the money comes from Lloyd George & George. It's my firm. I founded it.'

'Yes, but you're not there.'

'I'll be there in the recess. I'll be there if anything *interesting* comes up. You surely don't expect me to go rushing back there for all the piddling little local cases. Will can handle those. Besides, it's *my* name that brings in the clients, not his.'

'If only you had taken that money from my father we wouldn't *need* to keep asking your brother for cheques.'

It was the old argument. David was too proud to be dependent on the Owens. They had doubted whether he would be able to keep Maggie in the proper style. He would prove to them that he could, even if it meant in the short-term that the money had to come from Will. He also turned down an offer of a directorship with a Welsh drapery firm, and planned instead to set up a London office of Lloyd George & George.

Perhaps the Liberals would pass a bill to pay MPs. Perhaps David would become a barrister, for you didn't see barristers sweeping the streets. But something would have to be done, for Maggie was expecting another baby . . .

It was strange, though, that David, to whom it should all have been so foreign, found Parliament, big halls, powdered women, and the soft voices of the 'Oxford Street Welsh' – D. H. Evans, Peter Jones and John Lewis – the invitations and the admiration, so very much to his taste, while Maggie, who had been born, bred and trained for it in that posh Dolgellau school, just wished to be home.

He missed her. He liked his freedom, but he missed her. He missed the baby too. Furthermore he found that in his lodgings he was ill-fed, cold, and quite unable to provide himself with clean shirts or socks or drawers. Surely Mr Gladstone had clean underwear every night? And Lord Salisbury? And Randolph Churchill? Surely all politicians did, bar only him? But he could talk them into the ground when he was in the mood. He asked questions in Question Time, and elderly gentlemen nudged each other awake. He spoke at a meeting of the Liberation Society at the Metropolitan Tabernacle and called for disestablishment and was loudly cheered. And at the Manchester Free Trade Hall, where he pointed out that he was a native of Manchester, he attacked the proposal to compensate those publicans whose licences were not renewed. His speech was so charged with passion that there was a stunned silence for a moment before hats, handkerchiefs, sticks were flung into the air in wild enthusiasm. His maiden speech in the House was on the Local Taxation Bill and included attacks on both Randolph Churchill and Joseph Chamberlain. It lasted seventeen minutes and earned a respectful acknowledgement from Gladstone himself, who was said to be 'exceedingly delighted'.

But always he could make people laugh. On the principle, 'the Englishman never respects any fellow unless that fellow beats him: then he becomes particularly affable towards him', he laid into rascals and hypocrites wherever he found them, which was frequently on the same side of the House as himself. Here he is on Church of England dignitaries:

'They are the successors of Peter, the plain, bluff, honest old fisherman. If he had turned up at the Church Congress the other day, there is not a prelate, a prebendary or a dean among them who would not have shunned him. They might have handed him over to some convenient curate to be proselytized, who would have warned him against the pernicious habit of attending conventions to listen to an ordinary carpenter's son – a man without the true sacerdotal succession in his veins.'

In August he moved 'that £3,558 8s od be deducted from the sum of the Crown's miscellaneous expenditure, with reference to the following items: First, £439 3s 4d for the installation of Prince Henry of Prussia as Knight of the Garter. What service,' he wondered, 'has Prince Henry ever rendered to Britain? Or, for that matter, to his own country? Second, £2,769 4s 8d for equipping the Duke of Zetland with a wardrobe on his appointment as Lord Lieutenant of Ireland – plus £200 for a special steamer to send him over there. Though everybody knows,' he added, 'that the *real* governor of Ireland is Mr Balfour, and the Lord Lieutenant is nothing but a man in buttons who wears silk stockings and has a coat of arms on his carriage. And third, £180 to cover the funeral expenses of the Duchess of Cambridge whose husband has already received from a benevolent Exchequer a sum in the region of three million pounds! It is particularly monstrous,' he concluded, 'that while thousands of hard-working, thrifty men are living lives of hopeless, ceaseless toil we should be asked to spend hundreds in decorating a foreign prince and thousands in adorning a supernumerary.'

But all this was no more than swatting flies. There was still the disestablished princess tied to the tree to be freed, and the dragon called the House of Lords, stuffed with anglican bishops, guarding her, to be slain, before David could justifiably proclaim that he had kept his faith with those Welshmen who had voted the Boy Candidate into power. Everybody cared about Ireland, but nobody gave a leek for Wales.

Discussing the problem with Sam Evans, who was ardent for Home Rule, David concluded that nothing could be achieved without support from the Grand Old Man.

'He admires you,' said Sam, 'that's a start.'

'He pats me on the head,' said David, 'that's nothing. If I could only get to him face to face, I'd force him to recognize that the problem exists.'

'That's the privilege of Grand Old Men,' said Sam, 'they only recognize what they wish to recognize.'

'There must be a way,' said David.

'There usually is,' said Sam.

And there was. At David's suggestion the Engedi Calvinistic Methodist church and school organized an excursion to Hawarden Castle, Mrs Gladstone's inherited estate in Flintshire, of some nine hundred loyal party members, and at David's suggestion the Liberal ladies' section presented an address to Mrs Gladstone in person, and also at David's suggestion the date chosen was one when it seemed probable that the Grand Old Man would be in residence at Hawarden. The outcome was predictable. Mrs Gladstone, radiant among the summer glory of an English garden, clutched her roll of vellum and thanked the ladies' section with evident sincerity. And Mr Gladstone was pleased to make a brief appearance on the lawn and to say a few words about Welsh Home Rule.

He said that Ireland was the problem (it always was!). He said that Ireland was responsible for holding up a great deal of government business. He said that the moment Ireland was out of the way, the other problems would be reduced to trifling dimensions and the local problems of Scotland and Wales could be speedily dealt with. The visitors were gratified to hear it.

'I wish you goodbye,' said the Grand Old Man, and blackbirds accompanied his farewell. 'I hope you will enjoy yourselves: I am very glad the sky has been favourable to your visit.'

And then he shook a few proffered hands and turned to make his way back to the house. But David and Thomas Lewis, MP for Anglesey, shook their heads as though displeased with what they had heard. And David hurried after the Grand Old Man, having to break into a trot and then a canter in order to catch him before he vanished from sight around the rhododendrons. Gladstone looked down from his venerable height at the Welsh terrier snapping at his heels.

'I must point out, sir,' said the terrier, 'that there was one notable omission in your speech which has caused considerable disappointment if not dismay. Everybody expected some reference to Disestablishment.'

The Prime Minister was startled. What with the sun, the blackbirds and Mrs Gladstone's roll of vellum he had not anticipated such a challenge today. He felt quite tired. But he sighed and said: 'If Scotland was asking for Disestablishment I could give it to them in ten minutes – but how can I offer any early hope of it to Wales? The Welsh Church is part of the Church of England, with its bishops in the House of Lords. You must learn to consider the practical aspects. Wales is a very small place, you know – only twenty-seven members in the House. Suppose Yorkshire came to me and demanded Disestablishment?'

'That would be entirely different!' cried David indignantly. 'Wales is a nation!'

Gladstone nodded patiently. They came and they went, these lads. They had such brave ideas, such energy, such youth. Now what was this one called?

'Well, Mr Lewis – er – Mr George, I don't mean to discourage you. If you keep on pressing for it, it may come. One day . . . ' The sound of a distant Welsh hymn dissipated like smoke in the soft air. A small group of hefty young men elbowed David into a hedge in their keenness to get near their leader. Brushing himself down, David thought: The day *will* come, and sooner than Mr Gladstone expects. He, David, would see to that.

He would get back to his dark, gloomy dungeon after an evening in the House and he would work on a speech. He would work until his handwriting – spindly at the best of times – tailed off into an unintelligible scrawl. Then he would shake himself awake, dash some cold water on to the back of his neck, and remember that he had eaten nothing since lunchtime. He would search on the table until he found a door-step of bread, a hunk of cheese, an apple with a bite out of it quite brown where it had been bitten, the remains of a tin of biscuits. He would eat without registering the taste of the food, then push the plate back among socks and collars and half-written speeches. And then he would be seized with an onrush of loneliness and write to Maggie. She sent him fruit and news of Criccieth and he was grateful for that. He told her about his triumphant speeches and the things they were writing about him in the newspapers. He called her his faithful little Maggie and his old pet, and he felt better for writing. But the ache which could not be soothed was his longing to see little Dickie. 'Tell him not to forget his "Dada",' he wrote. 'Dada does not forget him.' And then he would stare out of the window at the sooty, stinking city and remember the freshness of the breeze along the front at Porthmadog, and the sparkling silver of the Dwyfor and the Tynewydd woods and the vast hulk of Cader Idris and the mysterious presence that was Wales. And he was filled with a sense of loss more grievous than anything he had felt before. What am I doing here he thought, what does all the acclaim and admiration matter if I never see my wife or my son? And he would tug off his clothes and lie awake. Why was he so alert when he longed for sleep, so tired when he longed to work? And he would think, supposing the phrenologist was wrong, supposing David Lloyd George is just deluding himself, supposing he is throwing away his youth and vigour chasing rainbows? His daughter Mair was born. And how he longed to be with her!

David felt that his fortunes were inextricably linked with the fate of the Liberal Party, and while in the spring of the year it had been easy to be swept along by the heady optimism of a radical party which reckoned itself at times almost divinely inspired, in the autumn of 1890 the Liberals were plunged into the deepest gloom by the Parnell scandal. For now the man who at the start of the parliamentary term had been triumphantly cleared of the innuendoes of a disreputable forger was exposed in the uncontested divorce case of O'Shea *v* O'Shea to be a man as intimate with fire-escapes and bedroom windows as with another man's wife; and he had lied publicly about all of them. The Tories said such behaviour was not to be pardoned. The Irish Nationalists said it didn't matter. The cause of Home Rule for Ireland, which Parnell championed in the House, could not be put at risk by such an irrelevancy. Gladstone disagreed. Parnell could not stay in the House if Home Rule were to remain on the agenda. The man at the centre of it all was unrepentant. David thoroughly disapproved of Parnell's conduct, and thought him a rascal and a bad lot. He didn't much care for the way he strutted about the House, 'as cool and as defiant as ever, puffing at his cigar like blazes'. But at the same time he could understand only too well the fascination of fire-escapes and hotel bedrooms – later in his career David was to become known as the 'Welsh Parnell'. Whatever David thought, Gladstone was determined to be rid of Parnell, although forty-five Irish MPs refused to accept his authority and repudiated him.

All of this was little short of disastrous for the Liberal Party: manna from heaven for the Tories. In the run-up to the general election David determined to concentrate on Welsh disestablishment and to leave the Irish to fight their own battles.

When David put it to William that Lloyd George & George ought to move to London he quite expected his brother to be thrilled at the prospect of the metropolis.

'Besides I'd be on the spot,' he added, gaining enthusiasm as he spoke – after all with the power of his eloquence he could sway everyone else to believe what he wanted them to believe, so why not himself?

'I could really pull my weight. I'd feel a lot better about it then!'

But William looked unimpressed, even angry, though there could be no cause for anger, as he replied: 'You must be out of your mind!'

'Why?'

'What about Uncle Lloyd? What about Mam? You know how bad her asthma is. But you obviously don't know how scared she is that her children will leave her. You obviously don't know that she opens my letters to see whether I'm planning to be off. Living in London, there's a lot that you don't know.'

Astounded at Will's strength of feeling. David asked: 'Well, what about Pollie? Couldn't she look after them?'

'I don't suppose you consider it of any relevance, Dei, but I don't want to go to London. I, personally, William George, do not *want* to go to London.'

'All right, no need to get excited.'

'I *like* it here.'

'*Duw annwyl*, you're just like Maggie.'

'I get on well with Maggie. I've got a lot of sympathy with Maggie. Why don't you open an office in London yourself?'

Which David did.

David was on form. It was a grand meeting. He had taken trouble with the speech, contrasting the Welsh nonconformist ministers, 'the successors of Peter, the plain, bluff honest fisherman', with a bishop in the House of Lords 'lolling on its scarlet benches, dwelling in a stately mansion with a host of menials ministering to his luxury, all this with the poor rotting in misery at his very palace gates'. And yet he had been able to depart from the flowery formality of this speech to put down hecklers and to answer questions with his own rich blend of scorn and whimsicality. He sounded good. He felt good. He looked good.

Catherine Edwards thought that he looked good. She had corn-coloured hair and looked good herself. She was a distant relative of Maggie's and felt aggrieved that her dowdy cousin should have landed the eloquent young MP while she had to make do with her tiresome Monmouth doctor. The world was unfair. And when your hair was the colour of corn and you had a separate bedroom from your husband the unfairness seemed bitter. Dr Edwards had invited David for supper after the meeting and Catherine found her hands trembling as she served the food. Her husband's name was David too. She dug her nails into the soft flesh of her palms and longed for him to be called out to a patient – something lengthy and difficult would be best, but with her luck . . .

Her husband was pumping David about the chances of disestablishment before the next election; slender, apparently with the Grand Old Man fully committed to Irish Home Rule, and a churchman, *and* eighty-four years old. David thought that if the House of Lords could be discredited over some other issue there might be an outside chance of getting a bill through, but the Irish would have to come first since it was the Irish not the Welsh who kept the Liberals in office.

And then there was this knock at the door, an urgent knock repeated several times. Catherine mumbled an apology and hurried out of the room, praying hard. She was in luck. Mrs Jones had started her baby. Doctor Edwards was required. It would be a long night.

It was a long night for Catherine and David too. He found it hard to decide whether he preferred corn-coloured hair or chestnut hair, but both, he reckoned, looked fine on a pillow.

In his sleep he murmured something about Home Rule. The baby was slowly but safely delivered.

David was prospering. He took a new flat in the Inns of Court and was very proud when Maggie came to town with the children. A third, Olwen, was born in 1892. At such times they were very happy together. He tried out his speeches on her and made her laugh. He told her about the magnificence of Ellen Terry's acting and the glories of the D'Oyly Carte operas at the Savoy. She washed his socks, cooked his meals and made a great fuss of him. But Maggie could never be at ease for long in the great, dark city.

The government was losing its nerve. In 1894 Rosebery, who preferred horse-racing to politics, had succeeded Gladstone who preferred politics to anything. The Parnell scandal had ensured that the next election would be a close-run thing, and having lost its popular support, the Party was now compromising on its radical manifesto. And as for Welsh Home Rule – 'Lord Rosebery referred to the Welsh people as "natives of the principality" as if he were referring to a tribe of Wahabees in Central Africa. I have been reading of how Stanley and his followers gave the natives empty jampots in exchange for goods. The policy pursued towards the "natives of the Principality" is also one of empty jampots. Others have the jam; we have the pots!

'During the past twenty-six years Wales has returned a preponderating majority of Liberal members to Parliament, but during the whole of that time Wales has not had a single measure of reform from any Liberal government dealing with the special topics which most affect her. Yet in recent years the Irish have succeeded, by monumental effort and in the teeth of a seething mass of prejudice and passion which we have never experienced, in having their grievances promptly attended to. If Wales wants similar attention Wales will have to follow Ireland's example. Do you really imagine that if we had a strong resolute independent party in Parliament like the Irish party, that any Liberal Ministry dependent for its existence on our votes would have dared to insult us by letting yet another session go by without fulfilling their solemn promises to us? We need such a party, and we need it soon. The agenda is a long one, and life is short.'

It was not to be expected that such views, so vehemently expressed, would be popular with the generality of the Liberal Party, but David had hoped that he might find support among his fellow Welsh MPs. He was disappointed. D. A. Thomas, Sam Evans and others accused him of betraying the party at a time when it was most vulnerable. Why, if he went on making such speeches, the Liberals – reeling from the Parnell business – might be counted out at the next election. But David was not concerned with the next election; it was as good as lost he claimed, and the battle was on for the election after that. What use were radicals who were terrified of losing their seats, any more than a party which was terrified of losing an election?

Sam grew angry – but he had always been returned unopposed to Parliament. D. A. Thomas grew angry, but he had a rich father prepared to meet his election expenses. David's seat was marginal, and it was problematic whether or no William would be able to help him out with money for the election. But that was no reason to compromise. Already he had refused the Party Whip on more than one occasion; now he flung himself wholeheartedly into Cymru Fydd, a Welsh Nationalist movement to rival the Irish. He also fought hard and long on behalf of the Welsh slate quarries, and against the Clergy Discipline Bill – yet more involvement by the state in religious matters.

When Rosebery's Disestablishment Bill failed to make its Second Reading, the Welsh MPs were faced with two problems. Could they continue to trust Rosebery and still retain the respect of their constituents? And could they really ignore the impact of Cymru Fydd, which was filling halls throughout the Principality. It may have been a David Lloyd George Admiration Society, but it certainly was a nuisance. It filled the papers, and it addled people's minds. The South Wales Liberal Association and the North Wales Liberal Association,

54

who had worked together for years in sleepy federation, were roused from their slumbers and declared that the man had to be stopped.

But the man would not be stopped. When the Registrar General noted that his census returns for 1891 could not be taken too seriously because such a large percentage of Welshmen claimed to be able to speak Welsh, David forced a debate in the House and moved that the Registrar General's salary be reduced by an annual £100. And when the LNWR Company sacked a number of their Welsh-speaking employees – and particularly those in responsible positions – David castigated them bitterly in and out of the House.

The meetings of Cymru Fydd continued and the more rotten tomatoes were thrown at David the more the newspapers loved him, and the more embarrassed were the Welsh Liberals, upholding, against their better judgement, a tottering regime.

Rosebery accepted the inevitable on 21 June 1896, when the Government, which preferred to go out with a bang rather than a whimper, was defeated in a vote of censure over cordite supplies, and in the subsequent election David found himself faced by his old enemy, Ellis-Nanney. In his home constituency the Boy Candidate had grown in power and influence, while Ellis-Nanney carried the expectation of defeat around with him like on old brief-case, Although there was a huge swing away from the Liberals, Lloyd George kept his seat with a majority of 194, compared to 196 four years previously when he had been opposed by the more-to-be-reckoned-with Sir John Puleston. He was relieved, but exhausted.

The election was a triumph for David, but not for Wales. With Salisbury back in charge Welsh Home Rule had no chance of succeeding. The Cymru Fydd League dwindled and died and David began to feel in his head what he had known in his heart for some time: Wales was too small to contain all his ambitions.

Betsy was dying. She was only in her sixties but she was very tired. She was not dying in Llanystumdwy where she had lived most of her life, but in Criccieth, where William had built himself a new house. She was not used to such large and airy rooms and the light dazzled her eyes. William was with her, and she was very fond of William, and Maggie was with her, and Maggie was a good girl and a good breeder – Gwilym had followed Richard and Mair and Olwen out of her womb and into the bracing air of North Wales. But David was in London, and she almost wished that he was a little less important so that he could delight her eyes before the light finally failed. But no, she could not and would not ask it of him. After all, he was running the country! At least she had his letters, and William could read the latest one to her.

' . . . Just you sit down in the coolest room in the house and boss the rest of them. I know they will be pleased to obey and if they do not, just give them that tongue a bit of which your eldest son has inherited from you . . . '

Maggie drew Uncle Richard into the kitchen, and spoke to him in a quite unnecessary whisper: 'Shouldn't we send for Dei?'

'She says no.'

'But shouldn't we at least tell him? He can't know how near the end she is.'

'He's in the middle of fighting the Agricultural Rating Bill. It's important to him. I wish I knew what to do.'

'How much have you told him?'

'Not enough.'

William continued to read to his mother. He felt David's absence most keenly. But you would not have known it from the way he read his brother's words: 'It is a good thing you have such a store of pluck to bear you up. I will back my good old mother against the whole lot of them. If you could get a nice place in an upland district to go to for a short time, then the moment the cool weather returns your appetite will improve and you will feel frisky as ever. My very fondest love to you. I got up just now with six others to speak, but they closured us. But I will pay them out. Your fondest boy, Dei.'

Betsy didn't like the idea of Davy being closured – she

didn't like the idea of being closured herself – but she knew he'd be all right. He'd show them. Will was a good boy too, but . . . she died.

David was on form again. He had castigated Balfour in the House, accusing him of using agricultural subsidy to line the pockets of landlords. He had attacked the Royal Commission set up to look into the matter, on the grounds that it was composed almost exclusively of landlords. He had blasted Ministers of the Crown who stood personally to benefit from the scheme by more than £67,000 a year. And to cheers from the Liberal benches and outraged howls from the Tories he had concluded: 'Having bled the farmer to the last drop of his blood, the landowners are now seeking to bleed the taxpayers, who are now to be driven in their turn into the landlords' leech-pond.'

David was on form. His speech had been a great success with Harcourt, Morley and Asquith, the powerful Liberal triumvirate. He had charmed those members of the House who were in any way susceptible to his charm, and now at Palace Mansions, Kensington, the grandest of a long line of addresses, he was enjoying a visit from a beautiful lady, who was in every way susceptible to his charm. She was the wife of Timothy Davies, a powerful man among the London Welsh. Her name was Elizabeth, her age twenty-six and her hair, oh, that was the colour of honey. David's hand was on the nape of her neck, his fingers toying with a few honey-coloured and charmingly disarranged strands of hair, when the telegram arrived.

Elizabeth thought she should go, said she would go, and even made the first few fidgets preparatory to going, but David restrained her. He said that on such a night he needed company. On such a night it would be heartless to leave him alone. Elizabeth stayed.

David was on form.

All these women. Each one of them meant more to him (at the time) than all the cheers and congratulations of his colleagues in the House. When he lay with each one of them he forgot Maggie and his little 'pets'. To feel each one of them against his skin was to be removed from the squalor of his grubby rooms, from the dusty air and the bitter arguments of crowded committee rooms, from the drudgery of letter-writing, the worries about money, the self-doubts. They gave themselves freely, so why not accept them graciously? And he was not obsessive about it, like Sam Evans. It was not essential to his health. It was just pleasant. It hurt nobody. It just . . . happened.

If only Maggie could understand that.

But Maggie would not understand. She had the children, and they were bonny. She had the new house in Criccieth, which was not grand but it was hers to do with as she pleased. She had a standing invitation to visit him in London, to meet his famous friends and iron his shirts. But no, she wouldn't come, or if she did she wouldn't stay, and she wouldn't understand. She claimed he spent half his time in London away from the House, visiting Lizzie Davies in Walham Green; which of course was stupid of her. He went to visit Tim Davies, who liked him and was not a man to be spurned. And if Tim was not at home, what did Maggie expect him to do? Turn his back on 'Mrs Tim' and walk straight out of the house? Anyway *she* came to call on *him* sometimes, and what should he do about that? He told Maggie to be reasonable, to curb her irrational jealousies, and then he said – and it was something of a conversation-stopper – that he was off to Patagonia in the morning.

Patagonia. The name had a good ring to it. If fortunes were to be made anywhere in the world surely they could be made in Patagonia. Impressed by the name and by rumours of gold in almost Aztec quantities, David had taken out a thousand shares in the Welsh Patagonian Gold Fields Syndicate Ltd, and had persuaded a reluctant William to take a further six hundred. The project had obstinately refused to get off the ground although a number of MPs, financiers, and others who should have known better invested their own money and encouraged their more gullible (and poorer) friends to do the same. Recently even Uncle Lloyd, with ten shares, and Margaret, with fifteen, had become involved in this desperate venture.

So now, with two friends, David set off on the R.M.S. *Clyde*, to see for himself what was happening in Patagonia and whether there was gold in 'them thar hills'. He had an interesting holiday on board ship, playing shovelboard and watching whales, being fêted and dined in Argentina, but never actually getting to Chubut, where the gold was supposed to be. A number of Patagonians seemed to have gone to quite a bit of trouble to ensure that he didn't. Back in Buenos Aires he became involved – the sun was hot, and so memories of the affair were naturally hazy – with the wife of a local grandee, was challenged to a duel, shaved off his moustache and hid in a small hotel to escape the confrontation. It had all been something of an adventure for the three Welshmen. They saw palm-trees and parrots, presidents, locusts and humming-birds. It was a shame that they never got to see any gold, but then one can't see everything on a holiday. The shareholders in the company watched their investments wilt, and finally – when the company went into liquidation in 1900 – fade away, although Lloyd George & George, as lawyers to the company, received legal fees for their onerous duties, because one has to live.

To David his lack of capital was an affront. He spent hours, days, weeks, writing articles, making speeches, in order to earn enough to buy a decent suit, while men of mediocre talent flashed their money around until eyes were dazzled. His failure to get rich in Patagonia did not therefore discourage him from other such ventures: rather the reverse.

It was a shame that Catherine's beautiful corn-coloured hair was so dishevelled and her eyes so swollen with weeping. But Dr Edwards was unmoved by the sight. He was very angry. When one finds one's wife pregnant although one has not slept with her for two years, anger is always on the cards.

'I know *when* it was. February the fourth. I was called out to deliver a baby – there's an irony. But what I want to know is *who* it was.'

Catherine continued to weep. It was a wonder where all the tears came from. She complained of a frightful headache. She begged to be allowed to go to bed. The more she wept, the louder her husband shouted. He didn't sound at all like a doctor.

'The name! I want the name! As God is my witness, if it takes me a *week*, neither of us is going to sleep again until you tell me who it was. It was Wilson, wasn't it?' Wilson was the local stationmaster. Dr Edwards was now shouting loud enough to stop the trains. '*Wasn't it?*'

'No! No! No!'

The doctor feared hysterics, and prepared to give his wife the recognized treatment for a hysterical attack – there would be some satisfaction too in slapping her face. But first he would try once more: '*Who was it?*'

Catherine stopped screaming. She lay back in her chair and closed her eyes. She said quietly: 'Lloyd George. Can I go to bed now?'

'No,' said the doctor, astounded, appalled, and – though he would never have admitted it – just a little thrilled. 'Not until you have put that in writing.'

He pulled her to her feet. He sat her in a chair. He thrust pen and ink in front of her and he dictated:

'I, Catherine Edwards, do solemnly confess that on 4 February 1896 I committed adultery with Lloyd George MP, and that the said Lloyd George is the father of the child, and that I have on a previous occasion committed adultery with the said Lloyd George.'

The statement was made on 10 August, and the baby was born nine days later, just two days before David left for Patagonia. By the time he returned, fit and bronzed, with his fine brown curls ruffled by the sea breezes, the scandal was public. At once he issued strenuous denials, making vital arithmetical calculations in his head. Surely it couldn't be true – and then it struck him that, no, by God, it *wasn't* true, the calculations were all wrong. One didn't need to be a doctor to know that if the baby was only six and a half months in the making, it wouldn't have been such a fine strapping infant as it apparently was. And yet the previous November he hadn't been anywhere near the woman. September, though, that would have been different. The bitch was evidently trying to shove the blame on to him, and to shield somebody else. Let her do her worst! But William was more circumspect. He pointed out that since a wife's confession to her husband was not technically a 'publication', David could take no action for libel or slander against the Edwardses, although if any newspaper printed the story . . .

'You should go down on your knees,' was William's helpful advice. 'If you get clear of this, it's nothing but luck. Or Providence. And for your own sake – if not for Maggie's – make up your mind to mend your ways. Your luck won't last for ever, Dei. Remember Parnell and Kitty O'Shea.'

But David's luck did not desert him yet. At the preliminary hearing his name was never mentioned and he was referred to merely as 'A.B.'. At the main hearing the presiding judge remarked tersely 'Mr Lloyd George is not a party to this suit. There is no imputation upon him at all.' Dr Edwards got his divorce and the stationmaster retained his good name, for he proved as doughty as David in denying that he had had any part of the lady's favours. The baby's father was thus officially 'a person unknown', and the only one to come out of the whole affair with dishonour was the baby, who had not been alive when the adultery took place. The law may be an ass, but it's no fool when it comes to protecting its own. And the rumours were kept from Uncle Lloyd. But Maggie was not so easily fooled. It wasn't just Catherine Edwards, there were others; there was Lizzie Davies, and little Richard had seen his father 'trying to eat her hand', as he described it.

'Shaking it,' said David apprehensively, 'just shaking it.'

'Do you think I'm stupid? In front of the child, too, there's no excuse for that. *And* she goes to your rooms.'

'Have you been setting spies on me now?' cried David. If only she had, he could legitimately attack her for disloyalty.

But Maggie's voice was contemptuous as she dismissed the idea, and added: 'What if I told her husband?'

'I can assure you there's nothing you could tell Tim Davies about his wife that he doesn't know already.' David was picking his words carefully.

'*He's* not worried because he's so keen on getting into Parliament. There are some very funny people in London. They seem to think that marriage vows are just words.'

'Maggie, I've had enough of this!' cried David. 'If you want to ruin me it's in your power. Go on, get it over with, do it! But don't put on that smug, self-satisfied, pharisaical air and preach at me, because I'll stand it no longer. I'm sick and tired of hearing about my marriage vows – what about yours? You promised to be a wife to me – to love, honour and obey! How many times have I entreated you to come to London and stay there? If you and the children were there I wouldn't want anyone else. I offered you Chelsea, or Ealing, or Acton – 'not good enough: the bad air'. I offered you *Brighton* – still not good enough! You leave me to come home in the middle of the night to a cold, empty flat. And then you ask if I think you're stupid. What do you call it – *wisdom?*'

Maggie felt, as she had often felt before, that there were signal disadvantages in being married to one of the most expert debaters in the British Isles. If she found him *in flagrante delicto* in the marriage bed he would probably be able to prove that he was the injured party. Nonetheless she had so say *something*.

'I'm very sorry, I'm sure, if you feel I've been a burden to you.'

'For the last time, Maggie,' cried David, beginning to enjoy himself, 'stop twisting my words and stop acting like a Christian martyr. I'm not complaining that your society is a burden to me: I'm complaining I don't get enough of it. Now for God's sake – and I'm in earnest – just for once look into your own heart and ask yourself if some of the blame doesn't lie there. When you married me you took over the charge of my soul as well as my body – if you had to answer to your maker tomorrow as to how faithfully you had carried out that charge what would your answer be? You have been a very good mother, Maggie. But you haven't always been a good wife. Even compared with some of those women you look down upon and despise, you have not always been a good wife.'

Maggie could no longer hold back her tears. She despised herself for crying in front of him, but it was not until she did so that his manner changed, and he put his arms around her, and made the promises she loved to hear. And so it was all right between them, until the next time.

When a man of talent and ambition determines to become Prime Minister he must get himself written about. If he comes from a cobbler's shop in a tiny village in North Wales and has a romantic presence and a powerful rhetorical style, one does not need to be a phrenologist to predict that he will get very close to the big prize. Politicians are no more handsome than the rest of us, nor are there many of them capable of engaging the passions of a large crowd. In any parliament of 627 members there are probaby 600 who for the lack of popular appeal could never attain the highest office. Of the other twenty-seven, twenty are likely to disqualify themselves through character deficiences, of which the most damning is laziness. There has only been one Prime Minister in this century who could truly be said to be lazy – and Baldwin was so charmingly lazy, lazy in such a grand style, that in his case it almost became an asset. David was neither ugly nor lazy, and, when he spoke, he spoke to the people, whereas most politicians speak to one another. He spoke everywhere and anywhere; and whenever he spoke the pompous, the hypo-critical and the time-servers shuffled their feet nervously. In a workhouse in front of old ladies in bonnets and pinafores he attacked the new Tory government for failing to honour their promise to bring in an old age pension. This is part of what he said:

'Go into any English village. You will see a gentleman driving a four-in-hand, with his two or three powdered footmen, through a large plantation populated with his pheasants and partridges. The government has already given *him* his old age pension – by the Agricultural Rating Bill they have added five hundred or a thousand pounds a year to the value of his estate. If you turn then to the village you will find on the roadside an old man, bent, broken, feeble with age and infirmity, breaking stones – work fit for convicts. This government solemnly pledged themselves to give him five shillings a week to save him from this degrading labour and from a pauper's grave. But once they were returned, did they use the resources at their disposal to redeem this pledge? No: they used them to line their own pockets and the pockets of their own class. The greatest, meanest and cruellest act of perfidy that ever tarnished the name of any land . . . !'

David was in Canada in October 1899 when the Transvaal and the Orange Free State declared war on Britain. Had he been content to remain on the back benches, he could have happily retired from the debate on the rights and wrongs of the war. But being ambitious he would have to be energetic on one side of the other. The only question was which.

The issues were clear enough. Since 1886 South Africa had been invaded by a crusade of rich and fortune-hunting 'Uitlanders', most of whom were British and all of whom had the sparkle of diamonds in their eyes, the weight of gold driving them forward. President Krüger of the Transvaal was sad to see the resources of his country exploited by foreigners, and taxed the colonists heavily. He also denied them the franchise until they had lived in the Transvaal for fourteen years (a requirement later amended to seven), which, since their numbers were equivalent to those of the indigenous Dutchmen, was not unreasonable. But it seemed most unreasonable to Chamberlain. He and all patriotic Englishmen still bitterly recalled Majuba Hill, when the British army had been put to rout by enthusiastic amateurs. More ill-will had been created when Rhodes and Jameson, representing all that was most admired in Victorian England, made an untimely and disastrous raid into the Transvaal, intending to put the stubborn Boers once and for all time under British rule. But the lion again had its tail twisted as Jameson surrendered 500 men to the Boers, and Sir Alfred Milner was sent as High Commissioner, ostensibly to press for reforms but effectively to impose diplomatically what Britain had failed to achieve by *force majeur*. Krüger remained as unimpressed by Milner as by Rhodes and Jameson.

And yet it was strange, was it not, for a great Empire to go to war on behalf of a handful of rich adventurers? And it was strange, was it not, for the British to believe what the politicians told them?: that the war was a patriotic indeed almost a sacred, struggle for justice and peace. David thought it was strange.

The Kaiser thought it was strange, and the French thought it was strange, and even the Tsar of Russia thought it was strange, but much as they would have liked an excuse to band together to drive the British out of Africa, there was no way they could do so while Britannia arrogantly and unquestionably ruled the waves.

David considered the issues carefully. If he directed his eloquence towards supporting the Government's action, as most of his fellow-Liberals did, he could expect his reputation to be enhanced. If, however, he spoke out for the Boers and against the Uitlanders, many of whom were Jewish (which did not endear them to David), he could expect to be vilified and berated: it was not the lazy way, but it had to be his way. He was sustained by ardent support from William and Uncle Lloyd.

In the corridors of the House of Commons they waited nervously for his return to see which way he would jump. When he told them, the Liberals were aghast, the Tories elated.

'Are you prepared to go and say these things in public to people who will have their sons out there fighting and dying for their country?' they asked him. 'Will you stand up in front of people like that and defend the men who are killing their sons?'

It was the sort of question that might not have been permitted in a court of law, but David did not hesitate to answer.

'I'm prepared to say it anywhere you care to name, to anybody who's prepared to listen, and to go on saying it as long as this lunacy goes on, and if they don't want to hear the truth, so much the worse for them!'

The trouble with proclaiming such principles – if you wish to be Prime Minister – is that it's not enough to proclaim them.

The first test came in Glasgow where, standing beside Keir Hardie, he spoke of what he regarded as the central issues.

'It is not President Krüger we are fighting. It's a poor, little weak state. Shall I tell you exactly *how* small? The total population of the Boer Republic is no greater than the population of Carmarthenshire! And what sort of people are they? They are simple hard-working farmers – very ignorant, it is true. Their only book is the Bible. They may be right or wrong, but they are finer men and godlier men than these Uitlanders we claim to be defending. And what kind of hypocrisy is it to insist on the Boers granting a franchise to these foreigners, which we haven't even given our people here in Britain?'

There were cries of protest at this, but David did not raise his voice. They were listening to him. He was convinced that they only needed to listen to him and they would have to accept the force of his arguments. People usually did.

'No? No. listen! If the Uitlanders wait seven years they will be allowed to vote even for the Upper Chamber, which neither you nor I will ever get the chance of doing! Besides, if you really believe our boys are out there fighting and dying over the issue of the franchise, then you understand very little about the realities of power. It is a question of the diamonds; it is a question of the greed for gold; it is a question of the forty-five per cent dividends.'

This was too much for the Glaswegians, or at least for the patriotic youths drafted into the meeting to raise the temperature of the proceedings. They booed and barracked. They sang the National Anthem and 'Rule Britannia' (painfully out of tune to the ears of a Welshman). They stormed the platform. They threw chairs. They punched heads. They were outraged to discover that their quarry had escaped by a side exit and followed him with sticks. They beat him about the hat (fortunately a good solid one) until he fell unconscious to the ground, which was the one argument that left Lloyd George, at least temporarily, at a loss for words.

Sharp blows to the head do not shake one's faith in the rightness of one's arguments. But David was shattered to learn that young Richard was being mercilessly bullied at his London school for his father's 'treachery'.

'Is it true,' the boy, tears stinging his eyes, asked his mother, 'that Tada wants our side to lose? He doesn't, does he?'

'He thinks the war is wrong.'

The boy considered this. 'But does he have to go around telling everybody? It only makes them angry.'

'If he thinks it's wrong, it's his duty to say to.'

Duty. It was not a word with which Dick was too familiar.

'Mam, have I *got* to go back there?'

'No, Dick, you don't have to. I'm sure Tada won't let you stay another day in that place once he knows.'

The boy sighed with relief, but he could still hear the taunts of the boys, still see the sidelong glances of the masters. 'Why does he do it? Do *you* think he's right, Mam?'

'I *know* he is. It's a wicked war. And it takes a lot of courage to do what he is doing. I have never been so proud of him in my life. And you must be proud of him too.'

Dick tried. He really did. But instead of feeling proud all he could feel was anger that his had to be the father to cause so much trouble.

David enlarged the scope of his attacks. He argued that each lyddite shell which burst on the African hills carried away with it an old age pension. Indeed the sixty million pounds which the war had cost by 11 April, when he addressed a meeting at Bangor, would have been enough to give an old age pension to every old man in the land. He pointed out that the Army was firing bullets which expanded on impact, and that these had been condemned as barbarous by the Hague Conference.

He referred to the appalling conditions in the prisoner of

war camps where infection was rife and the victims had to lie in the rain. He suggested that the great rush to get to Pretoria was politically motivated. 'No one in this House doubts that the lives of the troops have been sacrificed in Natal and and other places to political exigencies,' implying that a General Election would quickly follow the surrender of the Boers. He averred that the only people to benefit from the war were the armaments manufacturers. Kynoch, which supplied the army, had as its chairman the brother of the Colonial Secretary, Joseph Chamberlain. And Hoskins & Co, which supplied the Admiralty, included among its shareholders Mary Endicott Chamberlain, Arthur Neville Chamberlain, and Joseph Austen Chamberlain. He pointed out that the Uitlanders, for whom we were fighting, had raised barely a battalion from amongst their number, and preferred 'to lounge about the hotels of Cape Town grumbling about their losses while English homes are being made desolate on their behalf'. He argued that the war could scarcely be justified as a great Empire imperilling its prestige and squandering its resources to defend the poor helpless blacks, since the Kaffir labourers earned more money and enjoyed more freedom under the supposed tyrant Krüger than under 'the benignant patronage of Mr Cecil Rhodes.'

'It is true,' he said to his constituents, 'that at the end of this war we shall miss millions from our coffers. We shall miss many a gallant name from the roll-call of our warriors. But there is something infinitely more precious that we shall miss and that is the distinction of being the hope and shield of the weak and the oppressed in all lands, which was once the brightest jewel in Britain's glory. No true Liberal would have bartered that for all the gold in the Rand.

'I know that many of you do not agree with me. But it is the first duty of a Member of Parliament to give his constituents honest advice rather than to tell them always what they want to hear.

'Five years ago you handed me a strip of blue paper to give to the Speaker as your accredited representative. If I never again represent these Boroughs in the House of Com-

68

mons I shall at least have the satisfaction of handing back to you that blue paper with no single stain of human blood upon it.'

In London they hated him. He had only to appear on a golf course (his new fancy) for his clubs to be broken and thrown to the ground. But in North Wales his constituents had fallen out of love with the war. And in North Wales David was with his own people and spoke their language, and his fine head and thrilling voice was the most potent argument of all.

In the 'Khaki' election of October 1900 it was therefore no surprise to find that while the Unionists continued in office with a comfortable majority, David was returned by a healthy 296 over his undistinguished Tory opponent, Colonel Platt.

Then followed such scenes as made young Richard, now at school in Porthmadog, glad that he had suffered bullying for being his father's son, for the enthusiasm of the people gathered in front of Caernarvon Town Hall was something to keep bright in the jewel-case of memory.

A torchlight procession made its exuberant way to the Liberal Club and Maggie clutched David's arm and kissed him. They were standing in a brake; David was wearing a white hat, and Maggie could see nothing for her tears. Then at the end of their journey, David raised his arms for silence and said: 'I am more proud of my countrymen tonight than ever before. While England and Scotland are drunk with blood, Wales is marching with a steady step on the road to Liberty and Progress!'

And then the multitudes sang '*Hen Wlad fy Nhadau*' (Land of our fathers). Everyone there believed that the future of the world could be influenced by good men, that David was such a man, and that the world was in safe hands. And then they went quietly home.

However the war dragged on. Time and again the government had to vote itself more money and allot itself more time. There was no reason why the war should end. The Boers had plenty of food, and they captured stores of British ammunition sufficiently regularly to keep themselves supplied. Furthermore guerrilla tactics in their own terrain were extremely difficult to counter. All that the generals could come up with was a scorched earth policy, which had the effect of directing further attention towards the plight of the women and children who had been made homeless. Ironically the purpose for which Britain had ostensibly gone to war had been lost sight of. Instead of enfranchising the Uitlanders, it was now proposed that the population of the Transvaal should be disenfranchised and the territory should become a Crown Colony.

Many thousands of men had been killed, many millions of pounds had been wasted, and the damage to Britain's prestige was incalculable, yet still the war dragged on.

David began to feel that his voice was not loud enough to be heard by all those who ought to hear it. And if the Liberal Party were not prepared to amplify *his* voice by making it *their* voice, he had to find some other way of being heard.

So he bought the *Daily News*. This Liberal newspaper with a strong patriotic bias became overnight a powerful proponent of peace, just as a year previously the *Daily Chronicle* had been captured by the imperialists.

David's friends were most impressed. People who bought newspapers were usually megalomaniacs with more money than sense; David may have been a megalomaniac but there was never any doubt that he had more sense than money. He explained that after hearing that the *Daily News* was in financial trouble he had written 'a rather good letter' to George Cadbury, the philanthropic Quaker, emphasizing all that Cadbury had done for the nonconformists, for temperance and for peace, and asking for £20,000 as a contribution to a syndicate. He had extracted another £20,000 from J. P. Thomasson, and the rest had been plain sailing.

With the columns of the *Daily News* under his control and his continual baiting of Chamberlain in the House it was no longer easy to ignore David's arguments against the brutal and expensive war in South Africa. Probably the only influential person in Britain who managed to was Queen Victoria, and she only managed it by dying.

In April terms for peace which had been provisionally agreed between Kitchener for the British and Botha for the Boers were thrown out by Chamberlain, and in June Campbell-Bannerman, the Liberal leader, distressed by the mortality rate of 17 per cent in Kitchener's concentration camps (50 per cent in one camp), and the pointlessness of continuing a war when there was little left to play for, spoke out for peace, although Asquith remained staunchly behind the generals. And the war dragged on.

David's skill and agility in rhetoric and debate had ensured that he was a sought-after guest in town halls throughout the country. He had the gift of addressing each meeting as though it were the only one, his speech about the war new-minted for the occasion. He would flatter, beguile and seduce his audiences with the same blend of little boy charm and outraged innocence that was so effective when he flattered and beguiled and seduced his women. But there was one city in which he had not preached his gospel of disengagement, and that was the city which had grown fat on the production of armaments, the city which took pride in sending to Parliament Joseph Chamberlain around whose distinguished personage David had been running rings for many months. Not to speak in Birmingham would be to surrender. To speak in Birmingham might very well be to die.

The Birmingham Liberal Association was well aware of the danger. The two local papers had been attacking David venomously, and they gleefully announced the arrival time of the train bringing this unspeakable cad, this most virulent anti-Briton, to town and other provocative details, including the guarantee by the organizers to make good any damage to the Town Hall. Admission was to be by ticket only, but this impediment was removed by wholesale forgeries. A public holiday was declared, barricades were erected, and Alderman Cook, who was to have taken the chair, dropped out after demonstrations outside his house and threats to his family.

When David's carriage arrived outside the town hall at

half-past six, there were 350 policemen facing a crowd of 30,000. So intent were the crowd, many armed with sticks, hammers, knives and stones, upon attacking the police that they quite failed to recognize the determined figure pushing his way to the entrance. By the time the meeting was scheduled to begin a brass band was playing 'Rule Britannia' and so loud was the stamping, whistling, yelling and screaming, and so continuous the noise of knuckle against head and boot against shin, that there was no possibility of the main speaker of the evening making himself heard. Every window in the building was broken, the glass dome fell in, and after David had been narrowly missed by a brick tied round with barbed wire, the police made a truncheon charge from the front of the platform and the Chief Constable escorted the guests into the basement where the wounded were being tended by the St John's Ambulance Brigade. Two men were dead.

Birmingham policemen are sturdy fellows, big in shoulder and thigh, and David was just five feet seven and a half and delicately built. His wrists and ankles were entirely concealed within the policeman's uniform which the Chief Constable insisted he should wear for his escape. The helmet, however was if anything too small. A light in an upper window of the building was switched on as a diversion and David and a squad of policemen made their getaway to Ladywood Police Station. It was snowing. He survived unscathed, and was much admired for his courage, even by those who detested his views on the war.

Chapter Three

Wars end. On 31 May 1902 the Treaty of Vereeniging was signed, which brought the Boer War to an end after more than two and a half years. According to the government there was no way in which the war could be continued; in 1900 Balfour had estimated that there were 17,000 Boers active in the field, and since then Kitchener's despatches had listed 26,000 Boers as having been captured by the British Army, so it was remarkable that the war had lasted as long as it had. Who had won? Only the coffin-makers.

Wars take their toll. David looked older. His face was harsher, the eyes more deeply set, the hair and moustache greying, the cheeks lined. He was almost forty. And Maggie was thirty-six when she gave birth to Megan Arvon.

David burst into the house, his arms full of red carnations in tissue paper. The walk from the station had invigorated him and he felt like hugging the whole family. Mair, whom he loved so much it pained him to think about her, hurled herself into his arms. As he embraced her he felt a surge of jealousy for the man she would one day prefer to himself. Dick, square-faced and serious, looked on biting his lip. When David turned to him the boy's expression was so strange that all David could find to say was: 'How's school going?'

'Very well, thank you.'

'And where's Gwilym and Olwen?'

'Next door with Tadcu.'

'And your mother?'

'She's upstairs,' said the boy, and turned his face away.

Mair still had hold of her father's hand. 'She's bad in bed, Tada,' she said solemnly. 'But everything will be all right now you're home.'

David kicked off his shoes and lay down on the bed next to Maggie.

'Shoes off first, my lad,' she said. She looked her thirty-six years and more; but she seemed content.

'Isn't it a blessing, Dei that it's all over?'

'Did you have a hard time, *hen gariad*?' He stroked her hair.

'I meant the war.'

'Oh that.'

'They can see now you were right,' she said. 'It was all for nothing.'

'It's good to be back,' said David.

'Is it really over? They will get a treaty this time?'

'They already have and a decent one too. But us Maggie? Have we got a treaty?'

'A decent one?' Maggie was smiling at him, but her expression was wary and rueful.

'Can't get comfortable,' said David fidgetting. Then he added, taking her fingers in his: 'You know how I am about women. But there are plenty of husbands worse than me, fair play. Some of them drunkards as well. And Maggie, after fourteen years you must know none of those women means a damn to me, only you.'

'I know that now. I've given up trying to change you.'

'Yes, old love, that was the secret. That was when it started to mend.'

'No, that was only the half of it. You gave up trying to change me, too.'

David laughed aloud at this and the baby stirred in protest. But, being full of milk, she soon was asleep again.

'I don't think Dick's forgiven me; he was very cold when I got back.'

'He'll understand. It's not the war that upset him, Dei, not really. It was us rowing.'

'But we never did, not in front of the boy.'

'He doesn't miss much,' said Maggie, 'but he'll come round.'

He needed a new cause. The bitter dispute between the Bethesda quarrymen demanding a minimum wage of 4s 6d a day and the exclusion of outside contractors, and Lord

74

Penrhyn, the landowner, whose response was to suspend seventy-one of the workforce, had been continuing for some years, but David's suggested radical solution that the state should take over the quarries was several decades ahead of its time. Besides which, what would such a wrangle mean to Liberals in Bootle or Southampton, in Newcastle, Leicester or Slough? When at length David chose, he chose wisely. The Government's Education Bill of 1902 was to be the new battleground, and since the Liberals were outnumbered by the Tories (as the Boers had been by the British), it was vitally important that he learn new techniques, parliamentary trickery, guerrilla and commando tactics, that would leave the Tories and the House of Lords gasping for breath.

First of all it was important to be seen by the troops, so on the first day of the Committee stage he made three separate speeches. Then he studied the Blue Books, as successful generals study the manuals of military strategy, working out a plan of campaign and satisfying himself that he had mastered absolutely the technicalities that the civil servants had drafted into the Bill.

Gradually he became aware that the Bill was a formidable attack on all forms of nonconformist education, on nonconformism itself, and on Wales It would prop up an antiquated system of sectarian education in church schools in which 50 per cent of the pupils were nonconformists, and it would cost ratepayers two million pounds to do so, for the local authorities would be forced to pay for the Church schools whether or not they wished to.

But how to attack it? The Government were determined to see the Bill through, and had a healthy majority in the House to enable them to do so. Even if, by some form of divine intervention, the Government replaced the statutory clauses with voluntary ones, the Upper House in general, and the bishops in particular would never stand for it. *How* to attack it? David pondered.

All through the summer he was good as gold. Present at each stage of the Bill, present for all the debates, he moved helpful little amendments from time to time whenever clarification was needed. The Tories could not believe their good fortune. David was no longer 'demagogic' he was 'statesmanlike'. He had shown himself to be 'an eminent parliamentarian'. Some of the older Tories wondered whether it was golf which was having such a calming effect on the wild man from the hills. Those who saw him and heard him could scarcely believe it was the same man who had ridden his white charger at the head of Cymru Fydd.

He still spoke with delicate irony about the grievances of the Welsh people over their children's education: 'When they want to select a teacher under this Bill, suppose they get three applicants. The first man comes up – first-rate testimonials, splendid experience, first-class certificates. The Board of Managers says: "This is first-rate." Then the parson says: "What are your views on the apostolic succession?" The Teacher says: "I have no views on it," so the parson says "You can go."

'The second man comes up: second-class certificates, second-class testimonials, second-class experience. They say: "That's pretty good." The parson says: "Can you play the organ?" He says: "No, but I can play the cornet." They say: "No, thank you, we don't think that will do." The third man comes up – third-class testimonials, third-class experience, third-class certificates. The parson says: "Can you play the harmonium?" He says: "Yes, like Paderewski." (I'm not sure that is the instrument he plays). However, Paderewski is appointed . . . '

But it was one thing to recognize the grievance and quite another to get it put right. After the summer recess, David continued his gentle amiability. He made speeches on the Bill, ninety of them, and everyone said how wise they were. He moved amendments, twelve of them, and everyone said how relevant they were. But they worried about him in Wales. And then late one night . . .

They lay, those that were left, slumped in their seats, chins deep in their waistcoats, so that they appeared very old, very wise, and in more than one case, very asleep. Their legs, crossed at the ankle, were stretched out in the aisles or on the backs of the benches in front. They nodded, as the debate continued, either to show that they were awake, or occasionally, being unable to help it, because they were asleep. David was speaking in tones so monotonous and flat that one might have thought he was deliberately trying to induce somnolence in those few members who were still manfully trying to follow the argument of this latest in a very long line of amendments, yet why should he wish to do that?

' . . . to propose in the interests of clarity and precision after line ten of this clause of the subsection of the Bill and following the words 'non-provided schools' the addition of the words 'provided it has been kept in a proper state of repair.' This would exclude such buildings which may have fallen into disuse or been superceded by later buildings . . .'

The Amendment was passed, the Bill was passed by the Commons, the Bill was passed by the Lords, and early in 1903 in an address published on his fortieth birthday David explained to the Welsh why the passing of the Education Bill was not the disaster for the nonconformists it had widely been supposed to be and why the county councils should administer the Act as it stood. This was puzzling indeed. How could it not be a disaster if it was administered as it stood? Was Cardiff the capital of Scotland? Was Rugby football a waste of an afternoon? Was water dry?

'I believe', he continued, 'that they (the county councils) should capture the enemy's artillery and turn his own guns against him!'

Now these were stirring phrases, and not too ambiguous 'The enemy' must be England, the bishops and the government, or all three of them in unholy trinity, and the 'artillery' must be the clauses of the Education Bill – so much was clear. But . . .

'In particular, one Amendment which I successfully moved towards the end of the Third Reading. They will find that they are not required by law to take over and subsidize any church school which has not been properly maintained.

'Now, who is to decide whether or not a school has been properly maintained? Why – the council's own surveyors – at least I can find no provision in the Act to the contrary . . . '

Ah yes, now is was clear! For of course none of the schools was perfect. A broken window, an outdoor privy, a pile of rubble on the playground, a defective light fitment, headmasters had *so* much to think about and caretakers too, why it was pathetic to view the state of some of the old places!'

'Hundreds of sectarian schools have not even been treated to a coat of paint or whitewash for many years. It is for the councils to decide whether they are to be allowed to associate on equal terms with more decently-clad institutions.

'Of course the councils may decide to be lenient – I hope they will. They may freely negotiate any agreement to support these decifient schools out of the rates, but I would advise them to do so only on certain conditions, such as (a) that they are given control of the appointment of staff; (b) that they have public control of the funds for these schools; (c) that no religious or political tests be imposed on the appointment of teachers in these schools . . . '

It was prime. It was sublime. They loved him for it. And he thought that the pleasantest thing he had heard for a very long time was the triumphant sound of a whole nation laughing itself silly.

Besides the Education Act one had to keep after the government whenever one could. Chamberlain, so long the victim of David's savage wit, was 'not even worth hissing now'. The Cabinet was like a worm. Cut in two, both ends continued to wriggle 'blindly, I need hardly tell you'. And, as for the Prime Minister: 'Mr Balfour is like a captain who sends a marconigram from mid-ocean to say that a dispute has arisen among the officers as to the destination of the ship . . . that personally he has no opinions on the subject . . . but proposes drifting about until the victuals are exhausted.'

And of course the Licensing Bill, which was very much a landlord's charter, had to be opposed, and Chinese slavery, and an increase in tea duty, and the extravagant rates of railway companies, and this, and that, and the other.

One piece of good news was that his old friend Tim Davies was adopted as prospective Liberal Candidate at

Fulham. He deserved it, mind. But Tim thought that it was all David's doing and became quite embarrassingly grateful about the whole thing. How could he ever repay his distinguished friend? And Mrs Tim giggled secretly at that.

When Kitty and David were alone together – those snatched moments, how precious they had become! – she asked whether Tim would be elected at the forthcoming general election. David assured her that he would.

'Ah!,' she sighed and her bosom was as creamy, her honey-coloured hair as lustrous as ever, 'and what about you?'

'I don't know,' murmered David. His hair had so much grey in it, it made her sad to see it; such a busy man, so little time to relax.

'A seat in the Cabinet, for sure, if they've any sense of gratitude.'

David's throat was hurting him. It was still very sore from a recent operation. He tried to answer her, for there was much he could say on the subject of gratitude in politics, but it was too painful to speak. so he kept silent. Kitty put her head in his lap, and he could touch the glossy hair and admire the fine bosom at the same time – a rare treat, even for such a connoisseur. And she murmured something in Welsh which made him want to laugh – her Welsh always did – and then said that she had given the maid the night off which made him want to laugh all the more, irresistibly in fact, but when he tried to laugh, he could only cough, and when he coughed there was blood all over that honey-coloured hair. that fine, creamy bosom. Blood? Whose blood? His blood! Everywhere!

Within a very few minutes a doctor had diagnosed a throat haemorrhage. The recent operation and the pressure of work had almost done for him.

'Another ten minutes.' said the young Welsh doctor, conscious that he might have been responsible for altering the course of history, 'and he would have been dead. It's a very lucky thing, Mrs Davies, that you fetched me straight away.'

Kitty shuddered and put a hand to her face. The idea was too horrible to contemplate. And then an even more terrifying thought struck her. She raised a horrified hand to her face and muttered: 'Whatever would Maggie have said?'

Rumours of Balfour's imminent resignation reached William and David on a recuperative holiday in Italy. Italy had been very welcoming and very welcome, and at any other time Parliament Square might have seemed grey and bleak and not worth coming home to, but if Balfour went, the Tories would surely be replaced by a Liberal administration under Campbell-Bannerman, in which case David could expect a seat in the Cabinet. Nice for David, of course, but nice for Will too, since as a Cabinet Minister David would at last be earning some real money, and would be able to keep himself in the style to which he had accustomed himself.

So William went home on 2 December 1904 and cabled to David in Rapallo that the rumours were very much more than rumours, and that he must make haste to return. And on 11 December David Lloyd George, backbencher with an overdraft of £400, nonconformist Welsh radical and charmer, dressed in a frock coat, walked through the gates of Buckingham Palace and was presented to the King. When he came out of Buckingham Palace shortly afterwards he did so as President of the Board of Trade with a salary of £2000 per annum. But he was apprehensive. How much simpler it is to call for the goods to be delivered than to deliver them yourself! How much more satisfying to speak your mind from the back benches than to speak the Government's mind from the front bench! How much more natural to crave power than to exercise it! He may have looked impressive to the crowds as he smiled and waved to them in his fine frock coat, but inside it he felt a little foolish, a little inadequate and a little scared.

'I think you should be with him now,' said William to his sister-in-law. 'The way he's been living, well, a Cabinet Minister with buttons off his shirt . . . '

'Not all the year round?' Maggie's fingers curled tightly round a cushion on the sofa, as though by hanging on to the cushion she could hang on to Brynawelon, and her garden, Criccieth, Wales and obscurity.

'Besides he has help now.' And indeed he could afford a housekeeper and a maid at the house near Wandsworth Common which he had recently acquired.

'Well, you should be with him more than you have been. He's got to take things a little easily, and, if he's left to his own devices, you know what he's like. Besides there'll be a lot more entertaining to do now that he's a Minister.'

'I'm not cut out for that sort of thing,' said Maggie hastily. But William was not impressed.

'You'll learn. You can do anything you put your mind to. You learned to campaign and canvas for him – you must have been worth hundreds of votes to him at the last election.'

Maggie's memory was of bleak door-steps and hostile eyes, blank faces and conversations full of silences which she feared would never be filled. Had she really been of use?

'If I am useful to him here, all the more reason to stay. Besides it's nice for him to have somewhere to get away to where he knows he'll be safe.'

Safe. Safe from all those women, whom he didn't really like – she knew that now – except to flatter him a little and make him feel young. Safe with the children, whom he read to each night, regular as clockwork, always in Welsh, with that voice of his so thrilling that *The Three Musketeers* seemed to be clashing their swords in the very ruins of Criccieth Castle, safe to forget all that London cunning, all those hosts and hostesses with their calculating eyes, all the *pretence* and *hypocrisy*.

Mair had been listening quietly. She and William had decided on a two-pronged attack, only one could hardly think of 'prongs' and 'attacks' when one thought of the gentle Mair. Now she said: 'Mam, if we stay here we'll hardly *ever* see him now.'

Maggie sighed. 'All right, *cariad*. We'll go up soon.' If Mair and William both agreed that it was the thing to do, then maybe it was, but London was such a dirty, dangerous place, and Wales was so –

'Uncle Will, what will Tada *do* at the Board of Trade?'

'Well, Mair, he'll have a thousand men working under him, and he'll be responsible for the docks, the mines, the railways, the canals, the shipping and company law.'

Mair was impressed. It all sounded very glamorous and grand, but it just didn't sound a lot like Tada. Said Will: 'He's giving up the law practice to make more time. But he'll have to learn to toe the Cabinet line, which won't come easy to him.'

'No,' said Maggie. 'When Salisbury was in the Board of Trade, Dei was always telling him what he was doing wrong. He enjoyed doing that.'

'What worries me,' said Will, 'is how he manages with the Civil Service. Very set in its ways is the Civil Service; could make things difficult for him, the Civil Service . . . '

The Civil Service was called Sir Francis Hopgood and was tall, blond and elegantly dressed. The Civil Service was also scented, and spoke with all the easy assurance of one born to rule and educated to do so charmingly. Although it did not appear so to David, the Civil Service was also extremely anxious about the new Minister. The Marquis of Salisbury had not been easy to control, but this new man by all accounts ate Englishmen for breakfast. The thing to impress upon him, the Civil Service decided, was the importance of 'the usual procedure'.

At least the Welshman did not look very fierce. He was pallid and quite frail for a man in the prime of life. And his first request – after a comment that the office was big enough to contain the whole of No 3, Routh Road, wherever Routh Road might be – was reasonable enough; he just wished to familiarize himself with the most recent files. One was treading on egg-shells, of course, but so far it was all right.

'Do sit down,' said the Minister, 'I've studied the files. Now, what's the next step would you say?'

'You mentioned that you'd like to be introduced to all your Heads of Departments. I've pencilled that in for tomorrow morning, if that's convenient.'

The Minister raised an eyebrow. 'Here?'

'Why yes, Minister, isn't that what you meant?' Sensing trouble, the Civil Service added placatingly: 'It's the usual procedure.'

There was a pause before David said: 'That's fine for the first meeting. But, as soon as it can be fixed up, I'd like to visit them all in their own Departments. Much easier to judge a man on his own ground.'

'That can be arranged, certainly.'

'Good. Now about those files; what, exactly, is the Board's policy on canals and waterways?'

Canals, thought the Civil Service, that's an odd one. Do they have canals in Wales? Must look that up. The Civil Service said: 'I think you'll find the Department's last Annual Report among the documents I gave you on Tuesday.'

'That's not a policy, Hopgood,' said David, with a trace of asperity, 'that's just a record, and a record of decline, wouldn't you agree?'

'Isn't that inevitable, Minister? With the growth of the railways?'

'May be inevitable. May not. May be desirable. But what we must have in the Department is some sense of *direction* . . .'

'Well yes, that's a valid point,' agreed the Civil Service, still wondering why the Minister kept on about *canals*. 'But the fault does not lie with the permanent officials. Their function is not to formulate policy. To the best of my knowledge, Minister, there is no policy about canals.'

'Then we'll have to get one,' said David quietly, 'won't we? What would your reaction be to a Royal Commission?'

Sir Francis sat up straighter at that. A Royal Commission, oh yes, they were always excellent news. They did all the work and by the time they reported there was another government in power. A Royal Commission on canals? 'An excellent idea. The Department would welcome it.'

'Good. Now, these Consular Reports you gave me are all three months out of date. Why is that?'

Ah. Now that was a trickier one. Nobody had ever thought to raise it before. The Civil Service cleared its throat: 'The

Consular Reports go first to the Foreign Office, Minister, and there's always a certain amount of delay. It's the usual procedure. The fact of the matter is we've never had a very close relationship with the Consular Service.'

'But that's ridiculous!' David leapt out of his seat, and the Civil Service stood up too, respectfully. 'Good God, ninety per cent of Britain's transactions with foreign countries are commercial ones. And yet we've set up these elaborate embassies all over the world at enormous expense, stuffed full of braided ambassadors, envoys and officials, and the only Ministry they deign to communicate with is the Foriegn Office! The very least the FO could do is send along these reports as soon as they get them.'

By now the Minister was pacing around his office as though, thought the Civil Service, he was climbing Snowdon. In which case the Civil Service might as well sit down. It did.

'I did suggest to your predecessor that he should make representations. But it had no effect. The Foreign Office is very conservative in some ways.'

'Is it? Don't worry about the Foreign Office. *I'll* deal with the Foreign Office.'

The Civil Service was impressed. Though it was most unlikely that the FO would permit itself to be 'dealt with', the idea of somebody trying was extremely agreeable. But the Minister was not done with the Consular Reports.

'In any event none of these Reports tells us anything we need to know.'

'I'm afraid consuls are not appointed on the basis of their understanding of commerce.'

'No, just Latin and Greek apparently. *Classical* Latin and Greek. We ought to arrange for every consul on appointment to have a period of training at the Board of Trade.'

'I say, that's a damn good idea!' Pigeons pecking at crumbs outside the window of the office of the President of the Board of Trade looked up sharply at such a display from within. 'Do you think they'll wear it?'

'Oh, they'll wear it. I'll see to that.' Sir Francis permitted himself a smile. His job might actually become *fun*. The

84

Minister had taken up his position in the middle of the huge room and he spread his arms wide: 'You know some people think the only point of putting a silver-tongued orator in charge of a Ministry is so that he'll stand up in the House and put up a brilliant defence of the way things have always been done. But this time they've got the wrong man. My aim is to get things moving.'

Things couldn't move until after the General Election, which resulted, as expected, in a massive movement towards the Liberals. There were over four hundred Liberals and Lib-Labour members in the new parliament, with just 157 Unionists. Even Balfour, after twenty years service in Manchester, was out. David's majority was over twelve hundred in a ballot of some five thousand.

In the new session things did move, but quite quietly, quite peaceably and quite gently. The Department took up so much of his time that he was uncharacteristically tame in the House. He introduced a Merchant Shipping Act and helped the Education Minister with his Bill, which was to put right the anomalies existing under the Balfour Act. There was no opposition to two Patent Bills, and a Companies Act and a Tonnage Act caused no fluttering in dovecotes. A Royal Commission on Wales was set up, but David seemed strangely deaf, considering old days with Cymru Fydd, to the urgent cries for Disestablishment and Home Rule. Wales must take its place in the Government's priorities, he proclaimed, and a more pressing need was to do something about the Tory-dominated House of Lords which would be bound to block any truly radical legislation on Welsh matters. It was only when dealing with the House of Lords that the voice of the old David could be heard, derisive and mordant.

After the Lords had done with the Education Act, he commented: 'This poor Bill left the House of Commons with a good majority to speed it on its way. It has been stripped and wounded and left half dead. I am sorry to say that the priests and Levites did not even pass by; they joined the freebooters . . . The road from the people to the throne must

85

be cleared. It is intolerable that every petition that comes from the people to their sovereign should be waylaid and mutilated in this fashion.'

The King was furious at David's repeated attacks on the Peers. His supporters were relieved that David still had the ability to anger somebody, even if it were only the King.

Nine months after the new President of the Board of Trade took office he had his first opportunity to take decisive action on a major national issue.

There was to be a rail strike. The Amalgamated Society of Railway Servants wanted better pay and shorter hours for its members, but above all it wanted to be recognized by the railway companies. The railway companies were unimpressed and in the traditional manner sacked a few Union officials. After a ballot the Secretary of the Amalgamated Society of Railway Servants, Richard Bell, MP, announced a stoppage; at the last moment David intervened by inviting both parties in the dispute to visit him at the Board of Trade Office.

When Bell arrived David had deserted his desk and the two men sat knee to knee in two armchairs. Bell was furious but it's not easy to remain very angry in an armchair.

'It's not a damn bit of use the Prime Minister complaining to *me* that a rail strike would cripple the country – it's the Companies he wants to talk to. And if they really believe the Union's only got a small section of the railwaymen behind it they've got a bloody big shock coming – and, by God, they've been asking for it! You talk about negotiating? Isn't that what I've been asking for till I'm sick and tired of trying? They wouldn't even meet us. Just laid down the law, take it or leave it . . . If you try to argue you're an agitator, sacked out of hand. And for *years* this has been going on! Well, I'm sorry, Mr George, but it's too late now. We're going to put the fear of God into them this time – it's the only way they'll ever listen to reason. I couldn't hold the men now even if I wanted to. And if you take my advice you'll keep right out of it – it's between them and us, and it's nothing to do with the Government.'

When the director of the LNER came to the Board of Trade office, David was back behind his desk, fingertips together, looking impressively solemn and important. But the director's anger was not to be effaced by the Minister pulling rank.

'I don't mean to be offensive, but I've been in this business for twenty years and I must ask you to give me credit for knowing a *little* bit more about it than a handful of civil servants can swot up in a week. And let me tell you this – if the day ever comes when a private company allows itself to be influenced by threats and bluster from a bunch of hot-headed windbags like Bell and his crowd, that will mean the end of all discipline, the end of any hope of efficient administration, the end of all the commercial principles that have made this country what it is today. We're told that this strike will cripple the country. In the first place, I don't believe there'll *be* a strike – I think they're bluffing. But if it comes, it comes; I would rather face it now, *whatever* the cost, than give in to this kind of blackmail. Because mark my words, this would only be the thin end of the wedge. One last word, Mr George. You call yourself a Liberal. If that means anything, it means you oppose any restraints on the freedom of commercial transactions. I hope you'll bear that in mind, because I think any attempt at ministerial interference in this matter would be a grave mistake and would be deeply resented by everyone concerned . . . '

'Is there *any* measure of agreement between them?' asked the Prime Minister hopelessly.

'Oh yes,' replied the President of the Board of Trade, 'they are both perfectly agreed on one thing.'

'Really? I'm delighted to hear it.' And Campbell-Bannerman sounded just that. 'Is it something you can build on?'

'They are both agreed that they want the government to keep well out of it.'

'Ah, I see. And will we?'

David didn't answer. But he smiled and his eyes twinkled.

Sundays at 3, Routh Road, Wandsworth, were precious days. In his big office, and in the House, David often felt bitterly how he had grown out of touch with Criccieth, with Wales, with Maggie, and with himself. As a Cabinet Minister he could rarely speak his mind. In the Board of Trade, despite his stand for freedom, he felt that he was the slave of the Civil Service, and in the House the young Welsh MPs regarded him now as too grand and even too English to share their friendship. What was he but an administrator and a mouthpiece? What was he doing that others with lesser talents could not do as efficiently? But at home on Sundays when the family gathered around the piano to sing Welsh songs, while Mair's fingers ranged smoothly over the keyboard, and while Maggie squeezed his arm, he felt that he was still Davy of Llanystumdwy, still the boy who had refused to recite the creed and catechism to the Diocesan Inspector, still 'Brutus', fearless observer of the political scene, still one for the girls. Ah, blessed Sundays!

On Sunday, 3 November 1907, while the Amalgamated Society of Railway Servants was holding a mass-meeting in the Albert Hall and announcing the result of the postal ballot, overwhelmingly in favour of strike action, David took Mair to the London Zoo. She had never looked as beautiful as she did that afternoon, her soft hair haloed by a parasol. David scarcely dared glance at her for fear of being dazzled. Whatever else he had done or failed to do, would do or fail to do, no one could deny that he had brought into the world, with Maggie's help of course, a child of grace and beauty. Mair took his arm proudly as they walked between the cages and sometimes when David was recognized, which was not infrequently, she whispered to him: 'You're famous, Tada,' and 'How does it feel to be famous?' and 'Aren't I lucky to have a famous father?'

'I'm the lucky one, Mair *fach*,' David replied, and took her to see the lion which the Emperor of Ethiopia had given King Edward as a birthday present. It was a fine beast, although the President of the Board of Trade confessed that, personally, he would rather have socks.

The following day he had to call on all his guile and tact to meet first the union delegation then the directors.

Sir Francis expressed his nervousness that these negotiations had been left to the very last moment. 'Not the usual procedure,' he said regretfully.

'Works both ways,' said David. 'If you're nervous how do you suppose they're feeling? And you've got the files ready? Good. How long before they're here?'

The Civil Service looked at its watch: 'An hour.'

'Good, so let's use it well.'

By the time the union leaders arrived the office of the Board of Trade had been ransformed. Instead of the imposing desk there were now just chairs round a low circular table. Cigarettes and ash-trays had been provided; cups of tea and biscuits were in readiness.

The railwaymen were bitter and angry. They were also extremely suspicious. David warned them that they were in for a long hard fight. The directors were in a mood of bloody-minded arrogance, and were not willing to give an inch.

'We can stick it out as long as they can,' said one of the railwaymen.

'Well yes,' said David, nodding, 'that's true. But the unfair part is that they can stick it out in comfort. And you've got the winter in front of you. And, of course, if things come to a standstill, there'll be thousands of others thrown out of work besides your own members. I can't help wondering whether the companies haven't deliberately brought this thing to a head in November just to suit their book.'

'Buggers,' said Richard Bell with feeling. One couldn't use such language in the House; it was a pleasure to be amongst one's friends.

'I was talking to the Prime Minister,' said David in the mildest of tones. 'He suggested using the Conciliation Act of 1896.' There were groans, cries and snorts of derision from the railwaymen. 'Yes, I quite agree with you. Dick here knows what *I* think of the Conciliation Act. It was no use to us when I was fighting for the quarrymen against Lord Penrhyn, and it will be no use to us now either. What we need is something really watertight with legal sanctions behind it, something they couldn't wriggle out of.'

'Too late for that now,' said Bell.

'Well, *is* it, though?' asked David. He noticed that one of the railwaymen was picking at his teeth with the tip of a pencil, and tried to suppress a momentary revulsion. 'We've got an overwhelming majority in the House for anything we want to put through. If you could just hold off till Parliament reassembles in January.'

Bell looked at his men. He saw in their eyes what he hoped they saw in his. 'January's no good,' he said. 'The strike is *now*. I can't ask the men to go back just for promises.'

David did not look surprised at this. But he paused a moment, and Sir Francis was impressed at the power of the man to keep a whole room silent while he thought (or appeared to think).

'If – supposing – if the companies agreed to set up permanent boards, consisting of men and management, to consider questions of wages and hours – '

'Set them up when?' Bell interjected.

'Immediately.'

'But they won't bloody talk to us at *all*,' cried a Union man passionately, 'that's what the whole bloody thing's about!'

'Hold on a minute, Tom,' and Richard Bell raised a moderating hand, 'he's obviously got something up his sleeve.'

'I'm going to ask them nicely,' said David, 'and if they don't agree to the setting up of such a board, I shall threaten to run over them with a steam-roller. But it'll not work unless we leave them with some shred of dignity. We mustn't rub their noses in it, Dick, or we stand to lose everything.'

'How many men and how many management?' asked Bell, who was like most good union men in that he felt happiest jotting figures down on paper.

'Fifty-fifty,' said David.

'Including trade unionists? That's essential.'

David said quietly: 'I think we could manage to write that in.'

'Fifty-fifty would probably mean a deadlock. What happens then?'

David turned to Sir Francis who had five files ready to hand.

These were passed to the five railwaymen. Each file had the railwayman's name printed on it.

'Here's the draft agreement, gentlemen,' said David cheerfully. 'Go away and think about it and I'll meet you again at four o'clock.'

When the room was cleared David said to Sir Francis: 'So much for the union conference, now for the board meeting. What we need is a well-polished boardroom table – oak, would you think? And a set of solid straight-backed chairs, blotters, glasses of water. Can you organize that?'

'Surely, Minister, but where will you be?'

'Changing into my pin-stripes, of course. Oh, and Francis, do you suppose you could get me some first-rate Cuban cigars? There's a great deal at stake.'

The directors of the railway companies were much relieved when they saw the President of the Board of Trade and smelt the smoke from his cigar. It seemed likely that they would be talking the same language. They took their places at the long table, therefore, in a mood of quiet optimism. But David's voice was grave.

'Gentlemen, I am sorry to have to report that I have made practically no headway. Bell in particular is in a very intransigent mood. I can only assume that that tremendous show of solidarity at the Albert Hall has gone to his head. They've really got the bit between their teeth now, and they seem to be quite reckless of the consequences.'

This news was received with great gloom by the railways. However, as the Great Western put it: 'I suppose it's no more than we were prepared for.'

David shot his cuffs and said: 'Anyone with the interests of Britain at heart must regard this as a major tragedy.' There were murmurs of 'hear, hear', and the London and North Eastern went so far as to bang the table with the flat of his hand. David continued: 'I've had some slight experience of running a syndicate and I can appreciate the damage this is going to do to the morale of your shareholders. And it's not only the railways. For hundreds of small private business enterprises up and down the country this will mean total ruin.'

There was much murmuring and shaking of heads at this, and somebody even suggested that a foreign power must be behind it all. The London and North Eastern spoke for everyone when he announced: 'We can't give way now.'

The President of the Board of Trade said that he appreciated their position, but pointed out that with the strike timed for November, when demand for coal and other supplies was at its peak, it would wreak the greatest possible havoc on production, and result in a substantial drop in revenue for the companies. Obviously Bell knew what he was doing when he timed the strike so mischievously.

The South Eastern Railway took his cigar out of his mouth and said: 'Hooligans!' quietly, then replaced the cigar.

David said: 'I've been discussing the position with the Prime Minister and he feels, quite understandably, that if this strike goes ahead the country will demand very drastic action to ensure that it can never occur again.'

'Lock up the ringleaders,' cried the LNER. 'That's the thing to do!'

'But we all know that the radical wing of the Party would never stand for that. No, the plan is to introduce a very strong measure of compulsory arbitration throughout the whole range of industry.'

'But he can't do that!' cried the Great Western Railway in the tone of voice of a schoolboy who has been told he must stay in over a holiday.

David said gently: 'We can hardly allow the electorate to feel that the country is lapsing into anarchy while the government does nothing about it.' The gentle voice became a little steely as he continued: 'The PM has given me a firm undertaking that if necessary he will introduce such a Bill as soon as Parliament reassembles in January.'

The railways began to look at each other's faces for outward signs of the outrage that each of them inwardly felt. One could not believe that the Welshman was serious. The LNER summed it up best when he said: 'Do you imagine for one minute that British industrialists would be prepared to lie down and accept government intervention on a scale like that?'

'Oh come now, gentleman, we've all agreed on the importance of discipline. Is it not a bit inconsistent to demand discipline from the workers and then threaten to revolt against the superior authority of a democratically elected government? If, on the other hand, the strike could be averted by a voluntary move on your part the necessity might not arise.'

'Well, we're not going to recognize the union,' insisted the GWR, 'so you can forget about that.'

'Suppose they would agree to go back without that . . . '

'They'll never do it!' cried the Great Western, and one might almost have imagined him bursting into tears of frustration. 'That's what the strike's all about!'

The LNER remained cool. 'Just a moment. What's the proposal?'

David tapped the ash off the end of his cigar, and looked into the faces of each of the men at the table. They were not the sort of faces used to conciliation, concession or compromise. However . . . 'I think it's clear to all of us by now that sooner or later talks on pay and conditions will have to be held. Now, if – *if* – I could persuade the railwaymen to agree that talks would not be with union officials as such, but merely with groups of your own employees on a fifty-fifty basis from which union members, or indeed union officials could not be excluded as individuals, but would not be present ex officio . . . ' There were clearings of throats and other small symptoms of powerful men at war with themselves. David put together a most successful smile which warmed the whole room and continued: 'I know you are all responsible men with the interests of the country at heart. And we have to be realistic, and recognize that Bell can't ask his men to go back unless he can offer them some kind of face-saver. So perhaps you'd like to examine this draft agreement at your leisure and come back at six o'clock with your comments.'

The rest was routine. The permanent boards of men and management could refer any deadlock to a central conciliation committee and ultimately to an independent arbitrator agreeable to both sides. Both union and management felt that they had achieved something permanent without any loss of face, (which David had recognized to be the most important issue in such disputes) and the President of the Board of Trade found himself the most admired man in the country. Even the King was impressed.

The gods give with one hand, take away with the other. For many years David was to wonder whether he had paid for this substantial triumph with the life of his beloved daughter. Mair returend from school feeling unwell, and five days later died from peritonitis.

David refused to return to Routh Road, refused to see Maggie, refused to see the children. He would neither eat nor sleep. Only William Clark, his secretary, remained with him. David thought of the years when Mair had been growing up in Criccieth and he had been living alone in London. Why had he not been with her? The years had passed so fast, but he had always promised himself he would spend time with Mair, get to know her, explain the world to her – for there was so much to explain. Only recently she had been playing in a concert and had invited him along, but he was fighting for a clause in the Shipping Bill and had said: 'I'll come to the next one, *cariad*,' but would he have come? Or would he have found some other clause of some other Bill? What did clauses matter? What did Bills matter? The whole country could go hang, if only he could have another chance to see her, to talk to her, to tell her . . . He had had so little of her. She had had so little of life.

He refused to go to Maggie. And when Will visited him and spoke of Maggie's quiet courage and patience in adversity, he inveighed against Maggie in intemperate language. And when Will spoke of putting his trust in God, he spoke as violently of God as he had of Maggie. He claimed that Maggie had stolen Mair from him while she was alive and that God had compounded the theft. Then he cursed himself for bringing her to London. His grief was so noisy that it sometimes seemed like a parade of grief, an actor's grief, and he was aware that this was how it must seem, but could find no comfort.

At times he felt that life without Mair was insupportable, and those near him feared for his sanity; at other times he could feel nothing, and regarded himself as a monster. Then he would tug at his hair until the pain brought tears, and would pretend that he was weeping for his daughter.

He left all the arrangements to Maggie, instructing her to sell the house in Routh Road, but after the funeral he accused Maggie of having her buried in 'a pauper's grave'.

'Why not in the family vault? Was she not good enough to go in it?'

Maggie, much distressed, could only stammer that, left to make the arrangements she had done the best she could. But every word she uttered enraged David more. He insisted that the grave should be re-opened, the coffin exhumed, and Mair put where she properly belonged, with a monument which would bear her last words ('He is just, and merciful . . . tell them . . . ') carved upon it.

And then he felt suddenly humiliated and clasped Maggie in his arms and begged forgiveness. It was proposed that he should take a holiday, and he went to stay in Lady Nunburnholme's house in Nice with his two sons. But it wouldn't have mattered where he had gone; atheism, nihilism, and self-detestation would have accompanied him. One night Mair appeared to him when he was asleep. She told him that his excesses were distressing her and begged him not to be so grieved. This marked the beginning of his rehabilitation He enjoyed the sun. He played a few rounds of golf. He took an interest in political matters. And in due course he came home, to a new house in Cheyne Place, and to a wife whose grief was scarcely less poignant than his, though you might not have believed it to look at her. David refused to believe it.

He found her complacent. He could never forgive her for having had so much of Mair. He could never forgive her.

Prime Ministers, once they realize that they too are going to have to die, often see some political advantage to be gained from dying in office. Political opponents always speak highly about one on such occasions, and the press, in particular, like no politician so much as a dead or dying politician. Sir Henry Campbell-Bannerman had had two heart attacks in November and while these had weakened his heart they had strengthened his resolve to stay in office. But by the end of February Sir Henry's health was declining so fast that the arguments for going were irrefutable. Asquith, whom David had described in the early 1890s as 'the hope of the rising generation of Radicals', was next in line, and had pledged himself to making no very substantial changes in the Cabinet for a while. But Asquith was Chancellor of the Exchequer, and, unless he was prepared to take on dual responsibility himself, something which only Gladstone had tried previously and without much success, there would have to be a new Chancellor. For a while that 'unless' looked very formidable to David, who had his heart set on the Treasury, for word went round that Asquith would *not* be moving over; but wiser counsels prevailed. The younger man had staked his career on the cause of the Boers, and had been justified. He had gambled his reputation on settling the railway strike and he had settled it. If he kept winning he had to be paid sooner or later. So Asquith paid him with the Treasury, vowing him to secrecy until the proper time came for an announcement to be made. David's excitement was great, but what use was such wonderful news if one couldn't tell anybody? He told Maggie, who said that it was only what he deserved, and was it going to mean another move, because she had taken such pains with Cheyne Place? But telling Maggie was unsatisfactory. She said none of the right things, seemed unaware of the great compliment paid him, of the power he would now enjoy, and of the implications for the future. She seemed only concerned with carpets and curtains and pantechnicons. What was the colour of the Downing Street walls? David was exasperated. So, begging him to keep the news to himself, he told the editor of the *Daily Chronicle*, who said all the right things, but then went ahead and printed the details, to Asquith's disgust. David was distressed that his tenure of office had started so discreditably and wrote to Asquith thus:

'Winston told me last night that some of my colleagues had rushed to you immediately on your arrival with the amiable suggestion that I had been responsible for the *Chronicle* list. I need hardly tell you that I feel very hurt at the accusation and I think I ought to know who it is among my colleagues who deems me capable of what is not merely a gross indiscretion but a downright and discreditable breach of trust.' As David wrote these words, he persuaded himself of their truth and worked himself up into a state of high indignation. It is a most useful gift in a politician to be able to disregard the facts and believe one's own instincts: David did so naturally.

Now at last he could institute some of the reforms he had berated others for disregarding. He would get money for the elderly through an Old Age Pensions Bill, he would make a grab for the wealth of the landlords, he would work for temperance reform, and he would get money if he could from the Army and Naval Estimates. And when it came to the Budget . . .

How pleasant it was to be able to exercise power, and how pleasant to be seen to be powerful. Women, who had rarely ignored him, now gravitated to him, and he sat to Sir Luke Fildes, RA, for a portrait commissioned by the Law Society. Sir Luke was a man of parts, and, as ill luck would have it, one of his parts was an interest in the Graphic Company which published the *Bystander*.

Thus it was that while Sir Luke was painting David the *Bystander* printed a rumour, take up by the *People*, that the Chancellor had been rather indiscreet in his personal affairs and had paid £20,000 to avoid being cited in a divorce case. It also suggested that he and 'a certain colleague' (Churchill) had been 'having a most uncomfortable time of it politically, as a result of certain queer intrigues conducted . . . in connection with a proposed reduction of army and navy expenditure.'

That much was true. Though they had failed to get any reduction in Haldane's Army Estimates, Churchill and the Chancellor had fought ferociously and slyly against the building of any more dreadnoughts. Four hundred million pounds were being spent each year on weapons of destruction, and David had had to call on all his reserves of political cunning to get his Old Age Pensions Bill, which would cost a mere six million a year, through all its stages. McKenna's original estimate of six dreadnoughts in the year was reduced to four, but with the proviso that a further four dreadnoughts could be built later should the international situation require it. Bitterly David reflected on how his well-intentioned intervention had resulted in a $33\frac{1}{3}$ per cent *increase* in the Naval Estimates. It was tough at the top. The Labour men argued that David's Old Age Pensions Bill was mean and pusillanimous. The men from the services put their hands in the till when no one was looking. And every cheap newspaper journalist . . . He was not going to stand for it.

'It's all lies, Maggie,' he told her again and again.

'Is it? *Is* it? How do I know it's lies?'

'Good God, because I'm telling you. Do you imagine for a moment that a man in my position could afford to risk getting mixed up in a thing like this? Co-respondent in a murky little divorce case? They don't even name names. What kind of a fool do you think I am?'

'I've lived with you, Dei, for twenty years. I know only too well what kind of a fool you are. Not that I care about the women – not the way I used to anyway. When I hear the way you talk about them afterwards I even feel sorry for them sometimes. Anyway, why would they publish it if there is no truth in it?'

'Malice, Maggie. Just what you'd expect from the Tory press. Why doesn't the man come forward if he's going to cite me?'

'Because he was paid not to.'

'Oh Maggie, where in heaven's name would I get twenty thousand pounds?'

'I don't know how much it was, nor where it came from. I know when the party offered you money to tide us over with expenses you wouldn't take it. Too proud. Yet in things like this you've no pride, no foresight, no self-control, no respect for yourself or me. They wouldn't write filth about you if you didn't give them filth to write about. God knows I try never to think about it because whenever I do – you *disgust* me.'

'You can be a very hard woman sometimes, Maggie.'

'It's not me that's hard – it's the truth you don't like hearing, and these days I'm the only one you hear it from. But I don't have to stay, Dei, I can go back home and leave you with your toadies and your climbers, your rich hostesses and your loose women, to wallow in their lies and their flattery and swallow it all whole. And God help you, Dei, because by the time they've finished there'll be nothing left of you but a political machine with a gift of the gab.'

'Maggie, I'm suing them for libel, and I can win. But even if I do, everybody is bound to believe the rumours unless you're with me in court. And I'd be finished this time, finished and done for!'

'You should have thought of that sooner.'

'Please, Maggie. I've got the biggest fight of my life on my hands with this Budget. But if you don't stand by me, it'll all be wrecked. Whatever you feel about me, you used to believe in the things I'm fighting for.'

'Oh not *that* one again! If it were for the country or for the Cause you'd keep out of these messes.'

'*Please*, Maggie. Please.'

'You're asking me to go into court and tell lies. I can't do that. I *can't*.'

'No, Maggie, you'll not be called. Just be with me, sit beside me, that'll be enough. I know I've been a bloody fool, but this time I've learned my lesson, believe me. If I get out of this I give you my Bible oath it'll never happen again, never, never.'

'But you're going to give your oath in court and swear that there was nothing in it. So what is the value of any oath you swear to me?'

'All right, if you want to destroy me. I suppose it's no more than I deserve. You do as you please. Only remember one thing: I love you, Maggie. You know I have never loved anyone but you. Whatever happens, whatever you do to me, nothing will ever alter that.'

And so, since Maggie loved David more than she hated him, she attended the court, and listened to him taking the oath and giving his evidence, and, whether or not she was convinced by it, the court certainly was, for they found in his favour and awarded him three hundred guineas against the Graphic Company, a sum which was passed on to the Caernarvon Cottage Hospital. The *People* settled out of court, a little rashly perhaps, for it was obliged to pay a thousand pounds, which helped to build a Village Institute in Llanystumdwy. David had got away with it again!

His first Budget often seemed to David to have become a vast and treacly lake in which he had been swimming for so long that he could not remember what the pure air felt like. He had spent six months preparing it, clause by revolutionary clause. He had spent six weeks defending it in front of his Cabinet colleagues. And he had spent three days and three nights putting the final gloss on what promised to be the most important speech he had ever made in his life.

In the event it was the worst speech he had ever made in his life, some said the worst ever heard in the House of Commons – the sort of claim which would need some substantiation! He started speaking at three o'clock, and by five his voice was quite gone. The House was adjourned for a half-hour, and then continued until eight. It was as though all David's energies had been consumed in the battle and none was left for the victory parade. The Budget deficit was rather over sixteen millions, nearly ten millions of which were those blessed Army and Navy Estimates, and six millions the Old Age Pension. How to cover it? An increase in income tax, the introduction of supertax, death duties, estate duties and stamp duties would provide seven million. Higher licences for publicans, more land taxes, increases on spirits and tobacco would do the rest. Such proposals in the name of the government – remarkable! In all, the Budget was six times larger than any previous Budget in the history of the nation.

Uncle Richard was a proud old man and remarked: 'Well, my boy, these are stirring times!' to his nephew.

'If they want to meet the real author of the Budget,' said David, raising his voice a little for his uncle had grown rather hard of hearing, 'they must come to Criccieth and look for a man called Richard Lloyd.'

And they did want to meet the author of the Budget. The Duke of Beaufort went so far as to remark that 'he would like to see Winston Churchill and Lloyd George in the middle of twenty couple of foxhounds'. The Duke of Somerset threatened to sack all his estate hands, and the Duke of Buccleuch cancelled his annual subscription of a guinea to the Dumfriesshire Football Club, because he was convinced that the Budget was speeding him into a pauper's grave.

The fury of the aristocrats, which was especially virulent in the matter of the land taxes, was not unexpected. But what was a pleasant surprise to David, and something without which he could never have introduced this 'People's Budget', was the loyal support of Asquith, his chief. For Asquith liked nothing better than a weekend house party in the company of the rich and inter-bred; after such a Budget he could no longer expect to be as welcome as hitherto, but he never flinched.

For months David seldom ventured beyond Westminster, guiding his Budget through perilous seas, dotted with over five hundred divisions, on the rocks of any one of which his vulnerable barque might have damaged its fabric. Beyond Westminster he had expected it to be popular and it had been popular, except with dukes; and although the publicans complained that they would be ruined few others thought so for brewery shares moved up. When at length he felt free to leave Parliament, David addressed a public meeting at Limehouse, and not only had his throat improved, but so had his spirit. He was back on form.

'We are placing the burdens on the broadest shoulders,' he announced, and it sounded more like boasting than justification. 'Why should I put burdens on the people? I am a child of the people. I was brought up among them. I know their trials; and God forbid that I should add one grain of trouble to the anxieties which they bear with such patience and fortitude. When the Prime Minister did me the honour of inviting me to take charge of the National Exchequer at a time of great difficulty, I made up my mind, in framing the Budget which was in front of me, that at any rate no cupboard should be barer, no lot should be harder. By that test I challenge you to judge the Budget.'

Wherever in the country the Budget was hated, it was hated more passionately in the House of Lords. And the House of Lords was in the unique position of being able to channel that hatred by rejecting the Finance Bill when the time came to vote upon it. This was something the House of Lords *never* did. but it became increasingly possible that on this occasion they just might. To David it seemed no bad thing that they should, for if they dared to take this revolutionary constitutional step it would mean a General Election, and one fought chiefly on whether or not the power of the Upper Chamber should be curtailed. Well, why not? Speaking at Newcastle David pointed out that a fully equipped duke cost as much to keep as two dreadnoughts, was just as great a terror and lasted longer.

'Of course,' he continued as the laughter subsided, 'if they want a revolution they will get it. The Lords may decree a revolution, but the people will direct it! Issues will be raised that they little dream of. The question will be asked whether five hundred men, ordinary men chosen accidentally from among the – unemployed –' (much merriment at this) 'should override the judgement of millions of people engaged in the industry which makes the wealth of the country. They have threatened and menaced like this before, but in good time they have always seen that it is not to their interest to carry out their futile menaces. I do not believe in their threats.'

If David meant what he said, he was unusually credulous. For he should have known that a peer fighting to protect his land would not give in readily. For every three members of the House of Lords who gave their support to David's monumental Budget, there were fourteen who voted against. The Finance Bill was thrown out.

Now the real battle could begin!

Chapter Four

The expressions on the faces of most of those gathered in the Cabinet Room on St Andrew's Day 1910 had been carefully composed for the occasion. A big constitutional crisis required a rather special sort of face, and the faces of the members of the Cabinet were suitably awestruck. Only on the Chancellor's face could be observed a sort of unholy glee, the face of a schoolboy who has planned a very special kind of mischief, and sees everything going nicely to plan. Once at the Llanystumdwy National School there had been a similar expression on his face. Those who knew him best, feared it most.

Asquith, who was presiding, was righteously angry. The game called Democracy could only work if the rules remained unchanged, but the Lords had changed them radically and unfairly. When one expected to go up a ladder, it was more than a little frustrating to find it suddenly transformed into a snake. But what to do? Asquith had no doubt.

'I must simply ask the House to pass a resolution condemning the action of the Lords as a breach of the Constitution and a usurpation of the rights of the Commons.'

'And then?' asked the Foreign Secretary, Sir Edward Grey.

'Adjourn immediately. And tender my resignation – no government can carry on in these circumstances – and ask the King to prorogue Parliament.'

'There's no question of his not agreeing to that?'

Asquith shook his head. 'He could send for Balfour, but what good would that do?'

Smiling wryly at the irony of the situation Churchill said: 'The Tories would be more hamstrung than we are. Maybe we can't get our Budget past the Lords, but *they* couldn't get one past the Commons! It's deadlock.'

David rubbed his hands together and said cheerfully: 'Well, it seems to me the Lords have done for themselves now. We'll never have such a chance again. There's only one thing to do, and we all know what that is. Either the Lords toe the line, or the King will have to create five hundred new Liberal peers, if that will be enough to outvote the present gang.'

David's eyes lit up as he thought of all those lovely new Liberal lords and how eagerly they would vote for Home Rule for Wales and Disestablishment. Oh, if they could only carry both houses!

'Have to, George?' asked Morley, the man who had been tipped to succeed Asquith at the Treasury, but who had deferred to David. The mention of the King had depressed the gathering somewhat, although not the Chancellor, who would have been happy to have licked the Lords before breakfast and dealt with the King before lunch.

Asquith said: 'He is very reluctant to get publicly involved. I have given my word to make every possible effort to keep him out of it.'

'Every possible effort – *short of surrender*. I hope that's been made clear?'

Asquith was too much of a gentleman to conceive of 'making things clear' to a king. So diplomatically he explained: 'The position I am taking is that even if re-elected we shall not assume office unless we can secure the safeguards necessary for carrying out our mandate.'

David was content with that. He could not imagine that after his Budget, which was effectively *their* Budget, the people would withold their support. Even the Tory press accepted that the government's popularity was high.

'Well, we must wait and see,' said Asquith, and sighed. It seemed an unnecessarily gloomy sigh to David. 'There's not much more we can decide till after the election.'

Not everything could be left in abeyance. Some of the taxes due under the new Budget had already been collected, but since the Finance Bill had been rejected the Treasury had had no legal right to ask for them. If required to, the Treasury would have to refund all that had been paid to them. If the people should realize the implications of the

105

situation, they could throw their tax returns on the fire, and nobody could touch them for it.

The possibility of such anarchy gave the Cabinet more to worry about. The Foreign Secretary said that the answer was to rush through a new Finance Bill at the start of the next session. If the controversial clauses were omitted there would be no opposition from the Lords. David would not hear of this; to pass the power back to the enemy – unthinkable!

Churchill's answer to the problem was bold, if unsubtle. Collect the taxes and to hell with the law. The British constitution required that the Commons controlled the state's finances, and if the law got in the way, then the law must be elbowed out of the way. This suggestion was received with delight by the radical wing, but the lawyers puffed themselves up and said that it would never do. David found himself uncharacteristically cautious. If they were to take on the monarch and the House of Lords, perhaps the judiciary should wait its turn. His proposal was to treat the rejection as simply what it was – a tiresome little temporary hitch. The tax returns could be issued on a voluntary basis, and the Treasury could make up the deficit by borrowing. The taxpayer would be given an option: pay voluntarily now or compulsorily later.

This was all very well, as David's old enemy, the First Lord of the Admiralty, pointed out, so long as the Budget went through. David was loved and trusted in the country – except in Birmingham! – disliked and distrusted in the Cabinet Room. And in Number 11, Downing Street? Well, there they were used to him!

It was a Welsh Embassy. Sarah Jones, cook, housekeeper and defender of the faith, presided over the domestic arrangements, leaving Maggie free to return to Criccieth and her garden. There were several maids, all of whom spoke Welsh, and little Megan, now eight, who revelled in having Tada living over the shop. Her glowing face and bonny smile could always seduce him away from those dusty old papers and into an impromptu song or a tale of magic and devilment more fantastic even than what was taking place in the House of Commons. She ruled the place like the dictator of some banana republic.

Uncle Lloyd was in Criccieth, of course, enjoying the reflected glory of his nephew's career, and Will was busy with the firm, while Pollie, poor Pollie, was nowhere to be seen, for, while David had been fighting for his Budget, she had been fighting for her life. Clauses could be amended, Bills could be redrafted but nothing could be done about the cancer, and Pollie submitted, and went quietly, and David paused for a moment when he heard the news, and wondered whether such things as land taxes and dreadnoughts and publicans' licences really mattered. But there were plenty to argue that they did, and it was too late to help Pollie now, so he went back to his committees and cabals and coffees, but with a heavy heart.

As always, it was Megan who lightened it. David's morbid conviction that he had neglected Mair until it was too late made him all the more passionately devoted to the baby of the family. By now Richard was at Cambridge, Olwen at Roedean and Gwilym at Eastbourne College, so Megan was all the more precious. And if she were a little spoiled, well, it was only natural with her famous Tada encouraging her to make all his important friends smile at her songs and dances. And when they were alone together Megan sat by him on the settee and asked him to explain why it was that there had to be an election, and why the House of Lords was called Mr Balfour's poodle, and whether he was going to get his Budget through after the election and lots of other nonsensical questions.

To King Edward VII the crisis was a beastly nuisance. When you're feeling a little dyspeptic and your gout is troubling you, the last thing you need is a Prime Minister demanding your active participation in something which Parliament should have been perfectly able to handle by itself.

'I don't like it at all,' the King complained. 'I don't like any of it.'

Asquith tried hard to keep the irritation out of his voice as he explained: 'But, Your Majesty, I understand it was an agreed thing, that in the last resort if we were re-elected, I could count on your backing.'

The King frowned and wagged a finger: 'I'm not convinced you've reached the "last resort" yet, or have come anywhere near it. Good heavens, all it neads is a bit of give and take! We've come to a pretty pass if two English political parties in the twentieth century can't resolve their differences without dragging the Crown into their squabbles. You're asking me to make a fool of myself, turning out peers by the hundreds, like a baker turning out buns. It would reduce the Upper House to a laughing stock. Besides, the place would never hold them all.'

Asquith tried to explain how the threat would be quite enough to make the Lords capitulate, especially if it came directly from His Majesty. His Majesty considered that and was unimpressed. He grunted and said:

'I'm not so sure. *I* never thought they'd be pig headed enough to throw out the Budget. I urged them not to – I suppose you realize that? No effect at all. Like talking to a stable full of horses. I blame Lloyd George: he goads them into it. Language like a guttersnipe. No wonder their hackles rise.' Asquith started to defend his Chancellor, but the King would have none of it. 'Don't pretend you approve of the speeches he makes, because I shan't believe you, and it will only make me cross. Now where were we? You're fighting this election on the issue of Lloyd George's Budget, that's so, is it not?'

'Yes, Your Majesty.'

'Let us suppose you win. Just because the people voted for the Budget, it does not follow that they would support an attack on the House of Lords. For that, you would need another election.'

'Your Majesty is asking for *two* elections.'

The King sighed. 'I am asking you to produce an unmistakable mandate.'

The Prime Minister felt that there was something to be said for a republic. He had always believed that the monarchy was a force for consistent and stable government in Britain, but there were times . . . 'Am I at liberty to say, if pressed for an answer, that given such a mandate . . . '

'You are at liberty to say, Mr Asquith, that I have given no undertaking whatsoever. I prefer to be left out of this. And we shall see what develops.'

'If you leave me so weaponless, one development might be that the Liberal Party would seek more aggressive leadership.'

At this the King sat suddenly upright and his muddy complexion took on the shade of a beetroot that has just been cut open.

'You don't mean a Lloyd George government?' he gasped. He had begun to gulp in great mouthfuls of air and was weakly massaging his chest with a flaccid hand. Asquith was much alarmed and came quickly to his monarch's side, but the King, leaning back and closing his eyes, seemed to be recovering. His voice was so faint, however, that Asquith could only just make out the words: 'You'd better go. But remember, no undertaking.'

The election of 1910 taught David a tough truth of British political life. No matter how much you put yourself out to help the working man, the working man is never as grateful as you expect him to be. David had been cheered so long and so loud at the end of his public meetings that he had supposed it was his policies and his Budget which were being cheered, instead of his oratory and charisma. The heady majority which the Liberals had enjoyed so gleefully since 1906 now appeared so thin that the merest gust of political wind might blow it away. Indeed without the support of the Irish Nationalists and Labour Members – or a decent majority of them – the government would have been unable to continue in office.

After the early results had been declared Asquith had been ready to accept defeat. Virtually all southern England had gone over to the Tories, who had also won all the marginal seats in Yorkshire. But later results from Wales and Scotland indicated that David's Budget had won some friends among the Celts. The Liberals could expect to continue in office for a while; but without the support of the Irish members there was little chance of getting the Budget proposals through the Commons, and without the support of the King and his willingness to create a large number of new Liberal peers, little chance of getting them through the Lords. Initially one had to have some sort of deal with the Irish Party, but the Irish Nationals, determined on an early Home Rule Bill, were not the easiest people to deal with.

Still, an attempt had to be made, and David and the Chief Whip, Alexander Murray, the Master of Elibank, left a Wimbourne House reception early – far too early for David, since his philandering reputation and political buccaneering had made him almost irresistible to a large number of bored, upper-class ladies – and made for a dingy rooming-house above a pub near Victoria Station. This was where John Redmond, leading Irish Nationalist MP, lived, and David looked about him in surprise and something approaching nostalgia for his own squalid but unencumbered days as a back-bencher. With Redmond was John Dillon, another Irish member, and they made their position very plain.

The Nationalists wanted Home Rule and they wanted it soon. Also they were not over-keen on the whisky duty. The Liberals wanted to get the Budget through the House without too many mutilations and they also wanted to curb the House of Lords by depriving them of their veto. Was an accommodation possible?

The problem was the sequence of events. If the Irish members were to help the government get its Budget through, the emasculation of the House of Lords would follow shortly, and the final barrier to Irish Home Rule would be removed. That was David's proposal, and he was prepared to manage without the whisky duty.

But Redmond had a nasty, suspicious mind, or so he said; he wondered what guarantees there could be that the Liberals, having passed their Budget, would not absent mindedly forget to do anything about the Lords. And Dillon, who had a cynical view of political deals, or so he said, made the counter-proposal that the Lords' veto should be disposed of first and then the Budget could be seen to.

David's frustration was very evident as he said: 'But it won't work that way round! We must pass the Budget first to prove we're capable of governing. And only then can we put the fear of God into the Lords from a position of *strength*.'

'But we can only put the fear of God into you when you're in a position of weakness,' replied Dillon with a wry smile. 'Like now.'

The Chancellor and the Chief Whip exchanged a few private words, and then David concluded sadly:

'It can't be done. It simply can't be done.'

A couple of weeks later David offered the Nationalists a compromise. The Budget could be taken between the First and Second readings of the Veto Bill. But Redmond was unyielding. At the end of March the government introduced three revolutionary proposals: that the Lords should have no power to control financial legislation, that their veto should be no more than an impotent symbol of dissent, and that the life of a Parliament should never exceed five years. These were debated and passed on the understanding that if the Lords threw out this Parliament Bill, and the King still refused to create enough new peers to get it through, the government would go to the country for a new and more effective mandate.

This was enough for the Nationalists, who were now prepared to support the Budget, and support it they did.

Indeed, since the alternative would have been to let the Tories in and throw away all hope of Home Rule in the near future, the only wonder was it had taken them so long. No sooner had the Budget received the Royal Assent than the King died, mortified perhaps at betraying his class by assenting to such inflammatory stuff and still undecided as to whether or not he ought to create a bundle of new peers.

Since he had not had to live to see a Lloyd George government, it might have been regarded as a merciful release. But it was certainly a constitutional embarrassment.

Meanwhile William had got himself engaged. David felt a twinge of jealousy. Anita Williams was not very young, but she was intelligent and attractive, and David was a little tired of silly women who couldn't control their emotions and cunning women who wouldn't control their tongues. So he congratulated his brother warmly, perhaps over-warmly, on his good fortune, which was good fortune for Uncle Lloyd too since Anita was a qualified nurse, indeed a matron. Then in a burst of fraternal good-will David offered to help with the wedding expenses, an offer which William politely turned down. Will had been financially independent – and David dependent – for so long that he regarded it as an immutable law of nature. There were those who earned money and there were those who spent it. Will had always been an earner. David, who used to spend what Will earned, now spent the nation's money instead.

'I'll tell you what, though,' said David, bursting with generosity, 'if you've got any cash to spare I could pass on a very good tip I got from Rufus Isaacs. Marconi shares, Will! I made a nice little packet last month and I'm thinking of buying more.'

'No, I don't think so,' said Will startled.

'In your mind I'll never live down those Patagonian gold mines.'

'It's not that, Dei. It's just – and I'm sure you know what you're doing – the stock market's not my style. Thank you all the same.'

'That's fair enough, William.' said David, a little hurt. He was to be more than a little hurt by the shares of the Marconi Company in the months to come.

But in the meantime Will had to be seen off.

The wedding was held in Criccieth in high summer and it was a spiritual holiday for the Chancellor of the Exchequer. Since George V's accession ('a very jolly chap', he wrote to

Maggie, 'but thank God there's not much in his head'.) things had become confused and grubby in Westminster. The Parliament Bill had not been forwarded to the House of Lords, who were sure to have thrown it out, because this would have subjected the King to a major constitutional crisis before he had even got his crown warm. Asquith had come up with a compromise, a constitutional conference, which would see out the summer and might, just might, enable the two major parties to settle their differences and decide what was to be done about the Lords. And David had produced his second Budget, a very modest and genteel successor to his previous earth-shatterer.

He brought a copy to Uncle Lloyd in Criccieth and inscribed it: 'To Uncle Lloyd, the real author of this Budget, with his pupil's affectionate gratitude', but the old gentleman was ailing now and kept it by him 'to study later', as he said.

One couldn't blame him. The house was noisy with the large family and the hustle and bustle of the wedding, but to David it was all he wanted. He flattered the old gentleman, was ostentatiously affectionate to Maggie, which surprised her somewhat until she realized that the display was intended to impress Dick with his father's sincerity (but she didn't mind, just having him there was pleasure enough), was jovial towards Olwen and Gwilym, and spoiled Megan every minute of the day. Megan knew well enough that half her father's love was for her dead sister and only half for herself, but she was too shy to explain to him that she understood, she really did, so she suffered his affectionate excesses patiently and kindly.

As for Dick, David found that here he had created a proper little gentleman. The two of them took a walk together through the woods, walking slowly, as one should in the height of summer, and breathing deeply. David inquired what the boy, recently down from three years at Cambridge, intended to do, and was alarmed to hear that his son had it in mind to sign up with an oil company.

'I'm sorry if I've disappointed you, Father, but I'm afraid I can't quite see myself as a politician.'

'You make it sound a rather disreputable vocation.'

'I didn't mean to. What term should I use, then? Statesman?'

'Politicians and statesmen are the same breed, you know, Dick. Like butterflies and caterpillars. Nobody ends up as a statesman without squirming through those first grubby years as a politician.'

'Gwilym's talking of joining the Union when he goes up to Cambridge, Father. I'm sure the place will do him a world of good.'

'Would you say it's done *you* good?'

'I think so,' said Dick, matching strides with his father and folding his hands behind his back, 'I was pretty unsophisticated when I first went up, you know.'

David felt the need to do something to avoid catching the lad's eye. To be caught laughing at him would have been disastrous. So the distinguished-looking gentleman in the cloak slashed with his stick at some weeds in the hedge, before turning back to his son and saying gravely: 'So you were, Dick, so you were.'

'Possibly even a little intolerant. I knew practically nothing about – well, women.' David blew his nose into a handkerchief, thus avoiding the necessity for any comment. 'And I would like to admit to you now, Father, that perhaps it is not altogether as simple a matter as I used to believe. At least – not for a young man.'

'I'm not entirely sure what you're telling me, my son, but it seems to bear some of the hallmarks of an olive branch.'

With this David extended a hand to his son, who took it after a moment's surprise and shook it a little awkwardly.

'I'll tell you something, Dick. It doesn't get any simpler.'

It seemed to David in Criccieth that distance did not lend enchantment to the view. In other words the more he considered the plight of the country and the way it was being run the more he became convinced that parliamentary democracy was not a very satisfactory solution. Without a clear majority the Liberals could achieve nothing, and nothing was being done about the House of Lords, about Home Rule for Ireland or about Disestablishment for Wales. Where the centre was weak, the extremes were strong. The simplest solution would be a few years of benevolent dictatorship; the only trouble was, if you proposed such a scheme, everybody instantly supposed you had it in mind to apply for the job of dictator. On the other hand a coalition between the leading members of the two main parties might well be acceptable. David set out a long memorandum to this effect.

'No party,' he wrote, 'has a monopoly of able and efficient men, nor has it a monopoly of duffers. No party commands the services of more than half a dozen first-rate men, and it has to depend for the filling up of all the other posts in the Government of men of second, and even third-rate, capacity.'

This document was not of course circulated to men of second, or even third-rate capacity, and the first-rate men who saw it considered it first-rate. Churchill was keen, for he had little patience with duffers and he had his own ideas about party loyalty. Sir Edward Grey, who had not always loved David with a bright, undying flame, thought the idea worth pursuing, and so did the Master of Elibank. Since it was David's memorandum, he preferred to believe that polite interest was something more and claimed to have made converts of Lansdowne, Cawdor, Curzon, Long, Austen Chamberlain and even Balfour himself. But Balfour was not at all keen. He remarked that the problem, as he saw it, was that too many MPs would refuse to support a coalition in which Lloyd George took a leading role. This David sidestepped neatly by suggesting that both himself *and Balfour* should take a back seat in such a federation. In that case, thought Balfour, Asquith would certainly not approve. Thus was the matter allowed to drop.

Shortly afterwards the constitutional conference broke up in disarray; the Lords threw out the Parliament Bill; the King, considered sufficiently experienced now to enter the fray, promised Asquith that he would if he had to (and he hoped he wouldn't have to) create as many peers as were necessary to ensure the passage of the Bill; and an election was set in motion, though, so far as the public was concerned, the issues were murky and the need for a new administration a little less than urgent.

In the event the voters did the sensible thing (as they usually do), the sensible thing being to do more or less exactly what they had done before. 'Tell Megan', wrote David to Maggie, 'that the people of England seem to prefer her to Austen Chamberlain's little girl.'

Was it all worth it? David, his throat wrecked by three weeks of electioneering in fog, rain and hail, began to wonder. The prospect of struggling and plotting and wriggling to get the Parliament Bill, Irish Home Rule, and Welsh Disestablishment – yet again! – through an indifferent House of Commons and a hostile House of Lords, was not agreeable, but at the thought of the battle that awaited him over his new protégé, the National Insurance Bill, his blood began to course more freely through his veins and his eyes to twinkle.

Churchill suggested he take a holiday to build himself up for the great days ahead. Criccieth maybe? Criccieth be damned! David settled on the South of France.

In Nice he operated on the assumption that attractive young French girls don't have husbands or if they do, they don't tell them; or that the husbands, if told, don't mind or if they do, they don't go to court about it. And in a way he saw it as being faithful to Maggie, rather than the reverse, for wasn't it better to flirt securely in the South of France than risk embarrassment for himself and humiliation for Maggie by philandering in London? He felt sure she would have seen it his way.

In September 1911 Megan was to go to boarding-school. She had been receiving special coaching from Miss James, a rather crusty governess, but Miss James gave in her notice, packed up her pencils in her pencil-box, and went off. It was quite lucky that Miss James went off – miraculous as things were to turn out – for she was a sullen creature, and consequently the idea of Miss James being succeeded by Miss James's sister, who was available, was not followed up. Instead, the headmistress of Clapham High School, which

Mair and Olwyn had attended, was asked if she could recommend somebody for the post. David remarked to Maggie: 'She should have somebody a bit more cheerful next time, and more intelligent. There must be plenty of young women who'd jump at the chance. I could interview a couple of them for you if you'd like.'

Maggie answered with barely a trace of irony: 'Oh, I wouldn't want to put you to all that trouble, Dei.' And then he saw the twinkle in her eye, and he shook his head sadly, like an old bear, for he was more like an old bear than an old goat, whatever people called him.

David interviewed the recommended applicant, a teacher from Allenswood Girls' School in Wimbledon, in the drawing-room at 11 Downing Street, in early July 1911. When he first saw her, he thought for a moment that she was Mair returned from the grave, but when he looked again her face was just a face like any other, though a personable and intelligent twenty-three-year-old face – and he cursed himself for being foolish and middle-aged.

'I'm very pleased to meet you, Miss Stevenson. Mrs Woodhouse was full of your praises. She has explained to you what's required, has she?'

'A tutor for your daughter?' said Frances Stevenson. Her voice was husky from nervousness; to be in Downing Street and in the presence of the Chancellor was bad enough, but she had heard him speak in the Welsh Chapel in Church Street the previous month and she had found him astonishing. Close up, he looked older, but his eyes were, well they were *awful*, and as for the voice, no girl could have listened to that voice, intimately lowered for her especial benefit, without feeling just a little strange. Frances felt distinctly strange and hoped that she didn't look or sound as strange as she felt.

'That's right,' said the Chancellor of the Exchequer, sitting down horribly close to her on the settee, 'just for three months. I think she needs a little general grounding before she goes to her new school. Can you teach French?'

'My mother was French – half French and half Italian. And I won a travelling scholarship from the Institut Français, so I spent a whole summer there with my grandparents.'

'A scholarship? Does that mean you couldn't have gone otherwise?'

'We're five children, you see, it wouldn't have been easy.'

'I can understand that,' said David, liking the girl more than he cared to admit. 'What about music? I would like Megan to be able to play the piano.'

'Yes, I can teach her that.'

'Good. And then just the rudiments of the usual things, I suppose. English, history, arithmetic?'

'Yes. My degree was in classics, but I'm sure I could teach those subjects to the required level.'

'Her last governess said Megan had a lot of trouble with her maths.'

'I know how she feels. I used to, too.' And then Frances hesitated. She had not intended to say what she was about to say, but it seemed to her that Mr George would want her to. Her instincts in these matters could usually be trusted. 'I don't think I'd ever have got the hang of it if it hadn't been for Mair. She was brilliant at maths.'

'*Mair?*' David's eyes no longer twinkled: they glared. His voice was hoarse, and Frances was scared for both of them. '*Our* Mair? You knew her?'

'Yes, very well. She was in the same form as I was at Clapham High School. She was very kind to me.'

'She was very kind to everyone,' said the Chancellor quietly. He seemed to be speaking to himself, and not to hear the girl when she added: 'I know. I liked her very much. We all did.'

There was a long silence. Frances felt that it was not for her to break it. She looked round the room; everything was on a grand scale except the man beside her, but he *seemed* enormous. She shut her eyes and quoted some lines of Horace to herself. At moments of stress it helped.

At length David said: 'What an extraordinary thing,' still in his private voice, and there was another pause before he took hold of her hand, squeezed it, shook it, and announced briskly: 'Well, Miss Stevenson, that all seems eminently satisfactory from my point of view. If you take the job, it would mean your spending the summer with us at Criccieth – if that would be agreeable to you?'

'It sounds wonderful!' cried Frances, radiant, fixing her eyes on a small French mantel-clock and thinking: *this* is the moment when it all began. The clock was showing exactly twelve minutes to four, and the sun was bright on the carpet. *This* was the moment: hold on to it.

'I'd better send you ahead, I think, to meet the family, especially Megan, before you finally commit yourself. I won't be able to get away myself for a few weeks.'

The moment was over. Frances found herself anxious to prolong the interview with this extraordinary man, to talk to him about other things, to engage his interest in her as something other than a governess.

'I shouldn't think you will be able to get away,' she said a little desperately, 'not after yesterday's performance in the House. I've been reading the parliamentary reports. Those Tories are no better than hooligans!'

'You have strong views, Miss Stevenson. Are you a Liberal?'

'I haven't joined the party yet, Mr George, but I've joined the Fabian Society.'

'A step in the right direction,' said David, smiling, and elated at the possibilities opening up before him. He was a little bit anxious about whether Maggie would approve of such an independent and attractive creature, but Megan surely would; and that, after all, was what mattered most.

What a summer that was, the summer of 1911! It was a summer for sleeping on top of sheets, for lemonade and midges, for just lying on your back on the scorched grass, covering your eyes with a brown arm and thinking about nothing at all. Too hot for politics, for love-making, or revolutions; just right for picnics.

One day there was a properly organized picnic in the hills, with tablecloths and hampers. Everyone came. Richard lay back against a tree, his panama tipped forward over his eyes, and dozed off and dreamt about cobbling. Even the insects, it seemed, could hardly manage a buzz, and the cuckoo sounded as though it was distinctly the worse for the heat.

Maggie and Anita were talking about household matters. Maggie enjoyed having somebody with whom she could gossip, though it was too hot for gossip that afternoon. They spoke about wasps' nests, and about how well Miss Stevenson seemed to be getting on with Megan. And then Megan chipped in and said that Miss Stevenson was 'topping', that they were reading *Ann Veronica* together, and that Tada had said it wouldn't do her any harm.

Tada meanwhile was discussing his Insurance Bill with William. They spoke of how iniquitous it was that the big companies had insisted on widows and orphans being excluded. They thought what a difference it might have otherwise made to Betsy, and how if it had not been for Uncle Lloyd, she would probably have had to go to the workhouse. It seemed strange on such a lovely afternoon when the whole world seemed to be taking things easy, to think that there were still workhouses full of widows and orphans. Better not consider them too closely.

Frances and Gwilym in a desultory way had been packing the remains of the picnic away in the hamper and discussing – although it was *extremely* hot – the contentious question of the suffragettes. It appeared, and Gwilym was shocked to hear it, that Frances was one of 'Pankhurst's gang'. Shocking indeed, for had not David become their public enemy number one, since he had voted in Cabinet for a Bill against woman's suffrage, and had had stones thrown at him, and been vilified and ridiculed.

'I'm not one of the "gang",' said Francis, 'I'm a member of the Fawcett Society, the constitutional wing of the movement, but I admire Christabel more than I can say.'

'You admire the breaking of windows and arson?' asked Gwilym.

'They've tried all the other ways. And when I think of the

things being done to them in prison it makes me sick. There now I've said it!'

She had said it so forcefully that David had heard her, and, no matter how hot the weather, he could not let such provocation go unchallenged.

'Any ordinary girl would tell you, my dear, that there are far better ways of getting round a man than heaving a brick at him.'

'You mean they ought to be flatterers and liars and sycophants. Why should they? What would you think of a *man* who tried to influence you that way?'

Frances looked so scornfully at him and spoke with such passion that it was hard to imagine that one was the Chancellor of the Exchequer, the other his daughter's governess.

'Miss Stevenson, I have fought for many causes that looked far more forlorn than yours, but the only weapon I've ever resorted to is words.'

'Naturally, because you're a master of words. But the suffragettes have tried words, and they have proved useless.'

'Not useless. I support women's suffrage.' Frances raised an eyebrow. 'So does the Liberal Party. All I ask is that it takes its place in the queue. We couldn't have tackled any reforms of substance until we'd curbed the House of Lords. And now there's the small matter of poverty. I worry a lot more over a child starved of food than a woman waiting a little longer for the franchise. Then there'll be Ireland. If that's not solved soon lives will be lost.'

'But in the Cabinet you voted against women's suffrage.'

There was a silence into which an exhilarating burst of lark-song exploded. Uncle Lloyd suddenly snored himself awake, adjusted his panama, and drifted off again into dreams of leather and nails. Megan, who had been listening intently to the conversation, trotted over to her father and took his hand, saying: 'He doesn't have to explain it to *you*, do you Tada?'

David squeezed Megan's hand, and spoke gently to Frances, as though to a friend rather than a political opponent: 'Listen. Give me a Bill that enfranchises *all* women and I'll support it. The one I opposed would have granted the vote to a small minority of rich, property-owning women, ninety-per cent of them Tories. It would have helped the Opposition regain power and set the causes of social equity and Irish freedom back for a decade. Christabel Pankhurst supported it because she's a snob, an authoritarian and a total reactionary, but you ask Sylvia Pankhurst what *she* thinks. She's the only one that of family who gives a damn about the poor. And she agrees with me about the Bill. Well?'

Frances was confused. She did not look at David as she said: 'I hadn't thought of it that way.'

'I don't believe you did much thinking at all if you could defend the kind of actions your friends have been indulging in.'

'I did think,' said Frances, and her voice was more confident, so much so that Maggie listened in dismay. 'I thought about the words of a great statesman, who once said: 'There comes a time in the life of a people suffering from an intolerable injustice when the only way to maintain one's self-respect is to revolt against the injustice.'

'What great statesman was that?' asked Gwilym. 'Was it Gladstone? George Washington?'

David was already roaring with laughter as Frances said: 'It was David Lloyd George.'

He was still laughing as he stood up and stretched himself and walked off towards a clump of trees with Megan skipping after him.

There is a mischief in the Welsh hills. They play tricks on people. Acoustically they are improbable, and it was improbable that David could have overheard a conspiratorial exchange between Gwilym and Frances which followed his departure, but he did. He heard Gwilym ask: 'Come on, Miss Stevenson, tell me the truth now. What do you honestly think of the old man?' And then, of course, he listened intently to hear Frances say: 'I think he's quite wonderful for his age, don't you?' David, who had put a finger to his lips when Megan ran up to him, made a sour face at this, but when Frances added: with a glance at the panama hat: 'It's amazing to think he still preaches in chapel every Sunday.' David hugged Megan to him, and moved further behind the amiable tree which was hiding him from the rest of the party.

'I didn't mean Uncle Lloyd,' said Gwilym, 'I meant my father.'

'Oh I *see*! But you said "the old man", and that's ridiculous – he's not old!'

At this David set his daughter on the ground, kissed her briefly, and loped off up the hill. Gwilym and Frances were completing the packing. William had joined Anita, who was lying back on a rug and fanning the gnats away from her face with a fern. Uncle Richard was still asleep. Maggie was standing alone rearranging her hair which had become dishevelled. It was a curious thing to see on such a beautiful afternoon, but in the eyes of this matronly and sensible woman was an unmistakable expression of terror.

Suddenly the silence was broken by a great burst of singing, and a fluttering of outraged wings from a dozen birds. They felt – and one could understand their feelings – that senior Cabinet Ministers rising fifty should not sit in the uppermost branches of trees singing 'Men of Harlech', no matter how cheerful they felt.

At the bottom of the tree stood Megan, her arms clasping its rough and lichen-covered trunk. She thought that Tada had every right to sing, though she was not entirely sure why he had suddenly taken it into his head to do so. But that was one of the things she liked best about Tada; you could never be quite sure what he would do next and when you *were* quite sure, he went and did something totally different.

In the mischievous sunshine of Wales all the problems that had been troubling David seemed capable of easy solution. One just had to be resolute and determined, confident that one was right, and then, with a majority in the Commons and a constitutional monarch, what could get in the way? But back in London nothing seemed quite so simple.

There was formidable opposition to the National Insurance Bill. The Friendly Societies were hostile, as David had anticipated, and so he bribed them by making them responsible for operating the scheme. More formidable was the opposition of the big insurance companies with their tens of thousands of agents and collectors. They too wanted to have a part in the running of the scheme and insisted that death benefits, widows and orphans be excluded. Then there was the British Medical Association, which concluded that the work would not be distributed equitably among its members and that the rate of four shillings, plus two shillings for drugs, was too little (the Friendly Societies had argued that it was too much). The Dowager Countess Desart and Lord Northcliffe, that scourge of the enlightened, led an attack on what they called the iniquitous 'servants' tax'. When one considered all the powerful personages summoning up powerful arguments for doing nothing on behalf of those who could do nothing for themselves, it made one despair of ever achieving social justice in Britain. But one didn't despair. One compromised.

Most significantly, even the public seemed doubtful as to whether the scheme could work at all. At least in a number of by-elections they voted against the government, which is the kind of rational argument no administration cares to ignore. Several of David's Cabinet colleagues began to speak to each other out of the corners of their mouths. But David was convinced not only that the Bill was a momentous piece of reforming legislation but that it must also prove popular politically, just as soon as the public understood what was involved. How to make them understand? How to convince them that the forces massed against the Bill – duchesses, businessmen, Tories, a devil's army of power and privilege – were activated by greed, self-interest, malice and stupidity? There was only one way to do it, and that was to explain it to them in person.

'Let me explain the purpose of the Bill,' he told the public. 'It is designed to help the people who are not in a position to save enough money to see themselves safely through troubled times – sickness, accident, or unemployment. They may have been unlucky, or over-burdened, or have left it too late. A man of forty-five, for instance, if he wants to join a Friendly Society, has to pay twice as much as a man of twenty because the risks are greater. So what am I doing about that?

'I am going to treat everybody as if they were sixteen years of age. I am going to make everybody young, to renew their youth financially. Everybody starts at the rate he would have to pay if he were a young man. Now that will create a great deficiency, and that is where state money comes in. The state puts a strong shoulder under that burden and carries it. It will have to carry it for a generation, and then it will vanish like the mist on our hills when the sun comes out. We shall then have six and a quarter millions surplus for the purposes of increasing the benefits to everybody!'

The public liked the sound of this. The words 'surplus' and 'benefits' were good strong words. But it was when the Chancellor explained that for every fourpence the worker paid, the employer paid threepence, and the state twopence, so that the worker was in effect getting ninepence for fourpence, they realized that he was talking their kind of language and cheered him to the echo.

The Bill went through with a large majority, and nothing could alter the fact that, as Winston Churchill, now First Lord of the Admiralty, put it, 'We are an insured nation,' adding that 'this tremendous step . . . can never be retraced, and you and your children, and your children's children – every class in the state – will pay the contributions and draw the benefits and be influenced and affected by this legislation every week of their lives.'

Patagonia rankled. It seemed absurd that the man in charge of the finances of the entire country chould be so inept when it came to managing his own. He was no longer short of money, but it was painful for him to see on the Opposition benches men of vastly inferior intelligence who seemed able by virtue of a helpful 'tip' here, a little influence there, to make money as easily as making water. Patagonia rankled. He had been so *green*. Consequently, when Rufus Isaacs, who had represented him in court in the matter of the libel action against the *People* and was now Solicitor General, had offered both David and the Chief Whip one thousand shares apiece in the American Marconi Company (of which Rufus's brother was the managing director) at a pre-market rate, he had jumped at the chance. After all, the *Titanic* had hit an iceberg four days before the launching of the shares and everyone was saying that the loss of life would not have been so serious had there been radio communication from the ship. The shares had risen sharply on the day they were launched and David sold half his holding for a comfortable profit. This was too easy! For a month thereafter he reflected on his good fortune, and then, greatly daring, purchased another three thousand. But it was too late. He had – the metaphor seems appropriate – missed the boat. When he came to do his sums over the two deals he was chagrined to find that he was actually a small amount out of pocket. How humiliating! And, as events were to show, how tactless! For a sister company, the English Marconi Comapny, was shortly to be awarded a large government contract, and the Solicitor General's brother, managing director of the one company, was chairman of the other.

What an opportunity was there for the gutterpress! Government Ministers, government contracts, Jewish financiers, unfair profits, why, a story as juicy as this one could be guaranteed to up the circulation dramatically. And what should those involved in the nasty rumours do about it? Issue writs and invite further disastrous publicity? Or ignore the rumours and hope they would go away? 'Ignore them,' said the Prime Minister. But they didn't go away. The Chancellor was mentioned by name, and George Lansbury, Labour MP for Poplar, brought the matter to the notice of the House of Commons.

A Select Committee was set up to look into the whole affair, but since it had a preponderance of Liberals and would take plenty of time to complete its investigations, it might well find that there was no case for the Ministers to answer. It was considered something of a paper tiger. But then a French newspaper published the story, naming names (though not David's), and the opportunity was taken in court, where the libel action was undefended, to try to set the record straight.

But with each disclosure, that Lloyd George and the Chief Whip had bought shares – albeit in the American Marconi Company – on two occasions, that nine thousand pounds of Liberal funds had been invested, as well as personal savings, and so on, public interest in the matter became more acute. David's claim to have lost money on the whole affair, and therefore presumably to be blame-free, was unexpected, but scarcely tallied with his plea that he was a poor man and was only trying to put something by for a rainy day. Better put the country's finances in the hands of a successful rather than an unsuccessful knave was the frequently expressed view.

No one seemed much taken with the distinction between the English and American Marconi Companies, nor was anyone interested to hear that the Ministers had had no prior knowledge of any contract, but the Select Committee *did* take note of these matters, and after three months of deliberations pronounced all concerned honest as the day was long (and the report was published in June). Unfortunately two of the Committee were moved to present dissenting reports, and one of them was no less a person than Sir Albert Spicer, chairman of the Committee.

All very unpleasant while it lasted, and those close to David noticed how hard he was taking it. He looked old, with plenty of white amongst his flowing locks, and some of the optimism seemed to leave his face, never to return. He was noticeably tubby too, a tubbiness which the Tyrolean cloak he customarily wore did little to hide.

To Maggie David pretended that pressure of work was what had been getting him down. He told her that he was thinking of appointing another secretary and that he had half a mind to offer the job to Frances Stevenson.

Maggie knew that look in his eye and felt a little tired, for she would have to play the old game again by the same old rules; and it was a game that she had no heart for, and *shouldn't* have to play, not any more.

'Is that usual? To appoint a woman to such a post, I mean?' was what she said.

'Oh Maggie, we must move with the times. Besides she's so competent. I've given her quite a few little commissions over the past few months, translation, research and that sort of thing.'

'Yes, I know you have,' said Maggie, and squeezed his hand. 'Megan will be disappointed though. Miss Stevenson was the only reason she agreed to go to that school. And now she'll be leaving.'

'I've not put it to her yet,' said David quickly. 'She may not take it.'

'Oh she'll jump at it. But, Dei, just two things to bear in mind. You do know, don't you, that she's falling in love with you?' Maggie couldn't help watching him closely as she said this, and what she observed increased her foreboding.

'You do talk nonsense sometimes, old girl. Why, I'm old enough to be her father.'

'Yes that's the second thing. You'll be fifty next month.'

'About time for you to stop worrying then.'

David had spoken a little sharply, but Maggie just patted him gently on the shoulder. 'My dear old wicked Dei. I don't really worry any more about you trying to make a fool of me. I'm not really taken in. I know by now you can't help it, and I know I'll still be here when you've got tired of them all. But I'm still afraid that one day you might make a fool of yourself.'

At this point she kissed him on the cheek, and they hugged each other for a moment, so that David was not sure whether he'd been given a ticking off or a free hand. Anyway Frances might say no, especially when she heard exactly what it was that he had in mind to offer her.

Good food, good wine, candlelight and starched linen. Gatti's offered all that with discretion included in the cover charge. Frances ate the food and sipped the wine; her skin was like alabaster in the candlelight and her hands lay on the tablecloth, naked of rings and vulnerable; David covered one of hers with one of his; he would have liked to have covered both, only then Frances would have been unable to drink her coffee, which she needed to steady her nerves. David had tried not to unsteady them. He had been witty over the hors-d'oeuvre, reflective over the Dover sole, and passionate over the grouse. When it came to the soufflé he asked the question which she had been dreading – not because she didn't know what she would say, but because she did. And now over the coffee he begged his own darling 'Pussy' – the nickname which the girls at school had coined for her – not to keep him waiting too long.

'You've already got a private secretary,' said Frances. 'What would happen to Mr Davies?'

'There's enough work for both of you, God knows. And you get on quite well with him, don't you?'

'Oh yes.'

'You're not in any doubt that you're capable of the job?'

'No. I think I could learn to do it, if *you* think so. But about the other thing – I don't know.'

David looked at her hair, and thought it was more beautiful than any of the others. It was the colour of gold. Then he looked at her eyes, which were unquestionably blue, and was startled by the anxiety he saw there.

'Oh God, Pussy, don't look at me like that. I've sworn to myself I'll leave you free to decide. There are a million words I could put my tongue to, but I don't want to influence you too much, and I'm holding them back.'

'You mean the advantages of the job?' Her blue eyes were very wide, and her throat was very bare.

'No, *cariad*, about my need of you. This is not like anything I ever felt in my life . . . but no, I mustn't speak in such terms. I've put the proposition to you and I've tried to keep emotion out of it. Just facts. And you must choose.'

'It couldn't be the job without – the other thing?'

'I'm sorry, no. I wish it could,' lied the Chancellor. 'But I couldn't even pretend to promise that, seeing you every day.

I don't think any man could. I'm trying to be honest. If the thought of it is horrible to you, you must say so, and it's finished.'

'You know how far that is from the truth,' Frances murmured.

A waiter on his way to the table with fresh coffee was intercepted by the head waiter and sent back to the kitchen.

'Well then?'

'What about your wife?'

'Maggie mustn't know.'

'Ever?' David shook his head. he liked to believe that Maggie would remain in ignorance. Better not to consider too closely how that might be achieved.

'So I would always be the one in the shadows?'

'You read the book I gave you about Parnell and Kitty O'Shea?'

'I take the point,' said Frances with a trace of asperity.

'I couldn't bear to wreck the Party.'

'This *arrangement* wouldn't wreck it?'

'Not if we were careful. But divorce *would*. People are happy to leave things unsaid so long as they have the choice, so long as there's discretion.'

'I *hate* discretion!' cried Frances indiscreetly, for a head at a nearby table turned in her direction.

'My darling so do I. But what else is there for us? As long as I am what I am and where I am. Should I throw it all up? Should we change our name and go abroad and live in the sun, growing olives and vines, doing no harm to anybody, but doing no good to anybody either? I'll do that if you like.'

'No, no, I wouldn't let you do that,' said Frances, but she was thinking: And what if I were to say yes?

'Well then?'

'I don't know. I'm going to Scotland for Christmas.' She didn't know. She *had* known. She had been going to say yes, *please*. She had been going to kiss his hand, but then he had spoken of Maggie and the deceptions they would practise on her. Now it was all confusion again. Finishing her lukewarm coffee she added lamely: 'I'll think about it. I'll let you know when I come back.'

While Frances was in Scotland David heard a rumour she was engaged to be married. An able, intelligent, musical Scotsman. A *young* Scotsman. A young Scots *bachelor*, who could offer her a gold ring, a home and children. The news threw him into the deepest gloom, coming as it did on top of his dreadful anxiety over the Marconi affair.

For several days he saw no one except Sarah, the housekeeper; he did no work, ate no food, and dragged himself around the house. At length a despairing telegram to Frances brought her to his side. She gave him his answer lying in his arms. It is not recorded how the eligible young Scotsman felt.

Chapter Five

Discretion is a fine concept. It turns guilt into sensitivity for other people's feelings. The only trouble with discretion is that from the outside it tends to look like secrecy. When they received Frances's letter in which she set out with infinite tact the nature of the arrangement she had made with the Chancellor of the Exchequer, Mr and Mrs Stevenson were not at all touched by David's expressed concern for their finer feelings (so discreet was he that he would have much preferred it had they been kept in lifelong ignorance). Rather, they were very, very angry.

David had thought that they might be and was more nervous about his first meeting with the outraged parents than he had been about anything in his life. School Inspectors haemorrhages, Birmingham mobs, suffragettes, Irishmen paled into insignificance when compared with Mr and Mrs Stevenson. Frances's mother had written to David and when he had touched the writing paper steam rose from the tips of his fingers.

Frances did her best to encourage him. 'I'm sure,' she said (though she wasn't), 'that once she's actually met you she'll understand. You know when you're really trying to be nice nobody can resist you for a second.'

'Mothers can,' said David bleakly. At which moment Sarah (who adored David and felt that he deserved more affection than Maggie offered him), agog with curiosity, announced the visitors to Number 11 Downing Street.

Mrs Stevenson was the daughter of an Italian father and a French-born mother, who lived with her even after she was married. She was small dark and tightly corseted and her eyes flashed like a knife-thrower's blades Mr Stevenson, who entered the room a pace behind his wife, was a tall, fair, Calvinistic Scot self-effacing and conscientious.

David was at his most urbane as he advanced across the

room, one hand outstretched in welcome. 'Ah! Mrs Stevenson! *So* glad you could come!'

The proffered hand was ignored. Mrs Stevenson held hers tightly against her corset. They were safer there. Adroitly David redirected his hand in the direction of Mr Stevenson, who accepted it gratefully and shook it gravely. Only Frances could tell how hurt he was.

'Good evening to you, sir.'

'No trouble getting here, I hope? Thank you, Sarah, that will be all. I quite thought this afternoon that we were in for some more snow.'

'It seems to have turned to rain,' said Mr Stevenson, smiling at his daughter. 'the streets are practically clear again now.'

'John,' said Mrs Stevenson in a voice to bend steel.

'Yes my dear?'

'What is all this about the snow? Is this what we came here for? To have a chat about the weather with Mr Lloyd George?'

'Oh, *Mama*,' cried Frances, fearing the worst.

David took a deep breath, and with chivalry, deference and all the charm he could muster, said: 'Mrs Stevenson, please believe me. I entirely appreciate the sensitive nature of the matter you wish to discuss and I promise you there will be ample time in the course of the evening for all of us to – '

'No!' cried Mrs Stevenson, in a very loud voice for such a little lady. 'Maybe, Mr Lloyd George, you think I am a woman to have one kind of feeling in my heart and another on my tongue. You think I will nod and smile. shake your hand and sit down and talk about the rain in the streets and the news in the papers. Then when I am eating your food you will start to talk about my daughter – my daughter, Mr Lloyd George – and you think perhaps by then I will be ready to go on smiling . . . ' David had to admire her percipience. That was more or less how he *had* mapped things out. 'But no! I am not that kind of woman. I say what I feel and nobody is going to . . . '

'Mama,' cried Frances. feeling she must say *something*, 'all

David means is . . . '

'That is quite enough from you, my girl. I have had this out with you already. And if you are keen to know, Mr Lloyd George, what I told her, I told her what any decent mother would have told her. I told her . . ' and here her voice trembled with the shame of a mother who views her daughter's degradation – 'I told her I would rather see her dead at my feet! And as for you, John, who call yourself a man, why do you stand there? You are her father. Tell him!'

'My wife is overwrought, as you can see,' said John Stevenson, 'but for a God-fearing man with a good religious background as I have always understood you to be, there should be no need for either of us to say these things. Your own conscience should tell you that what you propose is wrong.'

The matter was nicely balanced. In the one scale a social code refined down the centuries, and a moral code subscribed to by the entire Western world; in the other the eloquence of the Chancellor of the Exchequer, five foot seven in his stockinged feet.

'I beg you to believe this isn't a thing we are entering upon lightly. To me, Mr Stevenson, it is a solemn and binding commitment. My only wish is to devote the rest of my life to making Frances happy. She will tell you herself that I made no effort to influence her: it was her own free choice.'

'A free choice between honour and dishonour?' said Mr Stevenson sadly. 'What kind of a man would put a choice like that before an innocent young girl?' The solemnity of these sentiments impressed Mrs Stevenson; instinctively she felt that the point should be pressed home.

'And how can you *not* influence her? A man twice her age – more than twice her age! You take her into all this!' She gestured around at the drawing-room of Number 11 as though it were Bluebeard's castle. 'You give her presents! You tell her lies!'

This was too much for David. Tell Frances lies? He never would! 'No!' he cried.

'No?' And Mrs Stevenson advanced on him, prodding him in the chest. 'You, who talk about binding commitments, have you not got a wife? Where is your commitment to her? You talk about making my daughter happy. Will she be happy in going against the will of God? Will she be happy in breaking her mother's heart? Are you trying to tell me that that kind of life will bring a decent girl anything but shame and tears and heartache? You wish for her happiness? Then, in God's name, send her away, leave her alone!'

At last, and most appropriately, came the tears. First from Mrs Stevenson whose tears were profuse and impressive despite the tight corseting. And then from Frances herself, who was unsure *why* she was crying but wished that she wasn't because it seemed like taking sides. John Stevenson stared at the ground, deeply embarrassed and distressed. And David, moist with sweat, ran a finger round his collar and tried to imagine himself into the future when this frightful scene would have faded into insignificance.

It was not long afterwards, that David sent Frances a poem he had written for her:

> Beloved let us work so well,
> Our work shall still be better for our love,
> And still our love be sweeter for our work,
> And both, commended for the sake of each,
> By all true workers and true lovers born.

Like many Prime Ministers before and after him, Asquith wished fervently that he could have towed Ireland into the middle of the Atlantic, holed it below the water-line and watched it sink. But he couldn't, and in February 1913 he could no longer ignore it.

The Republicans wanted Home Rule, wanted it at once and had formed a new private army, the Irish Volunteers, to make sure they got it. The Orangemen were equally determined that Ulster should not be handed over to the papists, and consignments of German rifles in the hands of the Ulster Volunteers were a powerful argument in support of their demands. If civil war was to be averted a compromise solution would have to be found, but how does one compromise between an irresistible force and an immovable object?

Asquith had no answer to that but David was not one to be discouraged by the impossible and he took it upon himself to try to find a solution to the impasse. In a memorandum he suggested that the Home Rule Bill be passed but with an amendment allowing Antrim, Armagh, Down and Londonderry to contract out for the first six years. (What was to happen to County Fermanagh and County Tyrone he did not specify). Then, if the Unionists were returned at the next election, the contracting out would presumably become permanent; but if the Liberals won the majority of the seats, Ulster would be incorporated in the rest of Ireland. The subtlety of the scheme lay in the pointlessness of armed intervention when one stood a fair chance of getting one's way by constitutional means.

But nobody liked it. Sir Edward Carson regarded it as surrendering a vital principle; Redmond and Dillon and the Sinn Fein saw it as perpetuating a shameful betrayal. Sagely David commented that if anybody *had* liked it, there must have been something wrong with it. And nobody from a neutral position was able to come up with anything better.

Churchill suggested calling out the army, but when the British army had last been in Ireland, three-quarters of the cavalry officers, urged on by the Tories, had sent in their papers rather than confront the Ulster Volunteers. Asquith in any case was powerfully against imposing Home Rule by force.

When the pressures became too great David took to the golf course – usually Walton Heath - where he played a most erratic and immoderate sort of game. Since Frances was his other relaxation he undertook to build a house at Walton Heath where they could be alone together and at peace. In the meantime it was undignified and embarrassing for both of them, and Frances, toasting muffins in the drawing-room of 11 Downing Street, with the furniture shrouded in dust sheets (which was how Maggie liked it to be when she wasn't present to supervise things) felt that life with the man she loved was not as satisfactory as it ought to be. A brooch of diamonds and sapphires was a considerable help, of course, but she longed for the new house to be completed and for her irregular position to feel at least a little more regular.

The new house was all but completed when part of it was wrecked by a bomb planted by suffragettes. The suffragettes were better at theory than at practice, and other bombs concealed in the house failed to explode. Had they done so the house and the workmen putting the final touches to it would have been blown to pieces.

Bombs! There were to be plenty of those in the next four years, and more was to be at stake than a country house on the edge of a golf course. But David was shocked by the incident and took it hard.

On 28 July Austria-Hungary declared war on Serbia. Four days later Germany declared war on Russia, two days after that on France. The German army en route for France massed on the borders of Belgium. Europe, for obscure reasons of political and financial expediency, had decided to do the dance of death, and it was apparent that Britain had no wish to be a wallflower. Britain in this context was Asquith, Churchill, Haldane, Crewe and Grey from the Cabinet, most of the Conservatives, most of the newspapers and of course the big manufacturers.

Asquith thought war inevitable and his energies were concentrated on preserving unity on the parliamentary front benches. He anticipated that Germany would invade Belgium, with whom Britain had treaty obligations, and that such an outrage would be sufficiently blatant to make up the minds of the undecided; in this he was astute.

David had visited Germany in 1908 to study their system of state insurance, and had taken the opportunity to speak affectionately of Anglo-German co-operation and to call for armament limitation on both sides. They had wined him and dined him well, although the Kaiser had 'not been available', and he had thought that war with Germany was quite out of the question and consequently that McKenna's dreadnoughts were a wild extravagance. Since then it had been assumed that David's sympathies remained pro-German and, remembering his opposition to the Boer War, that he would be reluctant to consider fighting anyone, let alone Germany. If this were true, Asquith was not going to find it easy to take the country to war, for David's impassioned voice was by now quite as influential as the Prime Minister's.

Churchill came to call. He lit a cigar, poured himself a whisky and stared at his old friend as though he could convert him without the use of words, while Sarah drew the curtains against a sky heavy with storm-clouds.

'It doesn't matter about the others, the rest of the peace-mongers,' Winston said at length when they were alone, 'but it *you* resign the Germans will know we've no stomach for a fight.'

David remembered Winston's despatches from the Transvaal. He had been a young man in love with war; and obviously his thirst was not yet slaked. The Chancellor said nothing.

'What will you do if you do resign? Will you join Henderson and Ramsay MacDonald on the Labour benches? Will you campaign against the war?'

'No, Winston, I would not. I'd have no part in it. I think I'd return to Wales and practise law again.'

'You couldn't do it! I know you too well. Stay there watching the mess that the other fools would make of things and say nothing? Not in your nature!'

'You speak as though war is inevitable.'

'I believe it to be so. From now on the march of events will dominate us all.'

'I can't believe it. A week ago we were all in Number Ten worrying about Ireland. Grey was going fishing. You were off to Cromer. And now most of Europe is suddenly seized with this mad desire for Armageddon, and you come here to try to persuade me to turn jingo and join the rest.'

'There is no honourable alternative.'

'There is the alternative of an honourable neutrality. If others had stayed neutral it would have remained no more than a little Balkan quarrel. The Tsar need not have mobilized because Austria declared war on Serbia. Germany didn't have to declare war on Russia and France just because the Tsar mobilized, and what on earth do we owe to any of them that's worth spilling the blood of our young men for? We've got no treaties with France.'

'But we have with Belgium.' Churchill pressed home his advantage. 'And you could hardly call Belgium jingoistic. All Belgium wants is what you want, an honourable neutrality. Well, haven't you always been the champion of the rights of small nations? If not for Belgium whom would you go to war for?'

David said slowly. 'I have been living in a nightmare world these last few days. The thought that I should have a share in the horrors of war scorches my flesh.' And then with more spirit: 'It was only a month ago that Grey said peace was more important than justice.'

'Serbia's a long way off. The injustice to Belgium is on our doorstep. Besides Grey's changed his mind. At least promise me you'll not commit yourself for the next couple of days?'

You could not help but admire Winston. He was always so certain that he was right, no matter how many times he changed his mind. He had mobilized the fleet and sent Asquith notice of what he was doing: Asquith's refusal to congratulate him he then took as official approval of his initiative. Since the situation had become so critical, it was as well that Winston had acted as he did. Although by sentiment a Tory, he remained a man after David's own heart. Too arrogant to be a man of the people, David thought, watching him refill his glass.

There was a sudden burst of cheering from the crowds gathering in Downing Street. They were singing: 'We don't want to fight but, by jingo, if we do . . . ' but the way they sang it gave the lie to the words.

'Why in Christ's name are they cheering?' cried David suddenly. 'It's simple madness. The whole thought of what we're heading into sickens me to my soul.'

'But you did say "we"? You and I have been through a lot together in the last thirteen years. We've had disagreements, but I think I can claim no one's ever been left in any doubt of my respect and admiration for you. Even through that unpleasant Marconi business last year I was never one of those who doubted you for a moment.'

'I know,' said David. 'I appreciated that more than I can say.'

'But this is the crossroads! If you stay with us there is no man on earth I would rather see at my side: if you try to impede us I will fight you with all the powers at my command. It is our whole future as comrades or as enemies!'

No man is an island but Churchill is as near an island as dammit, thought David when the First Lord had gone. *He* seemed to have no obligations, no responsibilities, except to play the game with a great deal of spirit and a certain amount of flair, and the hope that luck was running his way. Not so David. Uncle Richard made it plain that if the government were hell-bent on this madcap war, David should no longer be a part of the government. The issues seemed straightforward viewed from a sick-bed in Criccieth.

Frances had no doubts that the sooner Britain entered the war the better. To her, loyalty to France and the entente cordiale and a treaty with Belgium required no less.

Under so many contradictory pressures David felt less like an island than a tiny dinghy afloat in a maelstrom. No man is an island and also, he thought bitterly, no island is an island, not any more, not where modern politicians and statesmen are concerned. Secretly he began to hope that Germany would invade Belgium, that something would happen to make his mind up for him. On 4 August 1914 his wish was father to the deed. The Germans advanced across the border, destroying anything which impeded them. Asquith sent an ultimatum which expired at eleven o'clock Greenwich Mean Time.

In the Cabinet room Asquith and his wife, Grey. Haldane, McKenna and David waited. They could just hear the distant crowds in Whitehall and Trafalgar Square. To David their cheers seemed fatuous, but perhaps it was as well to cheer while one had the spirit to do so. There would be few enough opportunities in the next four years. As the deadline passed with no answer from Germany, the Prime Minister announced that Britain was at war with Germany.

Suddenly Churchill breezed into the room, waving his cigar in the air and grinning. 'Well, we're in!' he announced happily, and the cheering of the crowds seemed to show that he had not been celebrating alone.

The immediate effect of the declaration of war and something which required David's most urgent attention, was the financial crisis in the City of London. Crises in the City of London are seldom to do with money which is usually to be found in vulgar quantities there if you know where to look, but with something that cannot be created artificially: confidence. So unconfident was the Governor of the Bank of England of the country's ability to pay for the war that some said there had been tears in his eyes when he begged 'Keep us out of it! We shall all be ruined if we are dragged in!'

Obviously impressive gestures were needed. David went into consultation with everyone who might have ideas to offer about bringing confidence back into Lombard Street, including two ex-Chancellors of the Exchequer. Their advice must have been good for the panic was halted and Lord Rothschild was moved to write to David congratulating him on 'the masterly way you tackled the greatest difficulty that has ever occured in the finances of the country.' But all this consultative work was undercover stuff, and David felt the need to make a public statement why the decision to go to war had been the correct one. Without such a speech he could have been accused of sacrificing his principles to political expediency. So he took great pains in preparing his talk at the Queen's Hall, and was much afflicted with nervousness before the meeting began, yawning and stretching and unable to relax.

'The message has *got* to be strong and clear,' he told

141

' rances, 'no vacillation. Now that we've gone into this war the only thing that matters is to win it.'

'What they want from you are the divisive things, the old class things. And you've got to show that you speak for everybody, that your purpose is to bring them together.'

'That I can do. But can I make them listen?'

Frances wondered what sort of a question that was. Might as well ask whether water was wet: 'You know you always have them spellbound.'

But David was full of doubts. In Swansea or in the East End perhaps . . . 'I can *entertain* them, I can *reason* with them, I can make them *laugh*, but can I reach their hearts? These are not my people. And I'll make an awful fool of myself if I try and they just sit there and fail to respond.'

'We want to be told,' said Frances with customary intelligence, 'that we're doing the right thing. And we want to be told *why* it's right. And you are the only one who can tell us.'

He told them.

'There is no man in this room who has always regarded the prospect of engaging in a great war with greater reluctance and with greater repugnance than I have done throughout the whole of my political life. There is no man either inside or outside this room more convinced that we could not have avoided it without national dishonour . . . If we had stood by when two little nations were being crushed and broken by the brutal hands of barbarism, our shame would have rung down the ages . . .

'The Prussian Junker is the road-hog of Europe. Small nationalities in his way are hurled to the roadside, bleeding and broken. Women and children are crushed under the wheels of his cruel car, and Britain is ordered out of his road. All I can say is this: if the old British spirit is alive in British hearts, that bully will be torn from his seat. Were he to win, it would be the greatest catastrophe that has befallen democracy since the days of the Holy Alliance and its ascendancy.

'They think we cannot beat them. It will not be easy. It will be a long job. It will be a terrible war. But in the end we will march through terror to triumph. We shall need all our qualities – every quality that Britain and its people possess – prudence in counsel, daring in action, tenacity in purpose, courage in defect, moderation in victory; in all things faith . . .

'May I tell you in a simple parable what I think this war is doing for us? I know a valley in North Wales, between the mountains and the sea. It is a beautiful valley, snug, comfortable, sheltered by the mountains from all the bitter blasts. But it is very enervating, and I remember how the boys were in the habit of climbing the hill above the village to have a glimpse of the great mountains in the distance, and to be stimulated and freshened by the breezes which came from the hilltops, and by the spectacle of their grandeur. We have been living in a sheltered valley for generations. We have been too comfortable and too indulgent – many, perhaps, too selfish – and the stern hand of fate has scourged us to an elevation where we can see the great everlasting things that matter for a nation: the great peaks we had forgotten, of Honour, Duty, Patriotism, and, clad in glittering white, the great pinnacle of Sacrifice pointing like a rugged finger to heaven. We shall descend into the valleys again; but as long as the men and women of this generation last, they will carry in their hearts the image of these great mountain peaks whose foundations are not shaken, though Europe rock and sway in the convolutions of a great war.'

That was one way – and a most successful way – of appealing to the nation. Kitchener tried another. The stern face of duty, the pointed finger of conscience and the slogan: 'Your country needs YOU.'

Your country certainly did. The news could hardly have been worse. The French armies, the Russian armies, and even the British armies had been put to rout. And in the Cabinet Room the new Secretary of State for War was being given a rough ride by the Chancellor of the Exchequer.

Why, he wished to know, had it been made an offence for Welsh volunteers to speak their native tongue on parade or in their billets? How, he politely inquired, did the War Office suppose that recruiting could be seriously undertaken in the Principality under such conditions? What, he wondered, was the purpose behind refusing to send nonconformist chaplains out with the troops? Who, he demanded, was insisting that common-law wives and illegitimate children would receive no recompense when their men were killed? (No, said the Archbishop of Canterbury, such women and such children must not be allowed to starve, but we can hardly treat them openly as deserving of relief.) And when, David thundered, was Kitchener going to realize that the war was, and had got to be a *people's* war, and not a war-game for gentlemen only?

More urgently serious was an acute shortage of shells, howitzers and heavy artillery at the front. David made twenty million pounds available for remedying the deficiency but the Master-General of Ordnance did not pass this information on to the armaments' manufacturers lest they became extravagant. The fashionable view was that the war would be over by Christmas, in which case there would be little point in forcing other companies to switch to armament-production. Consequently there was a calamitous inertia and incompetence from the official contractors, and the new recruits who had been mesmerized by Kitchener's appeal now found that there was only one rifle to every six of their number, and that though there were plenty of shell-cases, there were not nearly enough explosives to fill them and hardly any fuses to detonate them.

People always say that wars will be over by Christmas, and of course they are always right, so long as they remain vague about which Christmas they have in mind. This war was beginning to look as though it would outlast any number of Christmases and New Year's Days. If you take two armies and dig holes in the ground and put the armies into the holes and tell all concerned to hold their positions at any cost it's no use anticipating a speedy victory.

One possibility was that the war would have to end when there was nobody left to fight it; fatalities in the front lines were so heavy that the living were outnumbered by the ghosts, the stretcher-bearers by the dying, and those who lived in hope were fewer than those who prayed for an early release. David paid a flying visit to France and was told by General Foch to pass on a message to the Cabinet: there will be no more retreats. Would there be any more advances? David asked. The following day saw the start of the Battle of Ypres.

At sea HMS *Audacious*, a dreadnought, and three cruisers were sunk, but the German admirals were content to avoid any decisive engagements in which they would be seriously outnumbered.

The Russians were in disarray and the War Cabinet, anxious for almost any kind of initiative, threw its weight behind Churchill's Dardanelles campaign instead of David's plan for a Salonika expedition. A disastrous decision, which only went to show that the sagest policy in wartime is often to do nothing and let the opposing side make all the mistakes.

If the guns and the ammunition were in short supply the young men were not. They came forward and signed on cheerfully, keen to do their bit. The best in the land, they trained with broom-handles. The trouble was that they were shipped to the Western front, and given enough ammunition for just two hours out of twenty-four, which suggested that they were twelve times more likely to be shot than their German counterparts. Fixed bayonets against German shells: a strange idea the War Office had of 'economy'. David's idea of the War Office was that it was composed of stupid, smug, hidebound, sanctimonious, Whitehall Old Etonians, and that the sooner they got the Chancellor's boot up their backsides the better for all concerned.

Dick Lloyd George was an officer in the Royal Engineers. When he came home on leave he told Maggie what it was really like in the trenches. And then with such bitterness in his voice that it made Maggie weep to hear it he asked: 'What's *he* doing these days? Still making speeches about glory and sacrifice, is he? Still imagining that the boys go over the top with a song in their hearts and "God bless England" on their lips. Well, he ought to know it's not like that. He ought to know what the boys are really saying about England and England's government.'

David listened to Dick and knew that he was not exaggerating the position; but the intransigence of the War Office, Kitchener's complacency, and Asquith's indolence were formidable barriers. Years in politics had taught David that when you are in doubt you must propose a new Committee. Asquith agreed and a Cabinet Munitions Committee was formed with David in the chair and both Kitchener and Churchill excluded. Kitchener was displeased. If the new Committee had more than advisory powers, he insisted he would resign. David would certainly resign unless the Committee had teeth. And the war dragged on with rumours circulating daily about who was in, who out, when Asquith would resign, whether David would take his place, when a coalition would be formed, and so on.

Meanwhile David decided that something must be done about the amount of liquor being consumed by workers in armaments factories. He told the King about it and suggested that if His Majesty were publicly to renounce the bottle many loyal subjects would feel impelled to follow suit. The King considered the matter and then announced that not a drop of spirituous liquor would pass his lips until the war was over. Curiously, though, even loyal subjects of His Majesty turned out not to be *that* loyal. There are some forces in nature more powerful than any king and not many signed the pledge.

The crisis grew more acute. Refusing to accept the authority of the new committee, Kitchener set up one of his own. Sir John French, despairing of getting any ammunition for his troops out of Kitchener, made a personal appeal to the Chancellor; *The Times* and the *Daily Mail*, both owned by Northcliffe, set about getting rid of the Secretary of State for War. Lord Fisher, the First Sea Lord, watching his ships being sunk and hearing of Churchill's proposal to send two more submarines to the Dardanelles, resigned, and would not be comforted. Bonar Law for the Unionists announced that his party would oppose Churchill's retention at the Admiralty and proposed to David that a coalition be formed, since internecine squabbling at such a time would be fatal. David agreed and so too, with a mighty sigh of relief, did Asquith.

And in such strange circumstances was Churchill indirectly responsible for the emasculation of the Liberal Party, which never again held office.

The new Coalition was a hotch-potch. The idea that Kitchener might go was too much for the public, who venerated him with superstitious idolatry, but David took over that part of his office which had been most noticeably incompetent, the business of munitions. McKenna replaced David at the Treasury (but he had no objection to his predecessor staying on at Number 11) and Bonar Law, who had hoped to be War Minister or Chancellor, had to console himself as best he could with the Colonial Office. But if it was hard on him it was worse on Churchill: the punishment for Winston's expensive spree at the Admiralty, his fiasco at Antwerp and the disaster in the Dardanelles, was to be appointed Chancellor of the Duchy of Lancaster, 'an office boy's job'.

'You don't really care, do you?' Churchill resentfully asked his old friend. 'You don't care what this means to me?'

David looked at him dispassionately. He saw a little boy sulking because he had been cheated out of a prize.

'No', he said. 'I don't care about you. I don't care about me either. All I care about now is winning the war. Remember how keen you were to get me into it?'

It was true. David had apparently been moved a few rungs down the ladder of political ambition – and Maggie didn't at all care for that! But Dick's experiences in the front lines and what he had seen for himself of conditions there had inspired him with a zealous energy to get ammunition and weapons into the hands of the brave young men who were dying for lack of them. Asquith was touched by his Chancellor's selflessness and wrote to him:

'I shall never forget your devotion. your unselfishness, your powers of resource . . . These are the rare things which make the drudgery and squalor of politics, with its constant revelation of the large part played by petty and personal motives, endurable, and give to its drabness a lightning streak of notability. I thank you with all my heart.'

Mrs Stevenson, to her amazement, was becoming reconciled to her daughter's irregular relationship with David (just as Mrs Owen had some thirty years before). Frances wrote in her diary: 'She recognizes it as an honest love which will last and not just a passing passion.' It is not recorded what Mrs Stevenson wrote in her diary but David continued to exercise his charm and from time to time sent her baskets of fruit. Frances herself had never regretted the decision taken that night in Gatti's. 'It has brought me two years of happiness, and if fate wills will bring me many more. Sometimes I am so happy that I tremble for fear it will not last. Our love will always last, but there is the dread that he might be taken from me.'

Was it fate or was it Maggie that Frances most feared? There was no doubt now that Maggie knew about Frances. There are always good, kind friends ready to tell wives any gossip to their husband's discredit, and vice versa. But besides that she had seen them together. She knew David's predilections, and she could imagine how fascinating he must seem to a girl of limited experience like Frances. And if the relationship was longer-lasting and less hole-in-the-corner than most of his previous affairs then there were advantages in that too. Frances was single, intelligent, and, it appeared, discreet. She was far less of a risk to David's career and to his peace of mind than the predatory and nervous married women he had become involved with in the past. Maggie knew about Frances as much as she cared to know. But she didn't have to like the girl.

They met in the drawing-room of 11 Downing Street. Frances was busy answering letters when Maggie arrived from Wales, which she did rarely and reluctantly. Frances stood up to greet her with: 'I hope you had a comfortable journey?'

'Not very,' said Maggie coldly. 'The train was full of soldiers.'

'I suppose,' said Frances a little sententiously 'we must all be ready to sacrifice some of our comforts these days. It's little enough compared with what *they* give.'

'I'm the last person to need reminding of that, Miss Stevenson. My son has just returned from the Western Front.'

'My brother will never return.'

'I'm sorry,' said Maggie, disliking the girl for having a brother who had been killed, and disliking herself for such uncharitable thoughts.

'Yes. He was quite brilliant.' Frances felt that Maggie expected her to leave the room, go about her business elsewhere; however she was *very* busy, and she had territorial rights in Downing Street.

Maggie asked: 'Are you finding your work congenial?'

'Oh yes! Mr Lloyd George has so much on his mind these days. I feel it's so important that he shouldn't be distracted from his work by any unnecessary problems and disturbances and I think I can help in that way.'

'Don't let him work *too* hard though, my dear' said Maggie, trading blows. 'I hope you try to remember that he must have a *bit* of rest now and then. And then pressing home the advantage: 'Oh by the way, would this be yours by any chance?'

149

'*This*' was a small round tin of vanishing cream. Frances was caught off guard: 'It might be. I'm not sure. Where did you find it?'

'Oh, it was just lying around. But there, it might be anybody's, my husband has such a wide circle of friends. I might ask Mrs Tim Davies. I know he still sees her occasionally.

For a moment Frances was too angry and too upset to speak. It was fortunate for her that at this moment David strolled in and she was able legitimately to ignore Maggie's mischief.

'Could you sign these, please?' she asked David and as she handed them to him the expression in her eyes clearly indicated that he had not arrived a moment too soon.

'I was just telling Miss Stevenson' said Maggie, 'that you're not to be allowed to work too hard Dei. Why don't you go down to Walton Heath for the weekend?'

The trap was sprung. David said: 'That's not a bad idea, Maggie,' and Frances looked decidedly brighter until Maggie added casually: 'And I think I'll come down with you. I could do with a change of air.'

Frances was beaten and knew it. She had no weaponry against Maggie in this sort of mood. She hurried out of the room, and slammed the door.

David said: 'Maggie, that was wicked!' but his eyes were twinkling and he took hold of her hand and squeezed it; two old professionals.

As Chancellor of the Exchequer David had commanded a department of thousands; as Minister of Munitions his staff consisted of just two private secretaries: J. T. Davies and Frances. He had two tables and a chair until the Office of Works took one of the tables away. His immediate concern was to provide the troops with what the French had been using in the trenches with abundant success: high explosive shells and lots of them. The army had been demanding – and Kitchener had been suppressing the demands – 200,000 shells a day, but the army had been getting just 150,000 a week.

A visit to Woolwich Arsenal convinced David that the productive capacity of such a place was completely inadequate. There were three other royal factories, but they were old-fashioned and slow. He commissioned the building of another seventy national armaments factories by the end of the year. Wisely he had made plenary powers conditional upon his acceptance of the Ministry, so that now when Kitchener raised objections to the extravagant requirements sent out daily from the Ministry of Munitions he was arguing from a position of weakness.

Kitchener complained about everything, about David communicating directly with the Army commanders and about his extravagance. When Kitchener ordered 770 heavy guns, David added 600 to the order.

When Asquith questioned him David explained his reasons. The Germans were supplying sixteen guns to each battalion. Kitchener had requested two as a minimum and four as a maximum. The request was carried to David by Sir Eric Geddes. Using his plenary powers David instructed Geddes to take Kitchener's maximum, to square it to multiply it by two, and then to double it again. With sixty-four guns to each battalion Britain might even win the war. To the TUC he explained that the real war was being fought between the engineers of Germany and Austria and those of Britain and France and so far as the British engineers were concerned only 15 per cent of the factories were working a night shift. If he had to take steps under the new Defence of the Realm Act to limit the possibility of drunkenness in the munitions factories, then so be it. And if some of the munitions workers baulked at working night shifts then it was worth reminding them that their prewar comrades their brothers and their sons, all those who had enlisted and were fighting in the filth and mud of the trenches could not say: 'I have been in the trenches eight hours and a half, and my trade union won't allow me to work more than eight hours . . . ' More controversially he had to reconcile trade union leaders to the idea that workers would not be permitted to strike during wartime and would have to present their grievances to an arbitrator.

English trade union leaders, being gentle spirits, were agreeable enough to all these proposals; their resistance, such as it was, was brittle and easily shattered. In return David guaranteed that any excessive profits by employers would be heavily taxed. But in Scotland, particularly on the Clyde, the union leaders were less compliant. There David Kirkwood and Willie Gallagher mounted strenuous opposition to such recidivism. At a meeing in St Andrew's Hall a large audience of Clydesiders shouted down their eminent visitors.

Seeing David off at the station Willie Gallagher murmured: 'I'm sorry if we wasted your time brother ' but he wasn't and David knew that he wasn't, and Willie knew that David knew which was why they were both smiling

'Are you?'

'Och aye. For auld times' sake anyway. You were a great hero of mine back in the Boer War before you became respectable.'

'Perhaps if I could have got them to listen to me . . . '

'They'd not do that brother. They remember what you've forgotten, you see. They know that a bayonet is a weapon with a worker at each end.'

It rankled. Criticism from the establishment was meat and drink to David; he had built his career to the sound of pips squeaking. But these words from a man he liked a man whose opinions he admired though he could not always share them, a man *of the people* rankled.

Glasgow's socialist newspaper, *Forward*, was grateful for the opportunity afforded by David's abortive visit and reported that 'the best-paid munitions worker in the country Mr Lloyd George – nearly a hundred pounds a week – visited the Clyde in search of adventure. He got it . . . '

More pertinently it characterized the war as an imperialist exercise and called on workers in the munitions factories to down tools Subversive stuff which David decided must be banned though he hated giving Willie Gallagher evidence of his respectability so soon after his visit. He had to accustom himself to playing the villain.

He sought solace in hard work and worked as he had never worked before, would never do again. He worked to great effect. The shells, guns and rifles, the tanks, bombs and instruments everything which the soldiers had died waiting for was now being shipped to France in great quantity and at great speed. His modest office became hopelessly inadequate; he moved to the Hotel Metropole and took on more staff.

There were good times, moments when he could get away from requisition forms the smell of cordite the sound of axes grinding, and the dealing in death and dying. He would take Frances into the countryside and he would sing to her, dance to her and make love to her not passionately as in his young unfettered days, but gently and tenderly, finding in Frances's embrace the peace and security for which he was striving in his cluttered and over-worked Ministry. Such moments kept him from going mad.

'Did I tell you,' he asked Frances as they walked together hand in hand along a deserted lane, 'about the last time I nearly got certified? I was driving home from the Guildhall – big function, all the crachach - me in the full Privy Councillor rig, the knee-breeches and the silver buckles sword, cloak! Then the car broke down. Mostyn gets out and sticks his head under the bonnet, fiddling around there for about twenty minutes. And you must understand it had been a *very* long banquet, and the waiter had kept on refilling my glass the lemonade flowing like water. So I quickly slipped out of the back seat to go – you know – *dros ben ciawdd*. But before I was halfway through I heard the car door slam – gospel truth. Pussy – vrmm, vrmm, car going off in to the night. "Hey! Come back! Come ba-ack!" Gone! Hitch up the knee-breeches, straighten the scabbard, flourish the cloak . . D'Artagnan was nowhere in it. I tramped for miles and miles till I came to these great iron gates, extensive grounds inside. I didn't know what it was. Mud all over the silk stockings by this time. for a wind had sprung up. I rang the bell and announced: "I am the Chancellor of the Exchequer!" "Oh yes," they say, very soothing like, "come on in, Chancellor, the rest of the Cabinet have been expecting you! And Napoleon Bonaparte!" '

Frances laughed at the story, but more from relief at the exuberant way he told it. She worried about the demands being made upon him and knew that so long as he retained his sense of humour all would be well. But he sounded less humorous as he continued: 'Fact is, Pussy I might even have to go back there soon, recruiting. They're about the only places I haven't combed out. Another deputation coming from Lancashire tomorrow screaming for more manpower, and what can I tell them? We're scraping the barrel already.'

Frances stopped walking leant back against a gate and inquired: 'What about womanpower?

'Women? Oh no. that's Maggie's department. She's got them all knitting woollies for soldiers, and rolling up bandages, and – '

'That's all you think they're fit for?'

'No. They can be nurses and secretaries and all kinds of things. But you know what I'm looking for. Factory workers lorry drivers engineers . . '

'Well?' said Frances, 'Why not?'

David had done well. He had obtained for his Committee plenary powers and he had used them to get the government to place orders for significant supplies of munitions. He had had the factories constructed to make the shells the bombs and the rifles; and he had persuaded the workers (except in Glasgow) that it was their patriotic duty to work day and night and to go easy on the drink. Short of killing Germans personally there was not a great deal more that he could do to ensure victory. But government orders factories and industrious workers cannot make bricks with straw no more could they make high explosives without cordite cordite without acetone acetone without wood alcohol, or wood alcohol without timber.

The American producers had been Britain's chief suppliers, but even they could not meet the enormous demands being made upon them (and when they could, they were less than scrupulous in meeting their quotas raising prices *after* signing contracts selling their output twice over and behaving in so feckless a fashion that David would have taken them over at once had they been British firms).

The Germans had more timber than they could possibly need, vast forests of their own, and limitless reserves in Eastern Europe and if Russia surrendered, as seemed increasingly probable the situation would be desperate. Only David knew how desperate, for the newspapers continued to sell copies by reporting more glorious victories on the Western Front; a few hundred yards of duckboards and mud for thousands of young lives, if they had cared to tell the truth.

All David could do he had done already: he had set a number of leading chemists the problem of making acetone without timber and making it quickly. But chemists do not believe in magic; spells charms and incantations are not employed in the best-run laboratories, and without such aids they could only work away with their bunsen burners and pipettes, making calculations and bubbles and smells.

But there was one chemist who did appear to have magical powers. Just five weeks after David had outlined the problem to him, Professor Chaim Weizmann, born on the banks of the Vistula but a naturalized Briton living on the banks of the Manchester Ship Canal, came to see him with a solution. Was it magic? Weizmann claimed to be able to extract acetone from maize directly, from any cereal with a little adaptation, from horse-chestnuts, from, it seemed, almost anything, even perhaps David's moustache. Furthermore, the Professor claimed that the process was quick and clean and would need far less bulk of raw material than the wood alcohol process.

'Professor Weizmann,' said David, scarcely daring to believe that this remarkable man in the shabby black overcoat was going to make the dream of a land flowing with milk and honey - or at least acetone - a reality, 'I need hardly say that if this process proves effective you will have rendered a very great service to the state, and I shall make it my personal responsibility to see that it is adequately recognized and honoured.'

'There is nothing I want for myself.'

'There must be *something* you would accept.'

'I have only one ambition.' The Professor's heavily accented voice became passionate, but he did not look at David. He had heard that the Minister was an anti-semite, but nothing in David's treatment of him had suggested it. 'Of course, I attach no conditions - the process is yours. But I would like you to do something for my people. It is my most cherished dream to see a national home for the Jews in Palestine.'

David smiled and murmured: 'If I forget thee, O Jerusalem, let my right hand forget her cunning '
Then he spoke more briskly: 'I can understand your feelings about this better perhaps than you can imagine. I would be very surprised if my knowledge of the Old Testament were any less extensive than your own. In the country I come from, Professor, we meet every Sunday in buildings called Beulah, Siloa, Ebenezer Bethany, Nazareth. Study the names on the gravestones of my people and you will find engraved Seth and Abel, Rachel and Bathsheba, Jacob and Israel. Some believe that the lost tribe came and settled in Wales. When you hear our poetry and music and see the faces of our women it is possible to believe it. However,' and he stood up and escorted the Professor to the door, 'I'll have a word with Mr Balfour about this and arrange for you to meet him. He's by way of being a

scientist and will be deeply interested in your discovery. As for the Palestine project, that will be a job for the Foreign Office. But I do give you my word that it will be given serious and sympathetic consideration.'

'I am very grateful to you, Minister,' said Weizmann warmly, shaking hands as though the physical contact were a transfusion of optimism for the future of the world, 'that is just what I hoped for.'

Frances Stevenson had suggested to David that woman-power was one natural source of energy in Britain which was scarcely being harnessed at all, and David saw the sense in the suggestion. But he could see no way in which to mobilize that energy, especially since the women who were most likely to be receptive to the idea were the very ones who had been receptive to the idea of blowing up his house at Walton Heath. However here the principle obtained of putting a knife and fork in the hands of your enemy and converting that enemy into a friend. So he invited Emmeline Pankhurst to dine with him at a restaurant which was as discreet as Gatti's where he had charmed Frances into doing what he wished and a good deal less fashionable. Mrs Pankhurst's reputation would probably have been more damaged by being seen with him than his by being seen with her, but it would have been a close-run thing.

'You don't need to worry,' David assured his companion when the food had been ordered, 'they're very discreet here.'

'I'll take your word for that,' said Emmeline. 'I'm sure you would know about such things,' She was evidently every bit as sharp as any of his colleagues in the House, and a good deal better-looking.

'Mrs Pankhurst, if I may speak frankly as one politician to another – '

'I don't accept that term "politician". Our movement is a crusade. I have never sought power for its own sake.'

'A great deal of power has accrued to you nevertheless

which means your time must be quite as valuable as mine. We can't afford to waste it on recriminations.'

'I certainly won't be the one to initiate them,' said Emmeline, smiling grimly. 'I regard myself first and foremost as an Englishwoman: we must be prepared to sink all other differences until the war is over.'

'And you think that what I'm proposing is at least feasible?'

'Of *course* it is!' Emmeline spoke with such scorn that David was bewildered. When he was polite to these women they despised him, and when he was rude to them they bombed him. It was hard to know what attitude to strike. Emmeline continued: 'If it will be of service to this country, the women of Britain will go anywhere and do anything that's required of them. And I venture to say you'll find them quite as efficient as the men they will be replacing.'

'I'm glad to hear it, but not surprised.'

'In that case, Mr Lloyd George, why *did* you arrange this meeting?'

'Two reasons. One is that if *I* issue an appeal for women to lay down their knitting needles and go into factories and make munitions it's going to arouse a lot of indignation – polluting the fair flower of English womanhood, forcing women into unnatural behaviour, destroying their femininity, the usual sort of thing.' Mrs Pankhurst nodded at this. She was only too familiar with such phrases. 'The other reason is that I want above all to appeal to the most active-minded and vigorous women, because they are the ones with most to offer, but they are also the ones who have been encouraged, perhaps even persuaded, Mrs Pankhurst, into regarding me as beyond the pale.'

'I think I could arrange for that to be amended – given time.'

'There is no time. We have to exploit the situation as it stands. Mrs Pankhurst I want you to twist my arm. These women will follow you anywhere. What I envisage is that you should lead a mass demonstration of suffragettes into Parliament Square *demanding* for women the right to work.

Then I shall cringe before this spontaneous display of unity and determination. It will be my road to Damascus: I shall see the light! The women will storm in through the factory gates trampling over the sensibilities of wicked old Lloyd George, and Emmeline Pankhurst will have scored another great victory.'

Mrs Pankhurst let the waiter serve the food, ignoring both it and him. Nor was there scorn in her expression any longer when she looked at the Munitions Minister. Despite his facetious way of expressing himself there was much in what he said.

'I hope you realize, Mr George, that if once you uncork this bottle you will never again be able to put the genie back in. When the war is over they will never again return to their kitchens and their nurseries. There can be no compulsion.'

'Madam, the idea of my compelling any woman to go where she would rather not be or do what she would rather not do is absurd. I've never been able to manage that and never will. And I've got too much sense to start now.'

Emmeline Pankhurst smiled. She was beginning to understand why so many women had made such fools of themselves over this undersized man. And she was smiling too at the irony which dictated that it would take a combination of the German war machine and an ambitious Welshman to ensure the imminent reality of Votes For Women.

Chapter Six

In February 1915 Frances had fallen ill and had believed herself to be pregnant. If she was pregnant she miscarried. Her mother reacted angrily. Frances wrote in her diary: 'My people have been trying to separate us, trying to make me promise that I will give up his love. the most precious thing of my life.' She felt that she had made David happy, and he once confessed to her that he had known no real happiness between the ages of three and twenty. 'If I had to choose between dying the next day, and going back to three years of age,' he had said, 'I should infinitely prefer death.' And yet if she made him happy she caused much misery to the two people to whom she felt she owed the most. It was dreadfully difficult.

Easier, though, when she was with David at Walton Heath. There he was 'husband, lover and mother' to her and she was constantly amazed at the concern and tenderness shown her by a man much immersed in the great and anxious affairs of state.

That autumn David showed his concern for her wellbeing in a characteristically unconventional manner He suggested that a certain Captain Hugh Owen, who was liaison officer between the Ministry of Munitions and the War Office, and who was partial to Frances, should marry her. By being an adultress instead of a mistress Frances would become more respectable, thought David, and should she again become pregnant the matter could be passed off without a scandal. The curious threesome motored to Eastbourne to see in the New Year, and in May 1916 Frances's marriage was confidently expected by some of her friends. But she did not marry Owen, who, in the traditional way. went to the colonies and had a successful, if lonely career Mrs Stevenson wrote, a little tartly, to her daughter: 'I have known all along that you did not care sufficiently for

Owen to marry him. The pity is that you ever engaged yourself to him.'

By June 1916 the Ministry of Munitions was running itself and Asquith proposed that David and Kitchener should sail together and study the situation on the Eastern Front at first hand. It was vital that the Russian army should continue to hold its positions against the Germans, for should they collapse, the additional pressure which the Central Powers could bring to bear on the Western Front might well prove decisive. Supplies of food and ammunition had been sent to Russia but frequently these got no further than Archangel.

Although Kitchener would not have been David's choice of travelling companion, for he had recently become lethargic and something of an embarrassment at the War Office, where the power had shifted to Sir William Robertson, Chief of the Imperial General Staff, it promised to be an interesting trip, and the Munitions Minister quite fancied himself in a fur hat.

But events were taking place in Dublin which made Russia seem trivial. On Easter Monday, 1916, a handful of Irishmen seized the Dublin Post Office and proclaimed an Irish Republic. Pearse, a schoolmaster, was to be president. It would have been an historic as well as an heroic gesture if only the rest of the Irish people had believed in the possibility of victory. As it was the heroism was compounded by martyrdom.

The British troops over-reacted; a polite expression for murder and mayhem. Instead of placing the Post Office under blockade and starving out the rebels. a battery situated at Trinity College and another on a warship in the Liffey so bombarded the city centre that a square mile of it was reduced to rubble. Just about every building of any size was flattened with the *exception* of the Post Office. for the troops were as wildly inaccurate as they were murderous. And then the executions began, and General Sir John Maxwell instituted a series of mopping-up operations of such savagery that the Irish could be forgiven for believing that what they were up against were not educated and sophisticated Englishmen but insatiable and bloodthirsty pirates.

The necessity for a settlement – almost any settlement – became urgent. Besides the damage to Anglo-Irish relationships those Americans who had traditional Irish ties (which meant most Americans) were being antagonized by the butchery, and might think twice about entering the war with such hysterical allies.

Asquith asked David to forget Russia and to concentrate his mind on Ireland and negotiate a settlement on behalf of the government. It was not unlike being asked to uncover a wasps' nest and make peace with the wasps. Asquith assured David that it was a unique opportunity.

'A unique opportunity to bang my head against a brick wall,' commented David wryly.

Asquith knew that if anyone could do it, David could. and said so. David begged to differ then agreed on condition he had *carte blanche* to negotiate. Asquith said he was very sorry but certain members of the Cabinet . . . no, he could *not* have *carte blanche*. David reluctantly agreed to take it on anyway.

First he saw the Nationalists and proposed Home Rule directly, but with Ulster excluded until after the war, when a vote could be taken on the future of the six counties. Redmond. the chairman of the Nationalists spotted the fly in this ointment at once. If the South was independent it would lose its representation at Westminster and the Unionists would be able to vote for permanent exclusion from the Republic. Supposing the Nationalists retained their MPs in the House of Commons until a final agreement had been reached? Redmond scratched his chin over that one. It sounded all very fine, but . . .

It sounded all very unsatisfactory to Sir Edward Carson, the handsome Ulsterman and Unionist Member for Dublin University. With a Liberal majority after the war and the Irish vote, the government would be perfectly able and probably willing to hand the six counties over to Dublin anyway. Politics didn't come into it. It was a simple matter of mathematics. Carson wanted guarantees. But, as David pointed out, there were none anyway. If after the war the Commons voted for Home Rule, that was it.

'We can fight,' said Carson, and there was little doubt that he and his Ulster Volunteers would fight as bitterly as the Sinn Feiners had done (and with rather more hope of success).

'You can always do that,' said David. 'But this way at least there'd be a precedent for separation; there'd be an agreed boundary. Isn't that worth something?'

Carson agreed, but was naturally inquisitive to know where the boundary would be drawn, and what would happen to Tyrone and Fermanagh.

Well it was a start, and more than a start. Once one started to discuss details there was always a chance of settling them; a compromise would be possible, and David took heart at that. He should not have done. No politician should ever dare to congratulate himself over Ireland.

General Maxwell continued his brutal progress through the South, and each atrocity made any settlement less likely. But it was in the Cabinet Room that David came to realize what it meant to inherit a whirlwind.

Walter Long wanted to know by what right the Minister proposed handing over the houses and lands of those Protestants who lived in the South to 'a gang of papists'. The Marquess of Lansdowne was incensed that a Cabinet Minister should have been engaged in making concessions to 'terrorists and rebels', and Long and Lansdowne and a handful of other Unionists made it uncomfortably clear that they would secede from the government if any form of Home Rule was granted to the South.

In that case, David inquired – and with a legitimate sense of grievance – what had been the point of his conducting the negotiations at all? If his authority was to be retrospectively repudiated he would resign. John Redmond would never trust him again; he would have been better employed with Kitchener in Russia. (But he would never have got to Russia. The ship carrying Kitchener and his entourage struck a mine off the Orkneys and sank. Very few passengers survived.)

Should he resign? Frances thought he should. Ireland had always been the graveyard of reputations, she said. So why had he ever taken on such a hopeless commission?

'I suppose because if I'd refused they'd have said I was afraid.'

'But, darling, that's a schoolboy's reason.'

'Is it, Pussy? I believe that the first time a man turns down a job because he thinks it's too big for him, he might as well throw in the towel.'

'And if it ends in your resignation?'

Should he resign? A new Chief Secretary for Ireland was appointed and administration from Dublin Castle reimposed. Consequently the Nationalists thought that he had broken his promise of Home Rule to them and should go. And the Unionists continued to bay for his blood.

Should he resign? Everyone seemed to think so; but he didn't want to. Dillon and Redmond vowed they would never trust him again if he didn't. He told everyone that he would and eventually told Asquith, who at once promised that conscription should be extended to married men, an extension which David had been anxious to bring about, if he stayed on. David did stay on. And with Kitchener's death an alternative presented itself. Somebody would have to succeed to the War Office, a post which had lost much of its significance since David's War Committee had been set up. But it could again become a Department worth running, in the hands of a strong man, one who was nobody's fool.

David was nobody's fool, but, it seemed, with the exception of Bonar Law, nobody's friend Sir William Robertson had had Kitchener well-trained and didn't want a little Welsh Terrier snapping at his heels. The King certainly regarded his Munitions Minister as unreliable. And Asquith, who had been kept in no doubt as to David's increasing contempt for his Prime Minister, was reluctant to commit himself. But Bonar Law, alert to the danger that David might join forces with Carson, insisted on Asquith's sounding him out.

David drafted two letters setting out his reasons for not accepting the office of Secretary of State for War, then sent one accepting. But the matter of the demarcation lines between the CIGS and the Secretary of State remained unresolved.

'They give me house-room,' David complained to Churchill. 'They treat me politely. They give me these chairs, and I sit on one and put my feet on another and go to sleep. When they look at me they see only one thing, a civilian, and they don't like civilians in an old officers' home. Should I be rash enough to try to change anything they sneak off to Buckingham Palace and complain that I'm, "Interfering with Strategy". And in this mausoleum that ranks as the sin against the Holy Ghost. My function here is that of the butcher's boy who leads the animals to slaughter.'

Churchill was sympathetic. He had spent months getting the new caterpillar tanks perfected and the army wasted them in taking a couple of ruined villages on the Somme, so that the psychological effect of the new weapon was quite blunted.

'As far as I can see,' David remarked, 'there hasn't been a single plan conceived and carried out by the soldiers that hasn't ended in bloody failure.' Civilians could surely do no worse. As for the Cabinet, it was demoralized and indecisive, and when it did take action it was usually too little and always too late.

The failures of the past were bloody enough but as nothing to the failures of the present. During the week before David took up his position at the War Office, Sir Douglas Haig launched what he was convinced would be the last great offensive of the war. For more than twenty thousand men on the first day of the Battle of the Somme it was. Such glorious sacrifices, the generals thought, must not be thrown away, and the great offensive and glorious sacrifices continued until it seemed that there could not possibly be any more men or horses anxious to open their throats to German bullets or impale themselves on barbed wire. Corpses are not easily distinguishable in such conditions and the handsome face of the British Prime Minister's brilliant son was no more handsome, his death no more brilliant than a million others in that Battle of the Somme which the generals thought so glorious.

With the death of his son, the light went out of Asquith's eyes. He still chaired his War Committee but his authority had gone, and the bickering and buck-passing, the time-wasting and time-serving indicated that if the generals were incompetent to prosecute the war successfully, the government was no better placed to do so. Even the predominance of Britain's navy was threatened by a sudden increase in Germany's submarine warfare. David argued that there was no time to be lost. Shipping and food dictators with plenary powers should be appointed at once. He sounded as though he felt there was only one man capable of taking on such onerous responsibilities. And then there was the matter of who should be responsible for the newly created Air Board. Should it be independent or run by the Admiralty? With such skilled debaters as Balfour, Curzon and Edwin Montagu (who had taken over from David at the Ministry of Munitions) anxious to take a hand in the matter, the debate would continue until Asquith sighed and glanced at the clock and sighed again and suggested postponing the discussion.

There were rare evenings when alone with Frances David was able to sit and warm his toes in front of the fire, eat an informal supper, and express his frustrations and fears to someone sympathetic enough to listen and intelligent enough to understand.

'Oh, Pussy! All the fools and villains and muddlers I've been trying to do battle with! I can put up with it all as long as you're beside me, but, when you're not there I just want to scream and smash things and push them all out of the way and make a bee-line back to my dear girl.'

And then sometimes he would add: 'If only we could be married!'

A look of pain would shadow Frances's eyes and she would say quietly: 'It's no use thinking about that,' which was true, but no help. David would continue to think about it, because of his guilt, and continue to talk about it, about giving up politics, about giving up England, about . . . And this was foolish talk, as Frances was quick to point out, for without politics David would be wretched within a week and would blame his wretchedness on her.

'It doesn't do,' said Frances severely, for she was, after all, a schoolmistress by profession, 'to think about living any other way: it only leads to bitterness.' Things had improved for her since she had taken a flat in Chester Square and furnished and decorated it with considerable taste. Now she could enjoy a certain measure of privacy. She no longer felt like an intruder and David could visit her with a little more discretion and less fear of interruption than in the dust-cover days of the recent past. He loved both his wives, expressing his love to Frances more frequently than to Maggie, and in language which Maggie would have thought ridiculous. He said that he only wished he could have found her sooner and given her more, but she seemed contented enough. Did she not feel the lack of children, David asked her one day, greatly daring, for it was a subject about which he fancied she would be sensitive (in his experience women were). But Frances just said:

'Well, if there were children, I wouldn't be able to share your work the way I do now; I couldn't be so much help to you, I wouldn't feel so close, so perhaps it's better as it is.' And then added after a momentary hesitation, 'At least that's what I tell myself.'

David felt himself to be on safer ground when he insisted that if ever he were in a position to marry her, it would be the first wish of his heart. He took pains to make her believe him, and she did; she felt more secure and apparently quite content with her lot.

For some time there had been murmurings among the War Committee that, since it seemed increasingly unlikely that Britain would win the war, the wisest thing to do would be to sue for peace while we still had something to sue with. Lansdowne put such a proposal in writing and circulated it amongst his colleagues. President Woodrow Wilson, up for re-election later in the year, was keen to put himself forward as arbitrator, and the idea found favour with most of the Cabinet, Asquith included, but not with Bonar Law or David.

Rather than continue a private squabble, David thought to let the fresh air of public opinion in on the musty committee rooms and stated the case for continuing the war in an interview printed in *The Times*.

'Britain,' he was quoted as saying, 'is not prepared to stop the war because of squealing done by Germans or done for Germans. We must fight to a finish, to a knock-out blow. There can be no outside interference at this stage. Britain can tolerate no intervention. The enemy is whimpering and whining. With regard to the duration of the war there is neither clock nor calendar in the British army today. Time is the least vital factor. It took England twenty years to defeat Napoleon, and the first fifteen of those years were bleak with British defeats. It will not take twenty years to win this war, but whatever time is required it will be done!'

Who were the traitors? The ones who called for 'an exchange of views' or the ones who cried 'Fight on!' The result of the war would decide that. But in the meantime David's stock among his colleagues was about as high as Patagonian gold-mining shares. They said – they were bound to – that he was making a bid for the premiership. They threatened to make public his liaison with Frances, although few of the ones who were prepared to sling mud were sufficiently confident that their own nests were unfouled. (But they had difficulty in Wales keeping the rumours from Uncle Lloyd.) Two things sustained David through this difficult time: the loyalty of two good women, and the numerous letters from soldiers' relatives who supported him in his desire to ensure that those who were fighting and dying were not doing so in vain; in order that President Wilson be re-elected; or to spare the blushes of pig-headed and incompetent generals.

In November 1916 a politicians' conference on the conduct of the war was held in Paris. The train carrying the British delegation passed the war cemetery at Etaples, where row upon row of plain wooden crosses stretched away into the mist. A chastening sight for politicians. Asquith remembered his son, sacrificed for Belgium. So hard to remember now why they had thought it necessary to go to war, though it had seemed straightforward enough at the time. Raymond Asquith had agreed; he had been hot as mustard to get at the Germans and his father had been so proud of him. In later years Asquith was to write to Baldwin of 'the unsharable solitude in the position of Prime Minister who has to bear the burden not only of his own sins and his colleagues, but at times it almost seems those of the whole world.' He felt the solitude most bitterly now as the train added its steam to the morning mists of Etaples.

David watched the Prime Minister and guessed at his feelings. He too had lost a child and felt at times as though he had killed her. He too saw the crosses fading to infinity, and thought that the lives of the young men must not have been in vain. The war must be fought out to the end. He thought too of the speech which Asquith had asked him to write for the Conference. Asquith should have written it himself, or had one of his staff do it, but he had lost all confidence, and hoped that David's words would give him back his spirit. So David *did* write it, and told the truth as he saw it; that the generals were wasting ammunition, men and time, but that the situation was grave though not irretrievable if the generals could be made to see the error of their ways (but when did generals ever see that? You didn't get to be a general by admitting your mistakes). He wrote the speech, and then had to undergo the humiliation of hearing Asquith deliver it with its teeth taken out. This was the *children's* version. And, if this were not disheartening enough, it soon became apparent that the *real* decisions were being made at Chantilly where the generals had convened. And what had the generals decided? That 1917 should be like 1916 with another Ypres no doubt, and another Somme.

Once again David determined to resign.

On the way home he was violently seasick; the other sickness, the one that went deeper, would not be cured by coming ashore; that would only be cured in Frances's arms.

Maggie was adaptable; it was a natural talent with her. She had had to adapt to marrying a man not thought worthy of her, and then she had had to adapt to being married to a man she was not thought worthy of, and then she had had to adapt to all the gossip and the scandal and, worst of all, to the self-conscious 'kindness' of those who felt sorry for her. Now she had to adapt – and it was the most unnatural accommodation of all – to taking second place in her husband's affections. If her love for David had not been so deeply embedded it would have been extracted like a splinter from a sore thumb, leaving behind it soreness and a sense of relief. As it was she could live with it and even talk to him about it, almost without rancour. Maggie was indeed adaptable.

When David had toothache and Frances sent for the dentist it was remarkable how quickly the pain disappeared, so quickly that Frances was able to cancel the dentist's visit – twice! But when David complained to Maggie that he had toothache she made certain that the dentist came and pulled the tooth out and then she sat beside him and comforted him and told him how brave he was and sent Sarah off to make some cawl. And then she told him what she had observed about Frances, not out of jealous spite, but because it would be useful information for him to file under R for Realistic.

'If anything happened to me you would marry this one,

I know,' she said, and David did not dispute it. And then she spoke of Frances's deficiences: 'First, she will always tell you what you want to hear. And that's not necessarily good for you all the time. Like this thing with the dentist; if you were acting the strong man she would be afraid to spoil the game by calling you a big old baby afraid of a little needle. But it'll be a bad day for you, Dei, when there's nobody left to tell you things like that.'

'Well, *hen gariad*,' said David, surprised as he always was at Maggies' *niceness*, 'a lot of the time we're too far apart for even you to tell them to me. And that hasn't always been my fault.'

'I know you think when you climbed the ladder so fast I ought to have followed you up better than I did. Only remember, it's the votes from the Caernarvon Boroughs that put you in this place. I may not put up with all the gossip and cliques and things going on up here, but I still understand Welsh politics. It's just as well for one of us to be keeping the place warm for you. And the other thing I want to tell you about Frances is this, Dei. She wouldn't be any better at changing herself than I was. It's all right while you're living in the kind of world she wants to be in – plenty of excitement and money and presents and famous people – '

David could hardly let that pass. The corridors of power were draughty and uncarpeted in his experience. But Maggie, aware that she might be over-stating her case, hurried on.

'But if ever you lost it all, and there wasn't any money, and people had forgotten about you, do you think she'd still be there? There'd only be me then, Dei. You do believe me, don't you?'

David did not believe her. But he believed that she believed it herself, which was important. He answered her cannily, anxious lest he upset her: 'You've always been a shrewd woman, Maggie: you may be right. I'll have to bear it in mind, then, won't I?'

David was dictating to Frances his letter of resignation, with Frances's full approval, so that she was even more efficient than usual, when Davies announced the arrival of Sir Max Aitken. Aitken looked a little like a monkey – very rich men often do – and was already a self-made millionaire, his ambitions only being limited, it seemed, by the amount of money there was available to make. If Britain lost the war his ambitions would be sadly disappointed, which was not the only reason he had been seeing David. Bonar Law had been his protégé, but there was little chance now that Bonar Law, Colonial Secretary and leader of the Unionist faction of the House, would be acceptable in Number 10. If it was agreed that Asquith was no longer competent to run the war – and most MPs were agreed on that – David was the obvious choice and successor. Sir Max had decided to throw the weight of his newspapers behind the Secretary of State for War; he brought David the news that Bonar Law and Carson were Lloyd George men and that Curzon and Balfour were on the point of committing themselves.

David was much impressed. '*Balfour*.' If Balfour ceased to support him, Asquith would realize at once that his time had come. (Not so Mrs Asquith. 'Nothing but God Almighty will drive Herbert out of Downing Street', she declared, the sort of declaration one later wishes one hadn't made.)

'A great deal depends on which way *The Times* is going to jump,' said Aitken. 'It's been getting more and more vitriolic about Asquith and sooner or later it's going to have to put another name forward.'

'Northcliffe will never support me. He hates practically everything I stand for.'

'He also sees you as the only possible saviour of the nation. You've had three jobs since 1914, the Treasury, the Ministry of Munitions and the War Office, and you managed to supply the money, the munitions and the men. Who else has achieved anything comparable? Now we need morale most of all and you can supply that too.'

'I could do that from where I am just as well as from Number 10 if Asquith would give me the chance. I don't *want* to split the Party. If only he'd accept the idea of an inner War Cabinet with himself in the background, then we could get on with the running of the war. Just three of us, Carson, Bonar Law and myself, meeting every day could achieve so much more than this huge great committee, with Asquith slowing everything down from the chair.'

Together Aitken and David drafted a memorandum proposing just such an accommodation and sent it to the Prime Minister. Asquith considered it, tasted it on his tongue, and rejected it. How could he agree to accept no more than an advisory role in the running of the war? That was on Friday. On Saturday Asquith again turned the proposal down, stipulating that while a smaller war committee might be more workable than a larger one, he must insist upon taking the chair. David thereupon let it be known that he would be resigning the following afternoon, and on the Sunday morning Bonar Law told Asquith that he and his Unionist colleagues who had assumed that David was making a bid for the leadership would also resign, unless Asquith agreed to step down. On the Sunday afternoon the Prime Minister offered David a compromise. There *would* be a small War Council, and David *would* be in the chair; on the other hand Asquith would be free to attend it whenever he wished to, and would have the right to approve its proposals. David agreed, and the Prime Minister let it be known that the War Committee had had its day, and that it would be replaced by a War Council under Lloyd George.

On the Monday morning, Northcliffe took a decisive hand in the crisis. The leading article of *The Times* announced:

From the beginning, Mr Lloyd George has stood apart from the rest in unmistakable enthusiasm for vigorous war. The Celtic temperament is apt to concentrate on a single passion, and Mr Lloyd George has somehow succeeded in impressing even the bitterest of his old opponents with his compulsive abandonment of every other thought besides the passion for victory. It was only a question of time before he found it impossible to work under the old unwieldy system. No elaborate theory is needed to account for this revolt. Nor, for the matter of that, is the country at large under any illusions about it.

Together with some less than flattering observations about Asquith's energy and enthusiasm for prosecuting the war, Northcliffe concluded that Asquith would have to go. Believing that David had inspired Northcliffe's attack, Asquith took up the challenge. Let someone else try to form a government *if they could*. Bonar Law, no longer ambitious for power, preferred that David should seize the opportunity. David, who had not intended to make a challenge for the leadership – at least *not yet* – was miserable and indignant. But when the King sent for him (the King was beginning to wonder whether he might not have to assume power himself so reluctant were his Ministers to help out), David said that he would. He told Frances that he wished he could run away to the mountains and hide, but he didn't. Gradually he grew calmer. Maybe he couldn't take supreme power upon himself, but if he couldn't, he was quite sure that there was nobody else who could.

The in-fighting and back-biting had disturbed and distracted him, but now his mind became as sparkling clear as the waters of the Dwyfor. The phrenologist had prophesied it, and he himself had known it must come; the rest would be straightforward.

He was fifty-four when he became Prime Minister. No other Prime Minister before or since came from such improbable origins. Without the benefit of family connections, political influence, privileged education or money, he had done it. Attracting scandal to himself, as a Venus fly-trap does flies, he had survived calumny, vengeful husbands and wronged wives. And what pleased him most, what filled him with a secret and exhilarating glee, was that Uncle Lloyd had lived to see the day.

The old man was lying in bed and enfeebled when the telegram arrived. William opened it and came into the bedroom.

'Uncle Lloyd?' The old man opened his eyes, irritated at being disturbed. It was the wrong time for letters from London, which were what he chiefly lived for, and so it could only be some needless interruption, some tiresome question or worrying decision to be made. Will looked cheerful however as he passed on the news: 'Telegram from our Dei. He's formed a government. He's Prime Minister. Isn't it wonderful?'

Richard began to nod. His eyes, which were a little rheumy, moistened. He cleared his throat and after some slight hesitation declared: 'The man . . . is greater . . . than his office.' The he turned his head to look at Maggie, who was smiling and seemingly very proud. He reached out his hand and with some effort managed to close his twisted fingers on the back of Maggie's hand. This he patted twice, before lying back on the pillows and recovering his breath.

Cabinet procedure was the first item on David's agenda. If the war was to be won – and David had staked his reputation on it being winnable – decisions would have to be taken more swiftly and passed on for implementation directly. A War Cabinet of five was set up: David in the chair, with Curzon, Lord Milner, Arthur Henderson and Bonar Law, Chancellor of the Exchequer. The Chancellor would be the Leader of the House and answer for the government in all the debates, for David anticipated that winning the war would, and should, take up all his time. He instructed Sir Maurice Hankey to take minutes of every bit of Cabinet business, so that there could be no wasteful discussion about what had taken place at the previous meeting. An agenda would be required for every Cabinet and departmental experts would be ready with specialist information whenever it was needed. Any decisions taken would be recorded and circulated within twenty-four hours to those responsible for implementing them, and a check would be made each week as to whether any action had been taken, and, if not, why not. Oh, it was grand to be able to issue instructions and be assured that they would be acted upon. It was like conducting a brass band. In this respect it was a great deal easier to be Prime Minister, David thought, than not to be.

Unfortunately wives and mistresses require more than agendas, minutes and peremptory orders, and when there are both wives *and* mistresses in a confined area (like Frances's office in Number 10) the resentment is likely to be considerable, and the supply of oxygen inadequate.

Maggie was upset to find that Frances was already installed at Number 10. David had told her that a whole new secretariat was to be appointed and that it would be based in Whitehall Gardens; Maggie had assumed that Frances would be a part of that secretariat. Frances took unkindly to the idea that she might be separated from the man to whom she had become, she was sure of it, indispensable.

David agreed. He had never intended that his *personal* secretariat should be moved out; of course not. Frances was left with nothing to complain about but the ruinous effect on the dignity of the house of the cheap oil painting of Maggie's granny from Llanfairfechan which Maggie had hung on the wall.

Maggie, who was enthusiatic about chintz and cushion covers, was not likely to surrender to her daughter's ex-schoolmistress without a struggle, and called an urgent meeting of her own personal war cabinet – David and herself. There was only one item on the agenda. She sounded quite reasonable about it: 'I wish you'd talk to some of your staff. They'll be taking over half the house if you let them.'

'It *would* be a help, *cariad*, if I could accommodate a few more . . . '

'But what about our furniture? Margot Asquith didn't have to turn the whole place into offices, did she? Oh no, Dei, it's plain enough who's behind this.' And now her voice grew shrill, and it was clear that a vote of censure was about to be proposed. 'Anybody would think *she* was moving in, and we were just lodgers. If I'd known you were going to let her treat me like this!'

The Prime Minister put an arm around her and cuddled her. 'Maggie, old love. The rooms can stay just as they are.'

'All of them?'

'Every last one. All right?'

'I'm sorry.' Maggie *was* sorry. She had tried so hard never to give way to that most vulgar of emotions, jealousy, at least in front of David, but now she was *who* she was, now she was to live *where* she was to live, it seemed so hard to have to share it with – well, with *her*. She patted her hair, sniffed, and said quietly: 'There's been too much excitement.'

'I know,' said David, and continued to make a fuss of her, until the moment seemed ripe to suggest the compromise.

'Now, old girl, you won't mind sparing your old Dei a bit of the garden?'

Maggie broke away from his clutches, and narrowed her eyes. 'When will you have time for gardening?'

'No, not gardening. To put up some offices. Temporary ones. Sort of huts.' It was important to keep talking. A momentary pause and Maggie might fly right off the handle. 'Oh, *tyrd*, now, *ferch*! A couple of old kennels down the bottom of the yard is it? For His Majesty's Prime Minister of Great Britain and Ireland, for heaven's sake?'

Maggie began to giggle. When she giggled she looked just like the respectable Miss Owen whom David had courted with such merciless charm and determination. When she looked like the respectable Miss Owen it made David giggle, and they were both old enough to know better: it was just as well Hankey wasn't there taking minutes, for they both became rather foolish and behaved without very much dignity, considering who they were.

He'd made it, disreputably perhaps, but he'd made it. The crowds cheered, and told him he'd made it. The newspapers patted themselves on the back for forecasting that he'd make it. Great men, men who had been great when he first entered the House, came to see him when he sent for them, and he knew he'd made it. He no longer had to worry about money, and the way the girls looked at him, no question but he'd made it. But he was still insecure.

Asquith would never forgive him; wounds do not heal in the fetid atmosphere of politcs. And Asquith could always do a deal with Redmond and the Sinn Feiners, and then where would he be? Best not to cross swords with the man too often in the House of Commons; best let Bonar Law parry his thrusts. It became a rare event for the Prime Minister to be seen in the House of Commons. Asquith was an enemy, but an enemy in his midst, and one who was content for the moment to keep silent.

But in the meantime the best response to the irritation of Asquith's proximity and Northcliffe's pugnacity was to Get Things Moving, for his predecessor had not been noted for his energy or efficiency. The War Cabinet was a healthy beginning.

He appointed a Controller of Shipping, a Controller of Food. Choose the right man, and there was no virtue in limiting his powers, just so long as he was directly responsible to his PM. He summoned a Conference of Prime Ministers of the Dominions to discuss their contributions to the war effort. He let President Woodrow Wilson know that he would have no truck with German Peace Notes, or any other such defeatist rubbish. But there was one thing which he was not allowed to do, not for more than six months, and that was to bring Churchill into his Cabinet. The Unionists would not stand for it and Bonar Law refused point-blank to agree to it.

Churchill was hurt. He had stood loyally by David when the Marconi scandal threatened to wreck his career, and he had expected David's gratitude to be expressed more usefully than by invitations to breakfast and discussions about the progress of the war.

David tried to explain that tactically it was wisest to wait until the enquiry into the Dardanelles disaster had been completed; then he would set about reinstating his closest political friend – and, should it ever come to it, most formidable potential enemy. He made that a promise, and Churchill had to be satisfied. But Churchill's views on the war were worth hearing, and David agreed with them, at least so far as the necessity for a new initiative was concerned. Haig's obsession with breaking through on the Western Front was proving tragically expensive. Twenty thousand German soldiers and thirty thousand British soldiers would die, a half a mile of shell-holes and rubble would be gained, and a great victory would be proclaimed by the Commander-in-Chief.

David was romantically inclined to take Jerusalem from the Turks by Christmas; an easy target, and one which would delight the Welsh. Churchill recommended an assault on the Austrians whose hearts he believed were no longer in the war, and more support for the Italians. David tried to explain that Haig refused to part with any of his big guns to help the Italians or anybody else, and that while the Tories, Carson, the King, and most significantly Northcliffe, were convinced that Haig was a military genius, there was very little effective action he, David, could take concerning the conduct of the war.

At an Allied Conference in Rome at the start of the New Year, David discovered that not just Haig and the British generals, but the French and Italians as well, also believed in running the war much as it had always been run. The Queen of Italy gave him a book and he bought a marble figure and some corals, though little else was achieved.

But in other matters David's energy was astonishing. Within three months of taking office and despite vigorous opposition from the Tories he had pushed through legislation on adult suffrage and votes for women, had abolished plural voting and had secured a minimum wage for agricultural workers. He had also ensured that landlords would be unable to raise the rents of their farms, a Bill which struck most painfully at the hearts of the Tories (tucked for safe keeping in their wallets).

Richard Lloyd died in February, 1917, aged eighty-three. From the churchyard at Y Maes, on a hillside on the outskirts of Criccieth, in which he was buried, it was just possible to hear the trickling stream in which David had been baptized.

The day of the funeral was typical Criccieth weather, cold and grey, and David wept as he had not wept since he was a child. He had not known how quickly the old man had aged since the turn of the year. To William and Anita, who had nursed him, it had seemed as though David's appointment as Prime Minister had been all Uncle Lloyd had been waiting for. How he had revelled, though, in the last few years! Reporters and photographers had come to visit him and had spoken to him with such respect, it was almost like being Prime Minister himself. Sometimes David had spoken in the House just so that Uncle Lloyd could read about it in the papers the following day. And David had written to him constantly, with details of affairs of state, asking him for advice even, so that Uncle Lloyd had felt that in a small way he was helping to run the country. And whenever there was a question of morality . . .

'He was the keeper of your conscience,' said William without irony, after the funeral. The brothers were no longer as close: there was rancour between them. When they were alone together they had trouble filling the silences.

Anita said: 'When your name was cleared in the Marconi affair he went down on his knees here in this room and thanked God that justice had been done.'

'He said he always knew you would never do anything to make him ashamed of you,' said William. David noticed that Maggie was looking pointedly at him and busied himself stirring his tea. William continued: 'He had such high ambitions for us. It's good to think that one of us fulfilled them.'

'I don't think that's the right way to put it,' cried Anita with unaccustomed spirit. 'There's no telling how far you would have got if you had just walked out.'

'I suppose,' said Maggie mildly, 'they each made their choice.'

'I'm not saying any different. Only I won't have Will putting himself down. As a boy he passed his exams as high as Dafydd, or higher. But he gave up his life to his mother and Uncle Lloyd, and to help Dei. Only what he did was never rightly valued.' William, embarrassed, put his hand on his wife's arm. 'It's all right, Will, that's all I'm saying. I'll go and make a cup of tea now.'

Anita and Maggie went off into the kitchen, and fifteen-year-old Megan was left alone with her father and her Uncle William. She was disturbed by what she had just heard her aunt say, distressed at the notion (quite new to her) that her father's career had been built upon the bowed back of her uncle. How would it have helped the country if *both* brothers had stayed in Wales? And Uncle William might be cleverer than Tada, but Tada was the one people always wanted to hear. William explained to her that Anita had meant no harm by her remarks, had just been sticking up for her husband 'the way women do'. 'When you get married yourself,' he continued, 'you will understand.'

But Megan looked unimpressed: 'I'm afraid I don't think much of boys,' she said. 'Most of them are rather silly. When I've finished school I'm going to stay with Tada and help him with his work.'

David put an arm round his daughter's waist and drew her to him. She kissed him lightly, than ran her fingers through his great white torrent of hair.

'She's a very clever girl, you know, Will,' said David.

'She'll know how to vote then when the time comes?'

David smiled: 'She'll know. She'll know who got her the right to vote too.'

Megan was in her element. Her dream, unexpressed as yet, was to be allowed to campaign for her father, speak on his behalf, share a platform with him, tell the world of his marvellous exploits. In the meantime just being with him and William and hearing them discuss matters of state was enough to be going on with.

Later in the day she overheard things she would rather not have known about. Anita and Maggie came into the room to set the table and failed to see Megan, who was looking for a book in the shelves behind the sofa. The two women were speaking about Tada and Miss Stevenson, foul things, disgusting things, which they had no right to mention. If they were true . . . but no, it didn't bear thinking about. It was all gossip, must be, and Megan would have no part of it.

Despite Megan's presence, David found this trip to Wales almost insupportably sad. Criccieth without Uncle Lloyd, well, it didn't seem possible; nothing could ever be the same.

He had done it all for Uncle Lloyd. Ever since those debates in the village parliament at Llanystumdwy he had striven to earn the old man's approval. The People's Budget had been a kind of love letter to him. His approval of David's radicalism had helped to keep him radical. Without Uncle Lloyd there to spur him on, he feared that he might become a doddery part of the British establishment himself. Without Mair and Uncle Lloyd, there was only Frances – oh, and Maggie, of course!

Back in the sheds at the bottom of the garden of 10 Downing Street – 'the garden suburb' it had come to be called – the most urgent matter requiring the attention of the War Cabinet was the conduct of the war at sea.

In November 1916, after the German U-boats had sunk some 400,000 tons of British shipping in four months, David had made representations to Admiral Jellicoe, the First Sea Lord, suggesting that losses might be reduced if merchant ships were to travel in convoys with a couple of destroyers escorting them. Sir John Jellicoe was horrified at such a radical idea. It would not be possible, he argued, for the ships to keep close enough together; furthermore a convoy would offer too large a target to the U-boats. He seemed unaware that the second argument invalidated the first. He had plenty more arguments in reserve, but the one which carried most weight was to categorize David as a civilian and a landlubber who could not be expected to understand such matters. Perhaps he thought secretly, as Haig seemed to do, that high casualties indicated a high degree of activity, and consequently a high degree of efficiency. Forty-nine ships were lost in January 1917, one hundred and five in February, one hundred and twenty-seven in March, and one hundred and sixty-nine in April. In return, two U-boats were sunk in January, and four in February. Instead of Britain's naval power blockading Germany, it became increasingly apparent that Germany was effectively blockading Britain.

David took the matter up with Carson, now First Lord of the Admiralty, and was distressed to find that Sir Edward was disinclined to interfere with naval strategy. The trouble was that David could not afford to antagonize the leader of the Ulster Unionists. So he sounded out a number of young naval officers and was not surprised to discover that they had no great desire to be drowned, and could not therefore support Jellicoe's spineless adherence to the old methods. More importantly, Admiral Beatty was now converted to the convoy idea.

If David could have removed Jellicoe, he would have done so, but to remove Jellicoe he would have had to remove Carson, and to remove Carson would tear the scab off the Irish problem once again. It was Lord Milner, a typical ex-public school aristocrat, experienced in skulduggery, who came up with the inspired suggestion of promoting Carson by bringing him into the War Cabinet and making Geddes the new First Lord.

With Carson tamed and Beatty converted, David could now get the convoy theory tested (it had already proved successful in a small way on the French coal ferry) and the results were impressive. From that moment the losses in British shipping began to decline and it was possible to hope again.

In March 1917 insurrection in Russia caused alarm and despondency in the West. Rasputin and the Romanovs were scarcely lovable people, but the Eastern Front had kept a large number of German troops busy killing and being killed; now it was impossible to predict what might happen. Had democracy truly come to Russia? Would Kerensky prosecute the war more vigorously than Tsar Nicholas had done or would he sue for peace? Would he have any choice? It was not long before starvation in the provinces and disaffection in the army made it improbable that Russia would be able to continue fighting at all. David sent a telegram of greetings to Prince Lvov, the new Head of State, expressing 'profound satisfaction that . . . Russia now stands with the nations which base their institutions upon responsible government,' and the House of Commons greeted Kerensky and the Duma fraternally. But all the good wishes in the world would not help with the war effort, and David's Cabinet colleagues turned their gaping beaks to him for the worms of comfort they so desperately desired. David did his best:

'The position on the Eastern Front is totally unaffected,' he announced with more optimism than conviction. 'There's been a *de facto* ceasefire there for weeks. The Tsar's army was running out of ammunition, They've even run out of bread; they've been fighting on lentils. The whole country seethes with unrest. Truce or no truce the Germans can't afford to withdraw their forces from the East until they get a Peace Treaty. And Kerensky's certainly not going to give them that. Only one thing is certain. The Tsar won't be climbing back on to his throne again. And just look at the weapon *that* puts into our hands!' From the blank looks around him, David realized that the weapon he had referred to was still invisible to lesser mortals, and he must give it greater substance before they could appreciate how sharp was its blade, how potent its threat.

'Consider America's position. It's eighteen months since the *Lusitania* was sunk. During those eighteen months American ships have continued to be blown to smithereens, yet President Wilson stands by and does nothing. *Why?* Because from that side of the Atlantic this war has looked like nothing but a bunch of corrupt European dynasties up to their knees in blood as they slaughter each other. Hapsburgs on the one side, Romanovs on the other. What is that to the Americans? But look at it now! It's a war for democracy, a people's war, a war for progress, for a new and better world. And if *that* doesn't pull in the Americans I'm a Dutchman!'

Pulling in the Americans was one thing (and David's prognosis was correct; such an appeal was irresistible to them and on April Fools Day, 1917 they *were* pulled in), but convincing the British of the worthiness of their new allies and the assured triumphant conclusion of the war now that the situation had changed so radically was something else.

With the French being massacred at Verdun, the Russians *hors de combat*, the Americans dragging their feet, and the German U-boats still ruling the waves, the British might need some convincing. With Haig in charge of the army and Jellicoe of the navy new techniques of persuasion would be necessary if the country's morale was not to slide into its boots. David set up a new Ministry of Information under Max Aitken, and Max Aitken persuaded Northcliffe (who for some time had been an expert in propaganda at home) to take charge of propaganda in enemy countries. Since Rothermere was also a part of David's administration, the Prime Minister could congratulate himself on having three press lords in his employ. How many Prime Ministers before or since have been able to enjoy such a satisfactory exercise of power? David thought, reasonably enough, that if he could tame the British press so simply and effectively, the German army should prove a small thing. But it would not and it did not, as he was soon to learn.

185

1917 was not a good year for families. The war shattered them. It liked young men best. At the end of the year there were few families left untouched by the war. It was dreadful to see the havoc wrought in some families, and best not to ask what it was all for. Talk of archdukes and kaisers, revolutions and war machines, Belgium and the Dardanelles, was all very well, but it did nothing to ease the pain of shattered families. Better not to ask why: better to find comfort elsewhere, in sleep, in drink, or in religion.

The George family had had its tragedy when Mair died. Uncle Lloyd's death had been sad but inevitable. And in 1917 there were fears that Megan had contracted meningitis, but it proved to be measles and David, who felt that he could not have survived the loss of another daughter, uttered a prayer of thanksgiving. But Megan was growing wiser as she grew older and with wisdom came disenchantment. It takes courage for a girl to tell her governess, or even her ex-governess, what she thinks of her moral character, but Megan did. She said she realized now why Frances had dropped into her conversation frequent hints about the virtues of being broadminded, and she was afraid that Frances had underestimated her, Megan's, intelligence. She knew, she said, that her mother was middle-aged, provincial, a little old-fashioned, and so on. But she would not accept that that was a reason for *outsiders* – and she gave the word a particular emphasis – to butt in and mess up the family relationships. And it was *certainly* not an excuse, she maintained, for a younger ambitious woman to try to make a fool out of her father. She concluded: 'You may think that if you can hang on long enough she'll be dead and you'll have him all to yourself. But you're forgetting one thing, *Miss Stevenson*, I'm not older than you. I'll still be here when you're gone.'

Such things, once said, are not easily unsaid. Whenever Megan and Frances found themselves in the same room, they recalled those words which had passed between them (although Frances had said little enough, having only emotional arguments to advance, which don't come well from an ex-governess), and others in the room would be aware of something a little *wrong* in the atmosphere.

On 7 April Richard married the daughter of Sir Robert McAlpine, the man who had made a million pounds out of cement. Not a happy choice for Richard's father, who would have preferred him to have settled for Dilys Roberts, a nice local girl. The trouble was that Miss Roberts had had second thoughts about settling for Richard. Her father died on the day of Richard's wedding.

'She'll need to be an heiress, this Roberta McAlpine, if she's going to pay for Dick's drinking,' was David's uncharitable comment, but he felt uncharitable, for it was just the sort of match which would bring cheer to his political opponents. In Wales they said that Richard had been 'bought over'.

Ten weeks later Olwen married a young Welsh surgeon, which was better, but no surgeon could have stitched up the torn fabric of what had once been the closest of families.

A bad year for families.

At the Eisteddfod that year the bardic crown was presented posthumously to a young man killed in France just a week before the crowning. The crown was pinned to a black cloth draped over the throne; instead of the young man his regimental emblem was placed on the seat.

David spoke in Welsh: 'Keep on!' he cried, and his voice was rough with grief. 'Falter not! he cried, and the audience wept freely. 'We have many dangerous marshes to cross: we will cross them! We have steep and stony paths to climb: we will climb them! Our footprints may be stained with blood, but we will reach the heights. Beyond them we shall see the rich valleys and plains of the new world which we have sacrificed so much to attain.'

And still on the Western Front the carnage continued into 1918. Lenin and Trotsky had made peace with the Germans which enabled Ludendorff to bring his troops back from the East and launch an offensive on the Somme, intended to drive a wedge between the British and the French armies. It almost did. The British Third and Fifth armies were in disarray. The General Reserve, which David had planned to have standing by behind the front lines in case of just such an emergency, never materialized, and the French reserves were too far away from the Somme to help. The crisis occurred on Black Saturday (23 March) and David rushed to the War Office to take charge. There he learned that 40,000 men and 600 guns had been lost on the Somme. He did all that could be done, arranging for the available manpower in Britain – 170,000 men in all – to be sent to France without delay; for two British divisions in Palestine (where Jerusalem had been captured by Allenby a fortnight before Christmas to David's delight) and one in Italy, to be diverted to France; and for the age-limits for conscription to be urgently lowered from 19 to 18½ and raised from 42 to 50. A desperate appeal was despatched to America for the substantial help which President Wilson had so far failed to provide, and arrangements made for the British and French armies to be put under united control. It seemed as though the unthinkable was about to become reality, the impossible nightmare a tragic awakening. A second offensive by Ludendorff in the north added to the crisis, and British soldiers were killed and British positions captured with such savage speed that it was hard to perceive any light through the gloom of gas, smoke and barbed wire entanglements.

David was one of the few who knew the full extent of the calamity, and almost the only one to believe that it might be reversed. He had to believe that. He had announced to the world that if he became Prime Minister he would win the war; it would never do for a man in his position to break his promise. Had the Germans fully appreciated that, a lot of tears would have remained unshed, a lot of widows would have remained wives, a lot of children would have had fathers to bring them back souvenirs from the front lines and make them smile again.

Chapter Seven

There are particular problems for a man of the people engaged in prosecuting a war. All too often the 'people' fail
to see things with the clarity of the politician and are a little
bemused by the haste with which they are shunted off to
the front lines and the assumption that they will be keen to
make the supreme sacrifice. What advantage accrues to the
workers even in a successful war? Does it make beer cheaper,
coal easier to dig, employers less grasping, children less
hungry? It does not. How does a politician persuade them
that it does?

Early in 1918 a delegation of four officials from the Miners'
Federation came to visit David. They were headed by Bob
Smillie, a dour and determined president of the Federation,
and they tried hard not to be overawed by the mist of
authority that surrounded the Prime Minister's office. They
could hardly fail to be curious about Frances, however, for
they had read about her in the *News of the World*, and, if
what they had read was true, why then . . .

She certainly had a very superior voice, they thought, as
she asked them if they would mind waiting for just a few
minutes. Fancy a girl with a voice like that being in the
News of the World! It was evident that David had been
doing all right for himself. It was equally evident from the
way in which he bounded out of his inner office, beaming
a welcome, and, so far as could be judged, more than just
politely concerned in the wellbeing of each member of the
delegation.

The miners put their case to the Prime Minister forcefully. No sooner was a young lad trained and ready to take
his place at the coal-face than it was time for him to be
whipped out of the mines and off to France. A lad didn't
need special training to be shot, gassed or impaled on

barbed wire, so why not exempt the miners from conscription and keep them where they could be most useful?

David explained that the engineers had made similar complaints, yet had managed to come to terms with conscription. But, Smillie argued, the miners were a special case and could not be compared with *anyone*. In a factory the worst that could happen would be a loss of efficiency, a bit of wastage, but in a pit, if the lads were not properly trained you could be bloody dead. Before David brought in his new Conscription Bill everyone knew where he stood. Those in essential work enjoyed honourable exemption. In a mining village the only ones in khaki would be shop keepers, and there was no glory in that. But now with the requirement of fifty thousand conscripts from the mining industry, a few youngsters from each valley would come home in uniform and flaunt themselves in front of the girls, and soon enough a few more would sneak off and volunteer, and then a few more, and then . . .

Nor was it just the terms of the Bill which the miners found objectionable; it was the language in which it was phrased. 'Combing out men from the pits' was a terrible way of describing the government's intentions. 'Combing out' was what you did to lice, not men.

In short the miners were being treated with disdain and if they were to show their resentment by downing tools, it would be all up with the war, the government, the Prime Minister, and the country.

As Minister for Munitions David had proclaimed the importance above all else of the coal-miners' contribution to the war effort. Then he had emphasized that the factories depended on coal, the navy depended on coal, the country depended on coal, so now that he was removing fifty thousand men from the pits, the miners were entitled to ask, what had changed? Had the factories rediscovered the water-wheel, the navy the sailing-ship, were windmills to provide the power to keep the home fires burning?

'It seems to me,' Smillie concluded, 'that whatever job

you happen to be in, you expect the whole country to jump to it and help you make a go of it.'

At last David had the opening he had been waiting for. 'That's right, Bob,' he said quietly. 'And if I never expected it before I expect it now because the job I "happen to be in" at the moment is the job of winning the war, and one way or another the next few weeks are going to decide it.' This was no exaggeration with Ludendorff striking north for the Channel. If the Americans were slow to mobilize or the resolve of the British troops weakened, he would make it. 'I won't talk about defeat,' David continued, 'because I never talk about defeat – but at best it would take us *years* to recover from a setback like that. I'm in your hands, Bob, the whole country is. If you want us to lose, if you want to see the war dragging on into 1921 or 1922, you've only got to lift your finger and all the lives that have been lost in the last four years will have been thrown away.'

When they heard such an argument, when they realized that David believed what he was saying, and would say it to everyone if they defied him, they knew that he had moved beyond them, that they could no longer appeal to him as a man of the people, that they had lost. They carried on the debate, but without any heart for it.

David asked them to hold off for six weeks, by which time, he promised them, the world would see that the war was being won. They replied that their job was just to report back. They had no mandate to –

David said he knew what their job was. It was to wring every last ounce of concession out of him by pretending that they were sitting on a seething stockpot of revolution. He said he wasn't born yesterday. But he knew that they had the power to hold the men in check, for a few weeks at least. He asked them to use that power and in return they should have concessions. Tribunals should decide whether men be conscripted in cases in which the issue was cloudy. The Unions would be represented on these tribunals, with full voting powers, and so on and so forth.

The details were hammered out. The Prime Minister had triumphed yet again. But it was not the miners who had been sacrificed; it was a still, small part of himself whose voice had been silenced.

The miners had been outwitted, but they were determined men with long memories. All right, they said to each other, we'll give him his six weeks, we'll let him have his triumph, we'll let him win his war. But when he's done that and the Coalition comes to an end, why then, new rules would be drawn up for a new game. And a new political party would come to power, and this would be truly a party of the people, and the old men would have to retire to the sidelines and gasp with amazement at the things which would be done. At least that's what the miners thought.

The first meeting of the Supreme War Council at the Trianon Palace Hotel, Versailles, brought together Orlando the Italian President, Clemenceau, who looked like a walrus and roared like a lion, and who had replaced the more moderate Painlevé as President of France, and David. The agenda was less important than the symbolic nature of the meeting, for the real business of charting the progress of the war would be done by the military advisers, while it was vital that the three leaders reached a plausible working relationship. Clemenceau was the problem. He ate politicians for breakfast and was hungry again by lunchtime. David considered the matter at length before deciding that the way to tame Clemenceau was to have a good row with him on the occasion of their first meeting. The only question was what to row about. It needed to be an issue that was not really vital to Clemenceau's interests, and yet one which he would not concede without a certain loss of pride. If he could find such an issue, and force Clemenceau to back down, he would have gained a psychological advantage for life (which should not be long, for Clemenceau was very old and very choleric. He was younger at 78, however, than most of his French Cabinet colleagues!). It should also be a public-spirited confrontation, for the old man bullied everyone unmercifully and would be the better for a dose of his own medicine.

Clemenceau not only looked the part, he lived the part. His place in the conference room was at the end of a long and highly polished table in a chair much like a throne and flanked by obsequious secretaries and interpreters. To David it seemed more like an audience with the Pope than a conference with equals.

As taut as a bow-string and puffing at a cigar, David entered and launched straight into an impressively passionate tirade which surprised even members of the British delegation.

'There is one issue which I'm afraid I must insist we clear up before we go any further. When I finally managed to secure the agreement of all allied powers to setting up this Supreme War Council it was as an integral part of the Rapallo Agreement drawn up in November last year which committed your country and mine to offer some active if belated support to our hard-pressed Italian allies. I am astonished to find that certain highly-placed French spokesmen are talking of the Rapallo undertaking having to be re-negotiated, because it was signed by Painlevé, your predecessor, and not by yourself! If these solemn agreements are to be thrown into the melting-pot every time the French encounter another domestic political crisis they are a complete waste of everybody's time. I have made arrangements to return to London this afternoon unless you can assure me that the agreement signed by Monsieur Painlevé will be honoured in its entirety.'

He threw his pencil down on to the table, leant back in his chair, folded his arms, and turned away from Clemenceau, as though indifferent to whatever might follow.

Clemenceau waited for David's words to be translated to him, and then, instead of the anticipated explosion of sound, came a gentle 'D'accord'.

Signor Orlando was touchingly grateful to David for his intervention and the British Prime Minister found himself popular on all sides and able to negotiate thereafter from a position of strength.

His only regret was that the French chambermaids proved less susceptible to Welsh charm than he had been led to believe, and rejected his advances with a great deal of unnecessary noise.

Back in London he took Frances to a big social gathering organized by Sir Max Aitken. It was something he had wanted to do for a long time. To be seen with her in public (and to be eyed enviously by the men with plainer women on their arms) was balm to his soul. There was no logical reason why she should not have been escorted by him sooner, for it was common knowledge that Maggie preferred to stay in Wales; what more natural therefore than that he should take his private secretary? Frances's presence excited much covert comment but little rudeness, except from Nancy Cunard, and the experiment was considered a success. As the couple prepared to spend the night in Number 10 David remarked that Frances had been flirting and patently enjoying herself. Frances, who did indeed look particularly glamorous in a silk dress with a necklace which David had given her around her throat, remarked with a bitterness which she usually managed to keep out of her voice:

'It's always nice to be reminded that there are still people around who'd like to make an honest woman of me.' David rebuked her, and she was instantly contrite: 'I'm sorry, my darling, but it's nights like this when I find it hardest. Because it only shows how it could *always* be, if, instead of just a few people who understand about us and don't mind, it was all above board and we could go everywhere together. I feel quite black about it sometimes. I don't think it's ever going to happen. *She'll* just squat there in Criccieth growing older and fatter and smugger. Then whenever there's a bit of limelight, she'll suddenly *appear* and sit smirking in the front row, the virtuous, pious, devoted Mrs Lloyd George. And she'll poke her nose into every corner to make sure the coal bills are still being kept down and all the stupid incompetent servants are still here so she can talk Welsh to them in front of people who don't understand. And I shall always have to sneak out through the back door like a kitchen maid caught stealing the spoons. And she'll live to be a hundred, I know, I can feel it in my bones. She'll dance on my grave.'

Saying what is in your mind ought to bring relief, but when David sat silently in front of her, shirt half off, head down, fingers toying with a cuff-link, Frances felt worse than ever. If David had rebuked her she could have apologized; then they could have kissed and gone to bed. But in the face of his silence she felt doubly humiliated. She had stared boldly into the faces of those at the reception whose eyes had seemed to question her right to be there but it had taken courage to face it out. Now, listening to her petulant voice and knowing how her words must be hurting the person who above all others she wanted not to hurt, she began to wish (for the very first time) that she had accepted that nice and suitable young Scotsman who had only wished to make her happy.

'I'm sorry,' she said, tears embarrassingly trickling down her cheeks, 'I shouldn't have said all that. I probably repel you when I lose grip of my dignity like that, but you'll admit it doesn't often happen.'

'Come here, *cariad*,' said David gently, pulling a handkerchief that was none too clean from his pocket and wiping her eyes with it. Then he planted a kiss on her damp nose and assured her: 'You are my dear love and the heart of my heart whatever you do. You imagine you would feel better if you could hear me join in saying nasty things about Maggie, but you wouldn't really. You would think: "If he speaks of her like that behind her back how do I know what he says about me when I'm not here?"'

'I realize there's nothing you can do. Not in the position you're in. Not in the middle of the war and everything. I know it's not fair to, to . . .'

David clicked his tongue against his teeth and sat her on

his lap. 'My dear child, a hundred times in the last six months when I've had my back to the wall, with everything going wrong and enemies snapping at my heels, haven't I been unfair? Think of all the times I've snarled and growled at the sweetest little girl in all the world, because if I lost my temper with the people who really deserve it I might do irreparable damage.' Frances recognized the description and managed a misty smile. 'By the time a man has got this far in this particular job the number of people he can really trust has shrunk away almost to nothing. But I know I can trust in you absolutely, *cariad*. And if there wasn't somebody I could say that to, I believe I'd go out of my mind. I've got a splendid idea,' cried David briskly, 'let's go to bed!'

And they would have gone and sunk all their differences between the sheets, had it not been that while Frances was attending to one or two urgent little matters, David glanced at the early edition of *The Times*.

The early edition of *The Times* was seldom controversial enough to cause a Prime Minister who had been looking happily forward to a night in bed with his mistress, to rise vertically in the air, defying gravity, and to bellow like a stuck pig, but on this occasion it was. The Prime Minister checked the other early editions and discovered that what had so shocked him in *The Times* was in three other national newspapers as well.

The cause of such uncharacteristic behaviour was to be found in the letter columns. Major-General Sir Frederick Maurice, until recently the Director of Military Operations, had accused David of lying to the House of Commons about the strength of Haig's army, the figures which he had given being 'known to a large number of troops to be incorrect' thus 'breeding such distrust of the Government as can only end in impairing the splendid morale of our troops at a time when everything possible should be done to raise it.'

David suspected a conspiracy in all this. Sir William Robertson, Chief of the Imperial General Staff, and a man

196

who had vigorously opposed the Supreme War Council in general and the establishment of a General Reserve (commanded by a foreigner to add insult to injury!) in particular, was still smarting from having been told by his Prime Minister that he had resigned when he was perfectly convinced that he had not. His cause was espoused on military grounds by Colonel Repington, war correspondent on the *Morning Post*, and on political grounds by Asquith, who still saw himself as leader of the Liberal Party and rightful leader of the country. Furthermore, Jellicoe had refused to accept his defeat over the convoy business like an officer and a gentleman, while Haig remained David's *bête noire*, so it may clearly be seen that David had lined up aginst him a powerful faction. Conspiracy or not, it was a bold and contentious move for a serving officer in the British Army to accuse his Prime Minister of lying to the country, and one which could not be ignored.

David's fury was fuelled by the precariousness of his own position as the leader of a Coalition. Any previous Prime Minister could have counted on the support of a political party solidly behind him. But David had no such support.

An emergency meeting of the War Cabinet was summoned and David, pallid from a night spent poring over details of parliamentary debates in the pages of Hansard when he might have been cuddling Frances, faced his colleagues.

Bonar Law proposed that Maurice's breach of discipline be dealt with by the Army Council, and that the charges against the Prime Minister be investigated by two judges. But Asquith had already put down a motion calling for a Select Committee. This would have the advantage of meeting *in camera*, thereby avoiding passing valuable information to the enemy. It would also give the Prime Minister longer to prepare his case. If there was any substance to the charges, the defence must be the best that could be mustered. But David had had enough of Select Committees. It was a Select Committee which had kept him in such dreadful suspense over the Marconi affair.

'Look, we all know what's behind this! Maurice is one of those who has always regarded Haig as a military genius. Never mind the Somme, Passchendaele, and Ypres. Each of these disasters was to have been a brilliant strategic coup. And now that Haig has let Ludendorff through they're threshing around looking for a scapegoat, and they think they've found one.'

'Whatever your personal opinions may be, Prime Minister,' Milner pointed out, 'you cannot publicly denounce the C-in-C as incompetent.'

'Nor is it a matter that can be simply glossed over,' said Bonar Law. 'The atmosphere in the House at present is very anxious, very disturbed . . . '

'Yes, so it is,' said David, 'and do you know why? For the first time they think it's possible that they may lose the war, and they're running amok, screaming for heads to roll, preferably mine. The whole thing's being whipped up by Northcliffe and the press, and it's being exacerbated by the Opposition benches, who have been waiting for months for just such an opportunity.'

Curzon expressed the view that Asquith – since Asquith was obviously meant – had no intention of bringing the Government down. His purpose in tabling the motion was merely to occasion it some embarrassment.

'Oh, is *that* all?' cried David, much incensed and rather enjoying himself. 'He thinks it would be a helpful and constructive move, does he, to try to convince the country that it's being led by a cowardly, squabbling bunch of incompetent liars, whom, nevertheless, he wants to see continue in office. Just when the outcome of the war is balanced on a knife-edge, and we're asking the people for every last ounce of effort and sacrifice. Oh, no, I'll not buy that! If he really believes this slanderous load of tripe, let him have the courage of his convictions and tell us to go.'

As Leader of the House, Bonar Law felt it his duty to point out that no matter how unpatriotic and slanderous the charges, they would still have to be faced and answered, whether by Select Committee or not.

'All right! They want answers? They shall have them! But to hell with committees and tribunals. I shall face them in the House. Tomorrow! The thing must be settled within twenty-four hours, which is all the time I can spare and more than it deserves. If they want a debate, by God, I'll give them a debate!'

What in the event he gave them was not really a debate, but it was one of the most extraordinary pieces of theatre ever seen in the House of Commons. Asquith, in a most judicious mood, warmed up the audience. As a supporting act, his role was to recommend the setting up of a Select Committee, and then to leave the stage.

The star of the show made his entrance carrying piles of documents and volumes of Hansard which he slammed down on the despatch box with enough force to disturb the dust produced by centuries of dry debate. Then before the dust had begun to settle he started his tremendous tirade. Older members of the House nudged each other happily, and younger members sat up very straight.

'The demand put forward in this Motion, Mr Speaker, is absolutely without precedent in the entire history of this House. Never has it been suggested – even in a period of peace, when there might be time to give to it – that a Select Committee of the House of Commons should enquire into the accuracy of statements by Ministers. And what has led to this present demand?

'A general, a distinguished general, has felt himself impelled to write to the newspapers challenging statements made by two Ministers during the time that he was Director of Military Operations. But if his motive was indeed to bring the truth as he conceived it to the attention of the House and the country, it is very strange that he refrained from doing this until he had, for good or bad reasons, ceased to hold that office.

'General Maurice was in office for weeks after I delivered that speech. He attended a Cabinet meeting the very next day. He never called my attention to it, then or at *any* time, though I was in daily contact with him. In fact I was under the impression that he was a great friend of mine. Was it not his business then to come to me – if he thought this matter was so important that it justified a great general in breaking the King's Regulations – to come to me and say: "You made a mistake in the House of Commons; I dare say you were misled, but can you put it right?"

'Never a word was said to me! Never a syllable. I saw it first in the newspapers! I imagine that possibly he felt it his duty to discuss it first with his immediate superiors, the Secretary of State for War or the Chief of the Imperial Staff, so I made inquiries . . .

'But no! He spoke of it to no one until he had left office, and then proceeded to trample upon the Regulations of the King, and set an example of flagrant indiscipline to the whole army. Suppose a regimental officer, or a poor ordinary soldier, had acted in this way. After all, they have their views about their superiors: they may disagree as to the wisdom of certain actions. Are they to write to the papers and say: "Though I am a soldier, I am first of all a citizen, and therefore I am going to break the rules"?

'The issue is a very clear one. I said the fighting strength of the army had increased in the past year: General Maurice said it had diminished. Now I find it very strange that General Maurice of all people should challenge the accuracy of those figures. Where does he imagine I got them from? When I am asked for statistics about any given department it is not my custom to conjure them out of the air. I took those figures from the official records of the War Office. From General Maurice's own Department! If indeed they were incorrect he would be quite as responsible for the mistake as anyone else. But in fact they were perfectly accurate! I am going to read from the document issued by General Maurice's Department.'

Now came the first interruption. Lord Hugh Cecil was rash enough to ask: 'Is it not contrary to the Rules of Order to read part of a document and not to disclose the whole of it to the House?' A groundswell of murmurs suggested that there were plenty of members who would like nothing better than for the Prime Minister to be exposed for using a document unscrupulously, but David had not sat up all night for nothing.

'If the House wants this document from which I am reading I am perfectly prepared to put it on the table.' The murmurers were silenced. 'My Honorable friend need not be afraid. I am not going to shirk anything. I propose before I sit down to give all the sources of information and let the public judge. Otherwise I am only too well aware that no statement, no decision of any secret tribunal, would ever suffice to put an end to all the violence, all the virulence of that portion of the press which supports my Right Honorable Friend. It would simply go on the same as before. For the past two or three years, ever since I have thrown myself into the vigorous prosecution of the war, I have been drenched with cocoa slop!

'Here is the statement – from General Maurice's own Department! It will thus be seen that the combatant strength of the British army was greater on 1 January 1918 than on 1 January 1917! This confirmation comes from General Maurice's Department *nine days after* I first made that statement!'

There could be no doubt that David passionately believed in the rightness of his case. His sincerity shone out of his eyes and rang out in the vigorous tones of his beautiful modulated voice. There could be no doubt that David passionately believed in the rightness of his case *while he was on his feet and arguing it to such purpose in the Chamber of the House*. But in the early morning hours when he worked out his reply to Maurice's damaging charges, he must have known that he was deliberately misunderstanding the nature of those charges. Maurice's argument had not been that the British Army had been seriously depleted between 1 January 1917 and 1 January 1918, but between 1 January 1918 and 1 March 1918 and since 140 battalions had been disbanded during those months there could be no question but that Maurice's charges were well-founded. Had David contrasted the figures for 1 March 1917 and

1 March 1918 it would have been clear enough.

Even more seriously, the figures for 1 January 1918 which David gave in his speech to the House were inaccurate, for 86,000 British troops serving in Italy had been included amongst those serving in France, so that there was indeed a shortfall between the two January figures, *and David must have known it*. However, he knew too – as all successful politicians know – that it's not what you say which counts so much as the way you say it, and of that David was indeed the master.

In the next section of his speech the Prime Minister had more than rhetoric on his side: 'We come next to the allegation that the decision to extend the British section of the front line was forced on Field-Marshal Haig without his knowledge and against his judgement. Of *course* the Field-Marshal was reluctant to extend his line! We were just as reluctant. It was done only in response to enormous pressure from the French Government and from the actual facts of the military situation which Sir Douglas Haig could not resist and we could not resist.

'More specifically Mr Bonar Law stated in this House: "This particular matter was not dealt with at all by the Supreme War Council at Versailles." However General Maurice wrote to the Press' – and now David characterized the unfortunate general with a smug, mincing delivery, which was devastating in its satirical effect – ' "But I was *at* Versailles when the question was decided by the Supreme War Council." Oh yes, he was at Versailles; that is perfectly true. But not in the Council Chamber. I have looked at the official records. He was away in a building . . . ' (and here David twiddled his fingers at some ineffably vague point on the distant horizon) 'somewhere in the vicinity assisting a couple of generals . . . '

David could not proceed for the raucous laughter and relieved cheers from his supporters. He broke into the laughter just as it began to die with: 'The extension was never discussed at that Council at all; for the simple reason that it had already taken place before the Council ever met.'

In his peroration David's voice became solemn and minatory. He directed his remarks at Asquith, who was already finding the afternoon distressingly long and uncomfortably warm.

'The Right Honorable Gentleman has admitted that this action by General Maurice was a flagrant breach of discipline. He has admitted it; I wish he had also deprecated it. He cannot be unaware of the possible repercussions of such incidents on the war effort, since he was himself responsible for the conduct of the war for two years. If this Motion is carried he will again be responsible for the conduct of the War.' There were cries of 'Shame!' at this. Asquith's conduct of the war seemed no more competent in retrospect than it had seemed at the time. David continued at full throttle, his voice throaty and resonant: 'Make no mistake! This is a vote of censure on the Goverment. If this Motion were carried we could not possibly continue in office.'

At this the MPs could contain themselves no longer. They shouted and waved their order papers and became very emotional, although some of them were not entirely clear why they were reacting so powerfully. But in the general hubbub it scarcely mattered, for there was only one voice which the majority wished to hear, only one line of reasoning which the majority wished to have suitably concluded; nor did David disappoint them. He lifted a hand and resumed in the pained tones of a great man whose vast reserves of patience have been all but used up by a mob of unruly children: 'These controversies are distracting, they are paralysing, they are rending. Days have been occupied in hunting up records, minutes, letters and *procès verbaux*, in interviews, and in raking up what happened during a whole twelve-month in the War Cabinet. And this at such a moment!

'I have just come back from France. The Germans are silently preparing perhaps the biggest blow of the war, under the shroud of mist, and I was asked by the military for certain help. I brought home a list of things they want done, and I wish to attend to them. I really beg and implore, for the sake of our country, the fate of which is in the balance now and in the next few weeks, that there should be an end of this sniping.'

It was sufficient. The Opposition had anticipated the appointment of a Select Committee, followed by an enquiry, which would have given them plenty of time, briefed by General Maurice, to prepare their case. But the hurricane of the Prime Minister's rhetoric blew their ships clean out of the water. McKenna, who was down to speak next, made no attempt to do so, and it was clear that there was really nothing more to be said. Asquith's Motion for a Select Committee, which he was too proud to withdraw, was thrown out with over seventy Liberals voting against the Motion.

Maurice, realizing perhaps that *being right* was no more profitable in politics than it was in the army, gave up both and turned to journalism for which he believed that telling the truth was a proper qualification.

Poor Maurice! He had only been a newspaperman for five months (as Military Correspondent on the *Daily Chronicle*) when the pen was wrenched from his hand. The *Daily Chronicle* was bought by a syndicate with money from the Lloyd George Fund (swollen to huge proportions by the selling of honours – £10,000 for a knighthood, £30,000 for a baronetcy, and £50,000 or more for a peerage), and David saw to it that the man who had dared to try to blacken his good name was out of a job.

Had David won? It would seem so. 'He is complete master of the country if he only knew it,' was Northcliffe's comment. But the Maurice affair caused a rift between David and Asquith that could never be bridged, and this rift became so wide and so deep that the Liberal Party, unable to make up its mind which side it should be on, tumbled right into it, was concussed, and was never the same again. Which meant that David had truly *not* won. For though he was still leader of the country, his party could not sustain him for much longer. From which it may be concluded that David, for all his ingenuity and eloquence, had not won his battle against Maurice at all, but had lost, · and lost disastrously.

He lost that battle, but won the war, although it took time. For a while it seemed that Paris would be lost, France would be lost, everything would be lost, as Ludendorff thrust on towards Paris. But then the balance of power shifted as the bright young doughboys, eager for the fray, stars and stripes in their eyes, danced down the gangplanks of the troopships. The decisive battle involving 400 tanks came at Amiens in August.

In September Bulgaria sued for peace, in October Damascus fell to Allenby, and in the same month the German Chancellor expressed his willingness to agree to an armistice based on President Wilson's Fourteen Points, Four Principles, and Five Particulars. Lloyd George and Clemenceau were not as grateful as President Wilson had hoped they would be. Leaving aside the Four Principles and Five Particulars, the Fourteen Points were most unsatisfactory and Clemenceau remarked that Wilson was trying to outdo the Almighty, for whom Ten Points had been quite enough. David thought Wilson's proposals nebulous and he commented: 'We who have borne the heat and burden of the day are entitled to be consulted.' However, so long as it was clearly understood that the words contained in the Fourteen Points meant whatever it was that anyone concerned with the armistice wanted them to mean, David and Clemenceau were content to agree to them, and on this rather metaphysical basis an armistice was signed with Austria-Hungary on 3 November, and with Germany eight days later.

Outside 10 Downing Street the crowds cheered as they do on such occasions, while church bells chimed, ships on the Thames blew their horns and hooters, and a band, eyes misty with emotion, played 'Keep the home fires burning'.

Standing just inside the window, David sighed deeply.

His shoulders were bowed, his mouth was slack, and his lower lip trembled. He looked so old and tired that it was just as well that he was out of sight of the crowds. David was not thinking of victory. He was wondering where he was going to find the energy to fight *another* war, for one would have to be fought. The old enemy, Asquith, was undefeated: the Liberal army was in disarray; where would it all end?

Frances came up behind him, and put a hand on his shoulder.

'Isn't it wonderful?' she said quietly, and her eyes were shining. David adjusted his face before turning towards her.

'Oh, Pussy!' He could do nothing about his tears.

'I know. Me, too, laughing and crying by turns.' Her voice became brisk and businesslike. 'Now tell me who's to come to the celebration and I'll make out a list and let them know right away.'

'A list?' Frances nodded, pencil poised. 'Oh Pussy, I don't think I could celebrate. Not tonight. Not after so much slaughter, not after so much misery.'

'I know how you feel, but, David, we've won! Nothing can change that!'

'Later, of course, there'll be parades and so on, but for tonight, let's just thank God it's all over.

'Whatever you say.'

David sat down and ran his hands through his hair. He sat in the chair nearest to the window. He did not cross the room to his favourite chair.

'If Uncle Lloyd was alive he'd be down on his knees all night, praying and fasting.'

'I take it,' said Frances, anxious but smiling, 'you're not going *that* far?'

'Who, me? I'll barely have time for an amen, I must make plans for the election.'

'What, right away? Can't you take a rest first?'

'A rest?' David managed a rather bitter smile. Seeing it, Frances was wretched. She had seen too much bitterness in the faces of too many politicians. 'Let me tell you this, the war was child's play compared to what awaits us now. All the reconstruction, the peace treaties, the jobs for the home-coming troops, housing, the unions. If you'd told me a year or two back that the *police* would strike, well ... Ireland – oh, God, *Ireland*! And a thousand and one issues everyone agreed to sweep under the carpet for the duration, they'll all have to be dealt with. If I put off the election long enough to get involved in all that, they'll have me out of office for ten years.'

'I don't believe it!' cried Frances, but she began to. 'How can people ever forget all you've done for Britain?'

'Very easily and very quickly. Overnight.'

'But if things are going to be as difficult as you say, they're going to need a strong man, surely?'

'Yes, but that's not enough. A man needs a party, a team, a power base.'

'You've got a wonderful team! Some of the best brains in the country.'

Another bitter smile as David said: 'Too many Tories in it. Loyal enough while the war was on, but how long will that last now? Tomorrow, Pussy – make a note of this – *tomorrow* I want a meeting of all the leading Liberals. I must get to them before Asquith does. And then we'll draft a policy statement. And when I've done that I might go home for a day or two.'

Frances turned away from him. All the pleasure in his triumph, the distant cheers and voices singing: 'For he's a jolly good fellow', all was forgotten.

'Home?' she asked quietly. Then answered her question. 'Criccieth, I suppose. I hadn't realized you still saw it in that light. After all we've been through here together, somehow I hoped you'd begun to think of *this* as home.'

'Number 10? Oh, my dear child, that's the commonest delusion in politics!'

'I might have known it. And then *she* will find her way to London now it's all over. In time to be in at the kill. To share in the victory parades, the banquets, the bouquets.'

She would not look at him now. She looked at herself in an ornate, gilt-framed mirror, and saw his reflection approaching her from behind, the mouth already open to utter some honeyed phrase or other. But there were times when words were no help at all.

He put his arm around her as he spoke softly: 'And all you can share is my work. All my thoughts, my hopes and despairs, my mind and my heart, my days and my nights. Would you really change places with her, *cariad annwyl aur*?'

David Lloyd George had won the war. That was what Frances told him and that was what he wanted to hear. Of course his political opponents (those within the Liberal Party as well as those outside) disagreed; they had a vested interest in doing so. And of course Haig, Jellicoe, Robertson and Maurice, and other naval and military leaders, were unlikely to see things as the Prime Minister did. Civilians always took the credit when things went well, but the soldiers and sailors had to do the fighting. No one denied that David had done valuable work at the Ministry of Munitions, all credit to him for that, but to claim that he had won the war and to strut about like some tin-pot dictator, well really!

A prophet is not without honour save in his own country, and David's country was now England. The irony was that only in Wales did they greet him as a saviour, stretching out to touch him, smiling to see and be seen by him, happy and proud.

At Brynawelon, the new house in Criccieth, William quizzed David about his plans for an early election. The younger brother looked the older now, and since Uncle Lloyd's death he was the only man in the country before whom David felt the need to justify himself. It was strange how the Prime Minister of England could never face his brother without a twinge of guilt, a feeling of moral culpability that was as irritating as it was irrational. So now he tried to explain to William why he felt the need to prolong the Coalition, but even as he gave his reasons they seemed insubstantial, even specious.

His plan was to convince the electorate that the administration really did represent all shades of opinion. Those Liberals who had supported him over the Maurice affair were to be known as official Lloyd George candidates, and would not oppose friendly Tory candidates. There would therefore be constituencies in which Asquithian Liberals would be opposing Georgian Liberals. William didn't like the sound of it at all: an accommodation with the Tories, he thought, could only advantage the new radicals of the Labour movement, and damage the Liberal Party irreparably.

'Look, let's get this clear,' David said hopefully. '*I'm* not the one that wants a split. I made approaches to Asquith, and offered to make him Chancellor of the Exchequer, but he refused to serve under me in any capacity whatsoever. So what does he expect? That after all that's happened I should be prepared to serve under *him*?'

William heard him out, and was troubled not only by the dubious tactics which David was employing to stay in power, but also by the choleric way in which he defended himself. He talked to his brother these days as though he were addressing a political opponent; it should not have been like that. Gently William said: 'Uncle Lloyd would have been so proud. "A great work Dafydd has been called to", he used to say, "raising the poor out of the dust." '

'It's a more complex job, Will, than any of us imagined. I'm afraid it's impossible to carry it out without shedding some ballast on the way up.'

William wondered whether they all expected too much of Dei, whether the pressures of office were so great that it was virtually impossible for a Prime Minister to remain humble and compassionate. But nonetheless he was moved to say: 'Dafydd, when you are promising them a country fit for heroes to live in – houses, wages, and so on – I wish you could put in a word about what kind of men they should strive to be. To deserve to live in such a country, I mean, they need somebody to remind them that man does not live by bread alone. Nobody could do it better than you if you set your mind to it.'

'I'm a layman, Will,' replied David, feeling more and more uncomfortable. This was the sort of conversation he least enjoyed. 'Their souls are not my business. That's the job of the church.'

'But what *is* the church? Is it bishops and deacons? Or is it not rather *us*, its members? In the beginning it wasn't only the material standards you set out to change. Of course I can see how the war cut across all that, but . . .'

David said gruffly: 'If all the churches had done their jobs properly, there would have been no war.'

It was no sort of an answer and he knew it. But the issues were simple enough. If Britons were to benefit from winning the war, a strong man must be in charge. David was the only strong man who could do it. Asquith was out of office, Bonar Law disheartened (both had lost sons in the war), and the only way David could do it was with a clear mandate. Since one doesn't win votes by promising to mend souls so much as by promising to line pockets, souls must wait their turn.

Megan was loyal. 'He hasn't the faintest idea, has he, Tada?' she said.

But Maggie muttered darkly: 'There may be a lot William has never learned, Dei, but there's a lot you're forgetting too. And you may be sorry.'

The 'coupon' election held at Christmas-time, 1918, six weeks after the end of the war, was unlike any election before or since. For a start the electorate was three times as large as it had been in 1910. Under the Representation of the People Act, there was no longer a property requirement for a voter. All men over twenty-one were entitled to cast their votes; and women (who had never been enfranchised before) over thirty. *Would* they vote? One could not tell. *How* would they vote? The two-party system was in such disarray that it was possible that many would quite fail to understand what the candidates stood for. For the first time all polling would take place on a single day.

And the servicemen still in France would have news-papers sent out so that they could have their minds made up for them, plus ballot-papers on which to register their votes.

But the most unusual aspect of the 'coupon' election was that it brought into being a new political grouping that was neither fish, fowl nor good red meat. David's problem at the end of the war was how to convert the popular support for himself as a man into a healthy mandate for himself as a Prime Minister. Many of the traditional Liberals re-mained loyal to Asquith; David could only count on a rump from his War Committee.

After secret negotiations between Frederick Guest and Bonar Law 150 Liberals were guaranteed Coalition backing in the election. These 'Coalie Libs' – 'a stage army' – set up in opposition to the 'official' Liberal candidates in many constituencies.

David was extremely anxious about the outcome of the election. There were so many imponderables, and if he were shown to have misjudged the mood of the public there would be no climbing back. He decided to campaign in the big cities and the marginal constituencies.

When Maggie reminded him that the people of Caernar-von Boroughs had put him into Parliament and kept him there and deserved at least a sight of the great man, he felt momentarily ashamed.

Maggie said: 'They don't care about Asquith, the Tories or the Lloyd George Political Fund. They care about Uncle Lloyd's boy, Will's brother, Maggie Owen's hus-band, the lad who stuck up for the chapels and against the demon drink, who got them their National Insurance and Old Age Pensions. And if that is true of the old voters, just think of all the new ones, Dei, the shepherds and potato-pickers and the old women in cottages and chapels. Where you say Will sees things too simple, they'll see things simpler still.'

David smiled affectionately at her and said without irony: 'I ought to have a memo printed and framed on my desk: "Never underestimate Marged Lloyd George". It may be true that I've been taking Wales too much for granted. If I could think of a suitable deputy . . .' Megan looked up hopefully. If only Tada would trust her, he would not be disappointed. 'One who could carry my banner to any place in the country and charm the birds off the trees and strike all my critics dumb.'

I could do it, thought Megan, if he would let me. I would work day and night for him. But then he added:

'Maggie, if I organize a speaking tour for you, will you do it?'

Maggie looked suddenly coy. She was stout and she was middle-aged but the expression in her eyes was as it had been when David first courted her.

'Oh, *twt lol*! I'm past all that kind of thing.'

'Not you, Maggie. Do it for your old Dei.'

'All right. On one condition,' said Maggie, after a pause, and Megan tried hard to conceal her disappointment. David did not care much for the sound of a condition, but merely warned:

'Don't set the price too high, old girl.'

'Why? What are you afraid of?'

David coughed and asked Megan if she would mind going to see if he had left his cigars in his overcoat pocket. Megan pointed out reproachfully that at nineteen she was quite old enough to understand what was going on, which David accepted but muttered that he was not too old to feel uncomfortable about it, so Megan left her mother and father to sort things out together.

'You needn't have worried,' said Maggie with a trace of contempt, 'I'm not going to talk about your precious Miss Stevenson. I can guess what kind of advice *she's* been giving you. Anything to keep you in Number 10. She likes the reflected glory.'

This was a new twist. Maggie was prepared to undertake a speaking tour on his behalf, and yet *didn't* want him returned as Prime Minister. What could it mean?

'If you want me to campaign there are things I don't

understand. This Lloyd George Fund, for instance . . . '

'What have you heard about that? Look, Maggie, if I had any respect for the House of Lords it might be different, but as far as I'm concerned, since I clipped its wings it's nothing but a home for geriatric dukes and a dumping ground for the kind of snobs and social climbers who can't wait to get in there and hobnob with them.'

'And pay for the privilege?'

'Certainly. But this is nothing new, and nobody forces them to . . . '

Maggie looked grim. 'In the past they may have made contributions to the *party*, but now they are making them to the Prime Minister.'

'In the past it's always been the same thing! But if I hand the money over to the party, it's the same as handing it to Asquith, to stab me in the back with, and I'd rather chuck it in the Thames.'

'I told you once that if you had no money that woman would leave you. Is that what you're guarding against?'

'As God is my witness, Maggie, it's a *political* fund. I don't dip into it. But I have to have some freedom of manoeuvre. I don't want to spend the rest of my political life handcuffed to Bonar Law and the Tories. What we need is a new party, a centre party, the Lloyd George Liberals, the Labour Party moderates and a few of the enlightened Tories. But I must wait for the right moment It's going to need cash and organization to launch it. *That's* what the fund is for!'

Maggie's next question was a facer. She wanted to know why David had been going around saying 'Hang the Kaiser!' And the answer was that he had originally said nothing of the sort. The Coalition Manifesto, issued jointly by himself and Bonar Law, had spoken merely of 'a just and lasting peace' with a passing reference to disabled soldiers and sailors. However, the electorate, mischievously encouraged by the newspapers of Lord Northcliffe who was smarting from being excluded from the Peace Delegation, had been clamouring for revenge against 'the Huns' who must be 'brought to their knees'. David had nothing personal against the Kaiser but confessed to Maggie that he would happily hang him with his own hands if it would help to bring about a decent and lasting peace with the German people.

'Most of them,' he said, 'were no guiltier than ourselves, and they've suffered just as much.'

'But Dei, this is so different from what you say on the platform. And isn't this why people say you're two-faced and insincere? They never dared to say that in the old days. Why can't you do as you did in the Boer War? Stand up and face the people and tell them the truth as you see it, even if they hate you for it?' Obviously Maggie felt that she wasn't getting her point across, because she went on with some passion, clutching his arm in the hope that this would render her argument the more convincing: 'But why not? Break up the Coalition, go back with the Liberals while there's still a party to go back to.'

'Go back as second in command? Watch Asquith lose the election for us, as he certainly would?'

'The Party would survive. And you would go down with honour, and your turn would come again, Dei, and, when it did, people would remember that you kept your hands clean and love you for it the way they did before.'

'And you would bask in the reflected love the way that Frances basks in the reflected glory.'

'I see nothing wrong with that,' said Maggie a little stiffly, removing her hand from his arm at the mention of the forbidden name.

'You argue, Maggie, that power at any price is a pretty shabby slogan and advocate in its place the truth at any price. And suppose I do sacrifice everything for my spotless reputation, who would suffer for it? Europe would, not us. Our children and our grandchildren would. The issues seem clear enough to you here in Criccieth, Maggie, as they do to Frances in London, but I have to be in Versailles. Clemenceau wants revenge, he wants to tear Germany to shreds. Do you think Asquith could stand up to such a man, or Bonar Law, or Arthur Henderson? He would go over any one of them like a steam-roller. I don't even know whether I can hold him, but I do believe that I've the best chance.'

Poor Maggie! As soon as David talked of Europe and of great affairs she knew she had lost him. What could she tell him about Germany, about Clemenceau? She so much wanted to believe his arguments, but, more than that she so much wanted to believe that he believed them.

'Oh, Dei,' she said, 'I should have known that once I let you talk . . . '

'Talk? You think that's all it is? All I can say, *hen gariad*, is if I'm deceiving you in this, then I'm deceiving myself too. Perhaps I am. Perhaps the task is beyond my powers. But, Maggie, will you help me try?'

And of course she did. She was magnificent. It was as though David had left all his old eloquence hanging in the air above the Welsh hills and Maggie had drawn it down into her lungs, exhaling it as fresh and clear as it had been a quarter of a century before. She spoke in Welsh to her audiences of farmers and labourers, of housewives and children, she spoke of David and for David. And as she spoke she rediscovered her pride in him and her love for him and it shone from her eyes. Why should they vote for him?

'Why,' cried Maggie, 'because he has fought for you steadfastly from the beginning. For Wales. For the poor and downtrodden. For dignity and freedom from want in sickness and old age. For the freedom and independence of small nations, for justice and righteousness everywhere!' She believed most of it, and most of those who listened to her believed her.

The split in the Liberal Party marked the end of a long-standing but volatile friendship. Timothy Davies, with whom David had been so friendly when he first came to London as a young MP (he had accompanied this wealthy draper to Rome and on a Mediterranean cruise, as well as sleeping with his charming young wife and, so she claimed, fathering one of her children), requested that the Prime Minister support his candidature in the election. It was not easy for David to say no, but he had already said no to a handsome diamond pin which the Davies family had offered him 'as a token of their joint regard' just a few days before, and he managed to excuse himself by explaining that the government Whips had examined Davies's record and found it unsatisfactory. Davies must have been hurt and disappointed; David was much relieved.

The campaign, which David had hoped to run along respectable lines, claiming that the government's task was 'to make Britain a land fit for heroes to live in', was rapidly being discredited by the ferment of feeling against the Germans. It was no longer enough, it seemed, to speak of hanging the Kaiser. Geddes, for instance, proclaimed that the German lemon should be squeezed 'until the pips squeaked'. Many were the hecklers demanding that all aliens resident in Britain must be sent home. In the face of such fanaticism all David could do was deliver his regular speeches but *in a snarl*. It was amazing how vague generalities could be transformed into raging demagogy simply by the admixture of some good old-fashioned Welsh *hwyl*

'It must be a just peace,' sounded tame. 'A sternly just peace' sounded better. 'A relentlessly just peace' sounded fine. And with voice, arm and forefinger raised, one could curdle the blood in the veins of a receptive audience with this sort of thing: 'I do not want to pursue a policy of vengeance for its own sake, but we must ensure that men who feel tempted to plunge the world into war will know what is awaiting them at the end of it!'

It sickened David to have to do it. Almost for the first time in his life he could take no pleasure in his own rhetoric. But if it had to be done . . .

He believed that it had to be done.

As Maggie and Megan waited in Criccieth for the outcome of this most perplexing of elections, Megan raised that question which neither had mentioned during the hectic campaign, but which both had worried about secretly at night. What would happen if David's gamble paid off?

'They've got the whole of Europe to deal with, Mam, to carve it up and share it out. They've got to decide about the Balkans, the Rhine, Poland, Turkey, Austria. They've got to set up a League of Nations, a proper one with teeth, and sort out reparations and what to do with the German colonies. Whoever gets in will be spending, Heaven knows, six or eight *months* probably in Paris. And, if it's Tada, you know who'll be there with him, don't you?'

Maggie smiled. She found her daughter's high moral tone both amusing and touching. Besides there was only one thing to do to keep David sweet – years of practice had perfected Maggie's technique – and that was to Be There When He Needs Me. A potent weapon in the right hands.

'I know you've got the idea she's been having things all her own way,' said Maggie. 'But I happen to know they've had some terrible rows. The war hasn't done his temper any good, you know.'

'I hope you're not going to say you feel *sorry* for her?' Megan sounded scandalized.

'No. Oh no. She knew quite well what she was doing. She asked for everything that's coming to her. But it will come, you mark my words. She's thirty-one. From now on, she's going to dread every birthday . . .'

'I think you ought to go to Paris with him.'

'What good would that do?'

'At least it would cramp her style a bit.'

Maggie rang for the maid and ordered a pot of tea. Then she stretched in her chair and smiled at Megan.

'What would *I* do in Paris, girl? No, I've done enough rushing about this last month. I'll go up to London for the celebrations. But then I'll have a nice long rest.'

'If he lost the election he might come back here too,' said Megan.

'Not to stay. He'll never do that. Not now.'

'Or if he only had a *narrow* majority, he wouldn't be able to give so much time to Paris then. He'd be worried about the House of Commons. It could happen, you know. The unions have not been happy, and Asquith's lot . . . it *could* happen.'

But Maggie just smiled her placid smile and picked up her knitting.

The results of this most peculiar of elections were announced on 28 December, and they were the answer to the Premier's prayer. The exact figures were confusing with so many split loyalties, uncomfortable alliances, and usual enmities, but David's majority amounted to over 340. Never before had the country cast such a majestic vote of confidence in a single man. The Sinn Feiners captured 73 of the Irish seats (they only had 69 candidates, so it was rather Irish of them), but announced that they would boycott the proceedings at Westminster. Consequently the official opposition was in the hands of the Labour Party, who had some 60 seats, twice as many as the routed and humiliated Asquithians. Asquith himself was defeated, and so were most of those who had thrown in their lot with him. General Maurice had unwittingly wrecked those who had called upon him to help them; his friends suffered now as bitterly as his enemies had during the war.

Only David, who took no pleasure in Asquith's fate, could stand above all recriminations. His party was in ruins, but he was supreme. Europe was in ruins, but the politicians would sort something out. They would make sure that such a thing could never happen again, not at least within their lifetimes. That was their job. They'd think of something in their land fit for heroes.

Epilogue

Sometimes as an old man he wondered why he had done it all. They hadn't thanked him for it. He had brought in historic measures to eliminate poverty, old age pensions and national insurance, and yet poverty seemed to thrive. He had fought the war to end all wars, and struggled for a just and lasting peace in the face of those who grew fat on the taste of blood, yet within a generation they were at it again. Just wait until some more young men are grown to manhood, some more girls married, some more babies born, then will be the time for more organized killing, for young widows, unweaned orphans. He had wrestled with the problem which defeated Pitt, Peel and Gladstone, he had sought for a solution of the Irish problem where no solution existed. Briefly in 1920 it seemed as though he had confronted the immovable object and moved it. A settlement was signed. But within two years the Sinn Feiners were at it again, killing indiscriminately anyone, English or Irish, Protestant or Catholic. Just so long as they were solid enough to stop a bullet, a bullet would be found for them. They even killed Michael Collins, whom David loved.

Sometimes as an old man he wondered what it had all been for. When he had set out to change the world there were those in Wales who looked upon him as only a little lower than the angels. And amongst those hills, and sitting in the tops of those trees he had felt himself at times to be divinely inspired. He was loved because he was a good man and afraid of nobody. And when he told them that he would build them a land fit for heroes they believed him because he had said he would win them the war and he did. A land fit for heroes? All they could see was dole queues. In 1922 he made his last speech as Prime Minister. He spoke of 'the just and generous people who would not allow one who rendered them service in a dark hour to be treated shabbily'. He spoke of 'casting himself on the people whose cause he never betrayed'. He spoke of going 'into the wilderness'. And they listened sympathetically. But what David did not understand was that the sympathy was for the rhetoric and no longer for the man. They now saw through him. He was too ruthless for power: paying spies, manipulating the press, selling honours. Better an honest mediocrity than that, they felt. The diet had been too rich for too long and they hankered for plainer fare. They got Bonar Law.

Sometimes as a very old man he remembered Maggie. Dame Margaret – how she had enjoyed that! As the years passed and Maggie stayed in Criccieth and David became Lord of the Manor at Churt – it is true they met only infrequently, but their love had never been of the demonstrative kind; she loved and admired him for being great and famous and married to her, while he loved her for loving him.

And then one day at the tail end of 1940, after a meeting of the Women's Institute, Maggie slipped on the parquet flooring and fractured her hip. Her bones were too brittle to mend. By the time it was considered necessary to send for David she was dying. He set off from London in the Rolls. It came on to snow. Maggie and the weather grew worse. The Rolls ran into a snowdrift in Bridgnorth, and had to be dug out. It ran into another at Cerrig-y-Druidion and was completely buried. He could go no further that night than the local inn. The following morning Maggie died.

'She was a great old pal,' said David, sobbing as he heard the news. He was seventy-eight. Thereafter he aged rapidly. He lost weight, and his hair, but still his eyes flashed from the Opposition Front Bench at the foolishness of the young men with power. Nine months after his eightieth birthday he married Frances in the Guildford Registry Office.

Megan was almost hysterical with rage, telephoning her

father on the eve of the happy occasion to beg him not to insult the memory of his wife in so heartless a fashion. Richard's fury, though less ostentatious, was just as profoundly felt.

Sometimes as a very frail old man Earl Lloyd-George of Dwyfor wondered whether his life would have been very much different if he had thrown over Maggie for Frances when he was still young enough to start a new life for himself abroad – as a journalist in America perhaps, for he wrote with great facility and the Americans paid him with great generosity – or if he had employed another young governess whose eyes were not quite so seductive, nor whose brain so perfectly attuned to the Liberal way of looking at things.

Frances had brought him great joy and great sorrow. The great joy she brought him at some danger to herself. At the age of forty she had given birth to his daughter, Jennifer Mary. The great sorrow came shortly after Jennifer Mary (who was officially 'adopted' abroad) and was a highly respectable public servant called Colonel Tweed. Frances was rash enough to do with Colonel Tweed what David had been doing with housemaids and secretaries all over Europe for many, many years, but to David such an excuse was not at all to the point.

Frances must choose, David thundered, and Frances chose – wisely. if one took the long-term view and regarded marriage in a Registry Office to a rather frail and not always sweet-tempered old man as an appropriate reward for a lifetime of sexual servitude.

As a very frail and rather bitter old man he brooded about his long years in the wilderness. And since they were no longer keen to hear his speeches, not like the old days in the House when the benches had been so crowded there was scarcely room for a point of order, he wrote books, and the words poured forth with all the old fluency. There was a satisfying particularity and permanence about words.

As a very frail and rather disappointed old man David wondered if the system were to blame. Hitler, for whom he had more than a passing admiration ('a magnetic, dynamic personality with a single-minded purpose' and 'a great leader'), had not had to contend with all the irritations of the party political system as practised in Britain. Sometimes David wondered how differently things might have worked out if he had enjoyed dictatorial powers.

As a very frail and rather frightened old man David thought about dying and wondered whether it was as gloomy as presiding over the dissolution of the Liberal Party or losing one's authority. One might have thought that as a lifelong and dedicated nonconformist he would have had no doubts, no terror, but he certainly remarked to the Minister who was attending him shortly before the end: 'I wish I could have the blind faith of the Catholic.'

But at last he seemed to come to some sort of accommodation with his maker, for he smiled cheerfully at all his visitors and died between Megan, who was proving to be a most worthy politician herself, and Frances, with other well-wishers seeing him off in appropriate style.

At times this very remarkable old gentleman felt that his had been an enjoyable, varied, and not altogether useless sort of life. And many of those who decide about such matters thought so too.